EROTICA—FOR WOMEN, BY WOMEN

"RUBENESQUE" *by Magenta Michaels*
A literary luncheon at a grand San Francisco hotel offers a big single girl a new treat sans pantyhose—from a stranger under the table.

"THE JOURNAL" *by Roberta Stone*
A holiday in Provincetown provides an intimate view of a woman's fantasies about gay men—and an eye-opening encounter with woman-woman love.

"AT DOCTOR d'AMOUR'S PARTY" *by Carol A. Queen*
Like its progenitor, *The Story of O,* this tale of dressing up in leather and lace—and getting down to business—is free of guilt *and* inhibitions.

"CLAUDIA'S CHEEKS" *by Catherine Tavel*
No matter what her own sexual preferences are, men have an insatiable attraction to Claudia's derrière—until she decides to get back at them, and on top, at the same time.

. . . AND 24 MORE IRRESISTIBLY SENSUAL, SEDUCTIVE, VERY NAUGHTY STORIES

HEROTICA 2

SUSIE BRIGHT is a sexual and erotic writer and educator who edited the first *Herotica* anthology. She is the author of *Susie Sexpert's Lesbian Sex World* and *Sexual Reality.* She lives in San Francisco with her two-year-old daughter.

JOANI BLANK is a sex educator and therapist and the publisher of Down There Press, which specializes in sexual self-help and sexual-enhancement books. She has written several books about sex. She lives near San Francisco with her husband and teenage daughter.

HEROTICA 2

A Collection of
Women's Erotic Fiction

Edited by
Susie Bright and Joani Blank

A PLUME BOOK

PLUME
Published by the Penguin Group
Penguin Books USA Inc., 375 Hudson Street,
New York, New York 10014, U.S.A.
Penguin Books Ltd, 27 Wrights Lane, London W8 5TZ, England
Penguin Books Australia Ltd, Ringwood, Victoria, Australia
Penguin Books Canada Ltd, 10 Alcorn Avenue,
Toronto, Ontario, Canada M4V 3B2
Penguin Books (N.Z.) Ltd, 182–190 Wairau Road,
Auckland 10, New Zealand

Penguin Books Ltd, Registered Offices:
Harmondsworth, Middlesex, England

First published by Plume, an imprint of New American Library,
a division of Penguin Books USA Inc.

First Printing, April, 1992
10   9   8   7   6   5   4   3   2   1

 REGISTERED TRADEMARK—MARCA REGISTRADA

LIBRARY OF CONGRESS CATALOGING IN PUBLICATION DATA:
Herotica 2: a collection of women's erotic fiction / edited by Susie
   Bright and Joani Blank.
      p.   cm.
   ISBN 0-452-26787-0
      1.   Erotic stories, American.   2.   American fiction—Women authors.
I.   Bright, Susie, 1958-   II.   Blank, Joani, 1937-
PS648.E7H474   1991
813′.01083538—dc20   91-32142
                                                                               CIP
Printed in the United States of America

PUBLISHER'S NOTE
These are works of fiction. Names, characters, places, and incidents either
are the product of the author's imagination or are used fictitiously, and any
resemblance to actual persons, living or dead, events, or locales is entirely
coincidental.

Needless to say, this book is for Lisa.   S. B.

This book is for A. W., who will appreciate it someday.   J. B.

Thank you to Leigh Davidson, managing editor of Down There Press, for her support, patience and persistence.

CONTENTS

INTRODUCTION

When I first started teaching women's erotic writing classes in 1989, I didn't know who would show up. After all, who hasn't written—either in her diary or on the back of a matchbook—at least a few sweaty words, a love poem, or a passionate letter?

But teaching a class to women writers on the art of sensual penmanship indicated that something more was afloat than the inalienable right to serenade one's lover. Women's erotica, as it has come to be called, is a new genre of literature; it is fiction that illustrates the very real changes that have occurred in women's sexual interests and desires.

Women are thirsty, no, let's say ravenous, for sexual knowledge and erotic inspiration. They are offended by notions of romance that exclude or play innocent of sexual satisfaction; indeed, it's no surprise when a woman sings a hit song called "What's Love Got To Do With It?" We have a new understanding about our bodies' sexual responses. We experience sex in and out of all the traditions of love, commitment, marriage, and during and after child rearing. We make love with men and women, sometimes in fantasy, sometimes in real life. Sometimes we are a man in our sexual imaginations. We take the sexual signs of our times, be it X-rated home video, AIDS awareness, G-spot ejaculations, condoms, marriage burn-out, date rape, single motherhood, lesbian visibility, vibrator availability—we take the reality of sex in our era and we insist, indeed, we delight in including these slices of real life in our erotica.

I like to play a game in my erotica classroom. I ask everyone to write an initial erotic sentence, something easy like, "She touched her clit."

"Now keep on going," I say, "and do it in the style of a plain brown wrapper novel, the kind of book you'd find in the back of the sleaziest store in town."

Two minutes later I tell them to stop. "Now switch," I say, "and start writing as if this were a free-verse uninhibited love poem that you wrote on the cliffs of Big Sur." Then I have them switch again, two minutes later, to a supermarket bodice-ripper style: "Me Rhett, you Scarlett." Switch again, to a 1950s beatnik ultra-hip cigarette-after-the-screw style. No matter how unsophisticated the writer, each student has had some glancing experience with each of the styles I ask them to imitate.

Finally, I ask them to end their stories in one last genre. "Finish your story in a 'women's erotica' style," I tell them. And they jump right in. No one asks me anymore, "What are you talking about?" Despite the continual handwringing in the media that no one knows what women want, apparently women do have a collective sense of what they expect out of a sexy story, and it's so well known that I can even ask my students to give me a quick stereotype of it.

I used to have one impeccable standard for what made an erotic story female-centric: the woman comes. This single concept is so rare in traditional erotica that it overwhelms every other feminine consideration. Of course we've all read stories where a woman is overwhelmed with the size of her lover's penis—she screams his name and clutches his breast—but how many times do you actually get a her-point-of-view orgasm? We read about how he sees her responding to him, but we don't see inside her explosion.

I still believe a woman's climax makes a good bottom line for women's erotica. But now I have other angles to consider. There are other aspects of a woman's literary libido that show their colors just as brilliantly as any hot pink orgasm.

Femmchismo

I call the primary signal of the burgeoning women's erotica movement "femmchismo." Femmchismo is exactly what it sounds like: the aggressive, seductive and very hungry sexual ego of a woman. Like machismo, it embodies an erotic arrogance; for women it's clear this is a long-overdue case of conceit. Femmchismo has been a well-kept secret. Women have always talked among themselves in classic pajama-party bravado about their awareness of their sexual power and talent. Sometimes this boasting takes the form of dubious self-effacement. When sexual heroine Claudia "complains" in Catherine Tavel's "Claudia's Cheeks" about her enormous sticks-in-the-air bottom, she is only kvetching insofar as she lets us know that her posterior is the center of sexual attention wherever she goes. A woman would not typically brag openly about having a big ass the way a man might boast of his big cock, but she gets her message across by talking about the trials of being an object of such enormous desire.

Femmchismo draws on both a woman's desirability—the excitement a woman creates simply by being there—and also her sexual talents to influence and make love to her intended subject.

Certainly the stereotype of the female predator is not new; the spider, the manipulator, the schemer. The sex-negative caricature of woman's sexual aggression is that she is evil and that she seeks destruction and castration, not an orgasm. Her scheme of sexual wiles is to procure something *other* than sex. What's new in women's erotica is that when women describe their sexual courage and pride, their erotic satisfaction *is* their explicit goal.

To be sexually adventurous *for her own sake*, to not only feel her desire but also to direct it for ultimate satisfaction. Yes, this is femmchismo, and don't be surprised if its hard little clit comes rubbing up against your leg—purring, of course.

Femmchismo is emphatically not about falling in love or about "the very first time." It's about the value of a unique sexual experience, desire empowered by action.

Daily Details

Women's erotic writing proves once and for all that women are actually less romantic than men. How else can we explain that their modern erotic stories are filled with pertinent yet terribly unromantic details of daily life? In fact, in most women's erotica the traditional duties of women's housekeeping and caretaking are often juxtaposed with a fanciful or daring sexual adventure. In Maggie Top's "No Balance," Shelley is taking her mother for a drive in the foothills, but her daughterly duties are blissfully intercut with a sexual fantasy that conceivably would eject her mother right out of the passenger seat if she could read her child's mind.

Women's concerns for practicality and routine are satirically counterposed to their lust in many of these stories. In Jane Longaway's "My Pussy is Dead," Dido rebuffs the nudist colony director who wants her to be more comfortable: "It had taken an hour to put those white shorts on and for her money they could stay there." In "The Company Man" by Moxie Light, our heroine not only bathes and perfumes herself for a big evening, she also stuffs all her kitchen clutter into the oven and swishes out the toilet bowl before her date arrives.

Women writers are less hesitant, and are even enthusiastic, to integrate the limitations and risks that enter their erotic adventures. In "The Trojan Woman" by Angela Fairweather, a schoolteacher involves her lover in her pursuit of condom research. In "Wheelchair Romance" by Margo Woods, the author describes in detail what her lover's disability means in and out of bed.

Language—The Shape of the Feeling

When feminists and writers first started discussing the future of women's erotica, there was a call for a new women-centric language, a modern vocabulary to discuss women's sexual feelings. As an editor, I find that the language is there at the tip of our tongues. What is harder than imagining the words is saying them out loud. Street vocabulary is easily possessed by women who find no embarrassment in the shape of erotic women's language.

Street slang is just as your mother taught you: absolutely unladylike. But how many "ladies" under sixty haven't said "fuck" by now, in either anger or passion? What women have to cope with in employing four-letter words is not that they aren't suited to us; they suit us just fine. What we have to handle is being shushed by some double-standard.

Obscene words are powerful and forceful—that's why they are deemed unsuitable for "ladies," who are weak and delicate. When we have indelicate sexual feelings we get a little choked up because there don't seem to be ladylike words for lustful emotions. Ladies don't lust. Real women do, however, and it's perfectly appropriate for us to use strong language when the situation calls for it.

Most disputes over erotic language center on trying to find a perfect alternative to words. Is "vagina" too medical or too clinical? Is "cunt" too mean? I think we're wrongly splitting hairs over such quests for the ideal synonym. What's really missing in our erotic language are descriptions of women's arousal, from the first flush of desire and wetness, to the climactic loss of control, to the multiple sensations after orgasm.

In "The Shape of the Feeling," Daphne Slade explores some fifty ways she feels about her orgasms, and each one is a delight to contemplate: "My final orgasm always feels like an afterthought because I never know when to quit. I think the phrase 'you should know when to quit' was started by someone who knew exactly which orgasm to stop on."

When Women Look at Women

Lesbian erotica has been the fastest changing and most controversial aspect of the bloom in women's erotica. Lesbian sex stories have been around forever, but they typically were not written by or for lesbians. They were stories about breaking a taboo, about the sexual possibilities of manlessness. They were more about the men who were not there than they were about the women present.

When lesbians began to speak for themselves erotically, it was often in the context of a coming-out story, a woman discovering she likes women. Self-discovery is the key to the sexual excitement in a coming-out scenario; yet for women of any lesbian experience, one's first sexual encounter with another woman, though an important event, is unlikely to be the most satisfying and revealing experience she'll ever have.

With this in mind, *Herotica 2* introduces lesbian characters who are grownups—women who not only desire and love other women but also have the same sophisticated and diverse sexual tastes as any typical heterosexual female. So often, lesbian protagonists are ingenues, whether they're fifteen or forty, questioning their sexuality, yearning for the security of knowing themselves. Not so in "Seductions," where a middle-aged gay divorced single mom takes her first leap into lust on the rebound. She's nobody's fool; her lesbianism is a matter of course. Like any woman coming out of a long-term relationship, she has emotional reservations competing with a trigger-happy sexual appetite.

Sometimes the history of coming out plays a sweet second-fiddle to a mature love story. Pat Williams's "Ellen, From Chicago" makes poignant reference to the difference gay liberation has made in lesbian lives when two African-American women teachers traveling in the South find themselves boarding at a sixty-year-old woman's home. Their hostess treasures her photos of "her very best friend," an early aviatrix. Her generation lived a love that dared not speak its name, but the post-Stonewall lovers in this story hide nothing from each other.

So much of contemporary women's fiction is considered outrageous simply for being non-stereotypical. While daytime talk shows may regale us with the spectacle of "Black Lesbians" or "Lesbian Moms Who Like Porn," the new lesbian erotic literature is an understated command to *get over it*. Not only is there a lesbian under every bed, but she comes in every color, lifestyle, and political opinion.

The first revolution in lesbian erotic literature was writing from the lesbian point of view. That seems overdue and obvious enough to understand immediately.

But the second revolution in lesbian erotica is not really about lesbianism per se at all. It's about gender-bending and the vicarious experience of erotically placing yourself in another's shoes. In "The Journal," a lesbian novelist sets her hand to gay male porn, while in "There's More of You," one woman lover reads to another from a heterosexual bodice-ripper.

These examples are a complete departure from the closely held myth that lesbians are utterly divorced from any kind of vicarious masculine appreciation. Lesbian purity has been like the last white dress anybody could find to cover up the fact that sexual imaginations wander everywhere. Just because a woman has no interest in a relationship with a man doesn't mean that she might not fantasize about sex with a man, or perhaps imagine being a man. Our fantasies, like our nightly dreams, are not compromised in the least by who we live and love with in the real world.

More than any other group of writers, lesbian erotica writers have grabbed gender-bending by the genitals, taken the whole spectrum of masculine/feminine eroticism by storm. Radical lesbian sex writers took one of porn's most common questions and turned it upside down: why do so many men like to watch lesbian sex? The hip lesbian answer is, "because everybody can and does fantasize about anybody and anything they please." Lesbians can appreciate masculinity whether it's in the traditional form of admiring a woman's unusual strength and perseverance, such as the student/teacher infatuation in Karen Marie Christa Minns's "Amazon," or the "kinkier" aspects of cross-dressing and gender-mixing.

As lesbian sexual themes become less predictable, the uniqueness of a strictly woman-to-woman experience can become more specific, even startling. In Serena Moloch's "I Visit the Doctor," a young woman is growing up in a fascist future much like that of *The Handmaid's Tale*. She seeks out a woman doctor to alleviate her severe menstrual pain. Only women understand this kind of pain and its link to both our erotic and reproductive capacity. A lesbian relationship in this context is intimately explosive.

When a Woman Feels Like a Man

When an ostensibly heterosexual woman writes of her desire for a man, she can also defy traditional roles. It's not unusual at all to find a story where the woman dominates her male lover or the man services her. This fantasy has been seen many times, mainly because it's such a popular turn-on for men.

The rare female twist to this role-reversal is where the woman not only takes control, but she also takes on a man's feelings and prerogatives—which have less to do with domination and more to do with the masculine world. In "Taking Him on a Sunday Afternoon," Magenta Michaels describes turning the tables on her husband.

> He clamps up to prevent me from rubbing him there, but aggression has risen in me and I press on, massaging a moistened finger at his entrance. It's slick there and I can imagine the smell, which excites me; I know that he's concerned about the smell, too—how I'll find him—and this excites me even more.

It's the phrase "how I'll find him" which epitomizes the role-reversal. Traditionally, it is women who "get found," ladies who worry about what they smell like, and men who relish this vulnerability.

Sometimes women subvert male sexual excitement by making their own submission almost, but not quite, impossible. They thrive on exuding as well as seeking masculine energy. It's like a Valkyrie demanding her due. In Susan St. Aubin's "This Isn't About Love," we are introduced to Ilka, a virtual woman warrior, a commando self-defense instructor who revels in her ability to reduce any man to a pulp at the same time as she dreams of a man who could break through her defenses. One dream involves a gun:

"I was having an orgasm when I woke up," she says. "It was as though the gun that woke me started the orgasm. He finally gave me what I wanted."

"Death?" I ask. My fingers are clenched under the table. "How can you think you're in love with someone who shoots you?"

"But it was like being shot to life." Ilka looks at me and sighs. "He shot his power into me. I can't explain it, there are not words in any language I know. I'm not talking about love, Chris."

The language Ilka seeks is not about love, at least not the Valentine's-Day-card love that women have long believed was the greatest literary expectation our passion could reach. Women are approaching a new lover's language today, a tongue that relishes abandon and adventure, a roar that comes straight out of our undulating bellies.

Women's fertility is no secret, but our fertile erotic imagination has been locked up as if by an iron chastity belt for too long. Shoot it off, shout it out—here's women's erotic language for you, shot right out of a cannon.

SUSIE BRIGHT
San Francisco,
June 1991

No Balance

These wheels were not right. Four tires, purchased, examined, and static-balanced only two short hours ago, were as lopsided as her ex's tits, and now it was too late to do anything about it. Shelley had picked up her mom and left civilization three hours ago, leaving a balmy day in San Francisco for a baking hot dirty day in the Sierra Nevada. The steering wheel shook like a vibrating drill.

"Hold up the map for me," she said to her mother. Twenty more miles to Grass Valley. Twenty more miles of her mom squeaking, "Oh, Shelley, it's so hot!" After thirty years of driving her own 1967 VW Bug all over the country, Mom had decided she couldn't use a stick shift anymore, didn't feel capable of driving at all. Wasn't that a nice surprise. Fine then; she'd sit tight in the passenger seat and make temperature reports every three minutes.

Shelley decided that in twenty more miles she was going to pull up to the first gas station she saw and call the tire man back in the city. She'd ask him what the hell he thought he was doing sending an innocent girl on a 200-mile mountain road trip with wobbly wheels.

She wondered how consumer-indignant she could act with such

a handsome tire man. *"Un jeune homme hyper-mignon."* How could someone that sexy not have a secret passion pit somewhere back behind the tire stacks? She saw herself posing against the yellow Cougar in the garage yard, watching him work. She could see the outline of his cock through his denim coveralls. She imagined pressing her bare belly against it, feeling the wetness seep through to her lips, and wondered if he could smell her.

Fifteen more miles. Her mom was talking about Mr. Harding, who was building his own bed-and-breakfast place, by himself, out of the old Wells Fargo bank building. "Such a masculine man," her mother insisted.

Shelley thought about the tire man again; he would make a beautiful girl if he wasn't already such a beautiful boy. He had excessively curly long hair, made for wrapping round her fingers. She let her hands slide down his smooth chest; he wrapped his arms around her like a vise.

His wet mouth searched for the hollow of her neck. She'd never felt so soft. He wanted to taste her. She didn't know if she could watch. She pulled his face into her pussy, rocking her long legs around his broad shoulders. Lick me. His steady tongue made her clit as hard as a berry. She panted. It was too hot. He was too hot. Her head was bursting and that awful ache opened up in her cunt like someone howling. She needed him inside her Right This Minute.

She switched hands on the steering wheel and wiped the sweat off her palm. Her nipples hurt. Five more miles. Would her mother notice hard nipples on such a hot sticky day? Shelley squinted at the junction ahead and saw the tire man bending her over at the waist across a set of steel-belted donuts. He rubbed himself up against her ass. The coveralls disappeared. His hard-on pressed her cheeks apart and her legs started to tremble. Oh please, Mr. Tire Man, please don't stop. His cock head slid into her. Jesus Christ.

"Shelley, what are you doing!" Her mom jolted forward and grabbed the dashboard.

"Sorry, sorry, I thought I was hitting the clutch."

Mr. Tire Man stirred inside her like a heavy spoon. He pulled out almost all the way and her cunt lips begged him back. Fuck me. She whimpered. He pushed in again, so deep, to the tip of her womb. She flinched. If he hurt her again like that she would scream. If he hurt her again like that she would come. She squeezed her legs together and he pushed into her ass. She cried out and pressed her clit hard against the rubber rims. He held her fast, moving in and out of her sugar walls. She crumbled and clutched at him in spasms.

She hit a bump in the road. It was Grass Valley. A Union 76 on the right.

"Honey, that phone booth looks out of order, are you sure you don't want to just keep going on to Mary's?" Her mom didn't like this gas station. Every time her mom smelled urine in a public place she thought something was out of order.

"No, Momma, just stay here for a second and try to run the air-conditioning."

She dialed the number she had on the business card wadded up in her pocket. "For a Good Time, Call Seaside Tire." Okay, Mr. Tire Man, these wheels are as loose as marbles and I want your cock between my lips right this second. She tasted his cum— so sweet—and kissed him hard on the mouth.

"Hi, this is the girl with the MR2, you saw me a couple of hours ago. . . . The wheels still aren't balanced. Isn't it a little dangerous to be driving like this?"

It was very, very dangerous to be driving with an aching pussy, hard nipples, soaking wet pants, and a front-wheel drive shaking as badly as her thighs.

Shelley yelled over to her mom. "He says, 'don't worry. . . .' He says to bring it back when we get home."

She hung up. "I've gotta get a Coke." She unglued her legs. She was going to stand outside this piss-smell gas station just a minute or two longer and cool off.

Winn Gilmore

Boca Chica

Waves slid up Amara's legs, gently licking, kissing, then swiftly pulling their succulent lips away from her crotch like the ceaseless tease of a "find them, fuck them, flee them" lover. Still beggar at an empty throne, Amara spread her legs, dug her ass deeper into the yielding sand and moaned, waiting for the next ephemeral kiss of the salty ocean. Yemaya lapped up her long—and now very dark—legs. Here on this nearly deserted beach in the Dominican Republic, Yemaya, goddess of ocean and life, was truly Boca Chica, the Girl's Mouth.

Amara sighed and crossed her arms beneath her head. Her hair, hot-combed only three days ago, had taken a vacation of its own: it had gone all the way home. Once again, it was a thick bush sucking up the demanding Caribbean sun and golden sand. She smiled, white teeth greeting the snow-white sun, imploring it to drop down into the gap between her two front teeth and rest its heat along her thick tongue. She'd savor it before letting it slip down between her salmon-pink tonsils. Finally, she'd swallow it and stick her satisfied tongue between the gap as the sun, still pulsating and radiating, slid warm and wet into her stomach. Her mouth watered. She wondered what her lover, Yasmin, was doing back in California.

* * *

"Baby, I can't come with you," Yasmin had whined on their last night together. Wrapping her juice-soaked thighs around Amara, Yasmin had whispered in her ear, "But I'll be waiting when you get back." She turned Amara over, sliding like a well-greased seal down the pole of Amara's back, inhaling the strong sex scent. She pulled back from her lover to behold Amara's quivering ass. She lifted her own fingers to her mouth and moistened them, then spread Amara's shuddering cheeks.

Her anus was like a tiny whirlpool on a heaving ocean, the deep brown ridges twirling inward, daring Yasmin to come closer, closer still, to spin ever down and into a place without time, to the place before the beginning. "Lover," Yasmin whispered into Amara's anus, squeezing a cheek in each hand, "I've got"—and her tongue slid between the crack she'd opened—"too many clients this week." She moaned, catching the tiniest trickle from Amara's anus before it dropped, blessed, onto her clit. "I can't pull myself away," she purred into her lover's damp hole. "We need the money."

Before Amara could protest that *she* would be paying for the vacation, Yasmin jammed her tongue between the buttocks tightened against her entry. Like a swimmer breaking the surface of cold waters and emerging in unexpected warmth, Yasmin's tongue burst free. The back of her tongue constricted as the front lunged into her lover. Probing, stretching out as her mouth watered into Amara's pussy, Yasmin sighed, "Girl, I'll wait for you." She stretched her long arms beneath Amara and squeezed one ripe breast in each hand. She pinched the nipples between her fingers and Amara moaned, her mind slipping past the sadness of the upcoming vacation without Yasmin. She was lost to all but the gathering waves roiling deep inside her.

Amara screamed as the first wave of cum shot from her over-burdened pussy onto her lover's face. She trembled as Yasmin's fingers, like a rock thrown across the water's surface, skipped over her clit, slip-slide, slip-slide, then sank into her heaving ocean. Her body convulsed and she bit her lip, clutching a pillow to her soaked chest. She called Yasmin's name, wishing her girl, and her girl's mouth, were with her on the beach called Boca Chica.

The memory splashed over Amara's sand-caked body like a wave, and she shuddered as she rolled belly-over onto the sand. "That woman's priorities are definitely off," she said to herself. "So what if she had a week jammed full of relaxers, haircuts, tints, and such shit. Cancel them, I say," Amara mumbled as she stood, pulling her bikini top over her hardened nipples.

A merengue band approached, lightning fast da-ta-ta as she ran into the ocean that was barely cooler than the air. The gitarras and guiros cascaded over her, chasing her into the shallow ocean's warm embrace.

Her arms shot out before her, parting the water like a lover's legs. Amara darted forth, gliding past the tiny school of black-and-yellow-striped fish. Then she floated. She propelled herself by fanning out her arms then pulling them back against her waist. Fingers opened; she spread and caressed her curvaceous thighs. She flipped her head to the left, inhaling a bit of sweet salt water as she sun glittered yellow and green against her goggles. Amara stretched out one graceful arm and flipped onto her back, offering her tight, black belly to the ocean's surface and the sun's kiss.

Squinting against the sun, Amara exhaled and slipped her left hand beneath her bikini top. She massaged her right nipple, gasping in water and air at her delectable touch. Yemaya lulled her, gently rocking her in her powerful arms.

She squeezed her eyes shut, imagining Yasmin's long, strong fingers rooting soapily through some client's locks, massaging the scalp as she murmured, "Just let your head go. I've got you, sugar." Amara could see the suds lapping up her arms, Yasmin's eyes closed and mouth slightly parted as her eyes rolled back deliciously in her head. She remembered the first time she, Amara, was beneath those supplicating hands, the fingers digging into her skull like a sea farmer shoveling her fingers into the wet, black earth at the ocean's shore to test its impregnability: could it yield sweet clams and luscious oysters this season?

Amara stroked her pussy lips, then squeezed them together

rhythmically with each rolling wave. She dipped her head back into her ocean-lover's lap, and stroked her clit. She shot the salty-sweet water from her mouth as she came, fingers working furiously as her black body lifted above the otherwise smooth surface of the water.

Red, green, and iridescent blue blasted across her closed lids. The strolling musicians' merengue bolted across the water and pounced upon her, and she thrashed from side to side, moaning deep in her throat. Amara went limp, arms and legs stretched over the water.

Exhausted, she swam languidly for shore.

Back on her stretch of sand, Amara lay facedown as yet another merengue washed over her still-throbbing body. Her pussy pulsated staccato from her fingers' and the ocean's gentle lapping. She ran her tongue over her wet, saline lips and sank her torso deeper into the hot sand.

"*¿Ostiones, señorita?*"

Amara was nearly dozing when the cracking, melodic voice broke through to her.

"*¿O quizás caracol? Son bastante frescas, se lo juro.*"

There was something familiar in the young boy's tone; something too knowing, too assuming. Amara tugged her revealing bathing trunks higher over her firm ass, then relaxed again.

"*Si, hombre,*" she said slowly, hoping to summon more of her halting Spanish. If only Yasmin were here, she thought angrily. Count on her not being here when I need her. Her Spanish is perfect. "*Umm, me gusto una docena ostiones, por favor.*"

Only when she heard the blunt-edged knife prying into the shell did Amara turn over. Lazily, she looked out to sea.

Finally, the knife slid through the small oyster's shell. It popped open with a satisfying *pthlop!* and Amara watched, enthralled, as a bit of its juice trailed over the young man's deep pink palm. Unhurriedly, he chuckled and lifted his hand majestically to his lips.

Amara's eyes followed the motion, and shielded her unaccustomed eyes against the glaring sun's brightness. Her eyes trailed the strong arm up, then stopped, puzzled, at his midriff. It wasn't a man after all, because the oyster-shucker was wearing a woman's one-piece spandex bathing suit beneath men's swim trunks. She's seen a suit like that before . . . in the apartment she'd shared with Yasmin the past four years. Too much cerveza, she thought, eyes sliding back to the ocean before her.

"Perhaps you would also try this tiny clam," the shucker asked in stammering English. Amara's gaze was arrested by the hand squeezing clear liquid from a tiny lemoncito onto the oyster, splayed like a raucous lover before her.

The shucker's hand delved into the battered bucket and pulled out, almost reluctantly, a small, white clam. Expertly this time, the knife found the creature's muscle, popped it open, and the shucker held it out to her.

Amara slid back onto the sand as the shucker moved the still-live clam closer, its muscle standing up like a tiny clit. Her eyes followed the gentle, strong curve of the arm up to the offerer's shoulder, and, astonished, Amara called out, "You bitch! How could you do this to me?"

The shucker crumpled to the ground beside her and flashed a brilliant smile to Amara. "My love, mi vida," she crooned, "did you really think I'd let you come here alone? Let your fine, black self come to some Caribbean island with a beach called The Girl's Mouth? Get serious!"

"Yasmin," Amara said, shaking her head and smiling, "give me that clam."

Aurora Light

Bus Stop

My bus pulled away from the bus stop just as I rounded the corner. "Darn," I muttered to myself. Well, at least there was a bench, and it was still warm in the September twilight. A man was sitting at the far end, his face hidden behind the *Wall Street Journal*. I sat at the opposite end and crossed my ankles primly.

People and cars passed occasionally. I checked the time on my watch. The next bus wasn't due for twenty minutes. I wasn't in any particular hurry, but I sighed, already bored.

The newspaper rustled from the other end of the bench. I looked casually at what I could see of its reader. The top of his head was just visible, the hair dark brown and wavy. His clothes were definitely Brooks Brothers: a glen plaid suit; charcoal gray with a subtle deep red pencil stripe, dark gray socks and cordovan wing tip shoes.

I looked away, checking the time once more. At least fifteen more minutes. My eyes were drawn again to the stranger on the bench. I wished he would put down his paper so I could see his face. "Don't be ridiculous," I told myself. "Why should I care what his face looks like?"

Legs crossed, his thighs looked muscular. He shifted his paper again, but didn't put it down. He seemed totally oblivious of my presence, which for some unaccountable reason bothered me. I wondered if he had seen me when I'd walked up and sat down on the bench. And if he had, did he find me attractive?

I took out my compact and looked critically at my reflection in the mirror. I saw naturally arched brows under dark hair, blue eyes flecked with green, a short straight nose, and full-lipped mouth. Then, feeling self-conscious, I hastily put the compact back in my purse.

I coughed softly, and the paper rattled but did not lower. I wasn't used to being ignored. I looked at the hands holding the newspaper. They were well cared for, rather large and deeply tanned. Large hands, large cock. Was that it? Or was it large feet, large cock? Was I thinking about cocks because I hadn't had any for a week?

I checked the time; ten more minutes. I wondered how old the mystery man was. There was no gray in his hair. I shifted restlessly, crossing my long legs and unobtrusively inching my skirt well above my knees. Suddenly, he lowered the paper and looked directly at me. The eyes that met mine were dark and unreadable in the dusk. It was not a handsome face, but rugged, with a sensuous mouth. For a melting moment I fantasized his mouth on mine, our tongues touching. He couldn't have been more than forty. For an intense instant I held my breath, then he turned the page of the paper, and his face disappeared behind it again. My breathing resumed, slightly faster than before.

How rude he was, I thought. He didn't even smile, but then neither had I. For that second I had felt riveted by his penetrating eyes. Penetrating. Why use that word to describe his look? As I said it to myself, I felt warmth between my crossed legs. I was definitely aroused. What was it about this silent, unfriendly man that turned me on?

It was rapidly getting dark and the streetlights had come on. I wondered how he was able to read in the gloom. Perhaps he had not been reading at all. Maybe he used the newspaper as an excuse to avoid talking to me. Or maybe he was thinking about me, wondering what I looked like under my red silk dress. My cunt twitched with that thought.

I allowed myself to imagine him aroused, his cock beautifully large and hard. The thought made me squirm on the bench and uncross my legs. There were fewer people walking past now, and practically no cars on the street. I decided to give in to one of my favorite pleasures: secretly masturbating in a public place. I shifted my large purse, putting it flat across my lap. I pressed my hand cautiously between my thighs. I barely suppressed a sigh.

I increased the pressure of my fingers, never taking my eyes from the newspaper. When the paper rustled I jerked my hand back, my face hot. I had an insane desire to laugh at my reckless behavior. Once more all was silent at the other end of the bench. I squeezed my thighs together. An almost audible "oh!" escaped my lips.

I inched the full skirt of my dress up, keeping my hand under my purse. I slid a finger under the band of my bikini pants, imagining the stranger's cock rubbing over my slippery cunt, caressing my swollen clitoris, finding its way into my pink pussy. I clamped my lips tightly to stifle a groan.

My entire hand was now in my panties, two fingers deep inside my dripping cunt. I stretched my legs out and leaned back on the bench. Two men were walking down the block on the other side of the street. I pictured their cocks, one long, the other short and thick. But it was still the man behind the paper that I wanted to see, feel, suck, and fuck, his cock ramming in, pulling out, in, out. My fingers quickened their thrusting. Just one more minute and I would come. As my orgasm crept up my shaking legs I chanted silently, "Fuck, fuck, fuck!" I closed my eyes at the intensity of my climax.

When I opened my eyes I saw my bus less than half a block away. The object of my fantasy was looking at me, a slight smile curling the corners of his lips. I felt my face flush. I jumped up from the bench as the bus stopped and opened its door, letting me escape into its anonymous depth. I paid my fare with trembling fingers and took a seat next to the window. The bus started up and I looked out to see my inspiration, raising his hand good-bye.

Carol A. Queen

At Doctor d'Amour's Party

Of course I had seen you before at other parties: your wiry intensity, your black cat's grace. I had seen the way you moved through the crowds and it seemed to me you lived in a realm of sexual intelligence. I had felt your hands on me before, too briefly, and so I was pleased that, like me, you arrived early at Doctor d'Amour's party; that I would have a chance to know you without the distractions of a party in full swing, a dozen hands on me, two dozen pairs of eyes. I was pleased to finally know your name. I knew nothing more about you, but if Doctor d'Amour thought you were smart and sexy (and he does), that was enough for me.

We could never have talked about art at a big party. We would probably not have talked about sex either, even though sex was our reason for attending those parties: to watch it, to learn more about it, to have it. Doctor d'Amour's party was no different, but we were early, so there the three of us sat talking about sex and art all afternoon, as easily as if this were a coffee date. We shared a joint, making our talk thoughtful and hazily intimate.

When it neared the time for other guests to arrive we decided to get into our party costumes. I changed in another room so I could make an entrance. I come to these parties prepared to give it all up, to become a sacred harlot, a temple priestess, and the one thing I like to keep to myself is the transformation. It changes my sense of the party space and my sense of purpose when I return garbed in my chosen outfit. The room, the minutes passing, all of us are then ritualized. While I was gone, Aphrodite passed into me.

So I returned, dressed in black leather boots with pointed toes; black net stockings held by garters to leave my thighs, creamy, naked, exposed above them; black silk brassiere and french-cut panties, already trying to work themselves like a G-string between the peach-halves of my ass; and a black leather collar. A peep-show Venus, a slut of the sacred.

You and Doctor d'Amour were next to leave street-clad, then emerge transformed. The Doctor returned as an erotic clown, not an unusual persona for him. In your costume you might have been my consort. Tight black pants of shiny fabric clung to your body like a second skin. That was all: delicate pale feet below, smooth-skinned torso above, lean and muscled, nipples little rosettes that anyone would want to put a tongue to. Face all intelligence and dignity, so sexy. I noticed everything about you as if for the first time. You too were beginning your change, your habitation of ritual space, priest of love.

If we let it, the erotic unfolds for us gradually, like the petals of a flower opening to the touch of the sun. Well, here was another layer of that process. We had begun as strangers, our view of each other internal, subjective; the act of looking almost masturbatory until it was time to reach and touch. Then the diffused erotic in an afternoon of conversation. Now black cloth clung tightly to places we began to want our hands to go; I was dressed for you, and you for me. Noticing gathered purpose, as your black Lycra displayed your cock to me, my black silk invited you to run your fingertips along the length of my vulva.

The doorbell began to ring at last: other guests arriving at Doctor d'Amour's party. A half dozen of us joined in a circular embrace to welcome each other, and with that little ritual the party truly began. You and I were left in the center of the room in one anothers' arms, all that was left of the circle. We swayed, and the unfamiliarity of our bodies touching began to ebb into the realm of the not-remembered.

Body-knowledge established, touch gave way to feline rubbing. We were sex-cats retreating into another world, alone there though guests continued to arrive and the party surrounded us, a parallel universe to which neither of us gave much attention. We were too absorbed in the rising tide of pleasure, of desire. How well we fit together, leg between legs, hands on each other's asses, pulling our hips tight, your cock hard against me, my clit begging for its pressure. So we danced, and before long we began to talk to each other; ohhh, mmmmmmmh, low purrings and throaty moans. When at last we kissed, our hands full of each other's hair, the last vestige of our being strangers fell away and it seemed we knew each other profoundly, bodies already electric before our mouths met.

I was vibrating with our sexual energy, gasping, trembling, clinging to you. I was too aroused to be responsible for my sense of balance, so I slid us both to the floor. We drank the sweat from each other's bodies, and I unhooked my brassiere so the silken cups would be no impediment to your lips. The feel of your mouth on my nipples made me catch my breath: it was like your tongue was already licking my pussy up and down, teasing me into heat. The pressure of your knee, then your thigh, then your cock on my clit made it sing as we rolled and writhed, as I thrust into you as if we were fucking. My hands grasping your ass felt the muscles go tight as you worked against me. Those who scoff at frottage have never ridden a sexual swell the way we did that day, hovering on the curl of energy like surfers on a sea. You orgasmed like a waverider tumbling in to shore. I felt it in my cunt, your orgasm, sharing the energy as if we were old lovers.

We rolled on the floor like kittens, practically mewing from pleasure. Other party guests who lay near us began to feel their own tides. Our eyes met, moving us in an instant from infant's delight to deep, wordless speech. Only then did wonder intrude. Who are we, whom have we become, to meet and mingle this way? And the moment our arms tightened around each other the sexual surge had us again. I moved into you, felt your response, welcomed it with, "Ohhhh, yes," and kept murmuring "yes, yes" in your ear as your arms went tighter. As you lowered your head and your teeth began grazing my nipples, your hand also moved south, cupping my vulva and pressing tight. I knew you could feel its silk-clad wetness, the labial cleavage, the erect and humming clit. I rocked my hips forward for the pleasure of the feeling, my cunt in your hand. Then you began a rhythmic tugging on the silk panties, bringing the fabric up tight between my lips, pulling harder and harder. Your mouth and free hand teased my nipples, and I felt my body curling into the arc of a brewing orgasm.

But my cunt ached, empty. I wanted you to fill me and I gasped: "Oh, fuck me, please!" Your fingers slid easily in. I was the center of the universe then, and my cunt the epicenter, my conscious self near extinguished to the body's pleasure. I rode it as long as I could, trusting you to take me closer and still closer, until I couldn't bear the wait and reached for my clit, a few fast hard circles sending me over the cliff's edge, coming, riding waves in the air. And when we didn't slow our rhythm, my hand on my clit and yours deep inside me, the ebbing of one climax led to the first surges of the next.

On and on. Your fingers almost leaving me, then sinking deeply in. Full circle of energy from hand to cunt, from my eyes to yours, so absorbing that for some time I forgot that we were with others in a room, forgot the day and the year and every extraneous thing. I knew only you and the sexual free-float, my store of knowledge pulsing cellularly, nerve-endings lit like neon, orgasms whirling like high, dispersing winds through my consciousness.

When my awareness reemerged it was into my nipples, which were glowing like points of fire. You were pulling on them, the sensation of such intensity that it bordered on pain: you took me to another erotic level, testing how far I'd stay with you. I was amazed that you would test me then and I felt the wonder more in my cunt than in my mind. How far into the stratosphere was it possible to follow you? In a surge of desire I tasted your power and my own remarkable power to respond. And let it all be consumed by the physical fire, the writhing and response in which even you were all but gone and I became the breath that dwells within intensity. Going high and higher, breathing fast and faster, until you let go and released me into body and then mind again: it was a wholly different kind of orgasm. I wondered whether my nipples burned you where they touched your chest as our bodies were once again pressed tightly together.

I felt you for days.

More sex, more play as we came down from those heights. But we'd peaked, and it was finally time to join the revelry, sip some wine, see who else was scattered around Doctor d'Amour's apartment like Cupid's pick-up sticks. One woman was tying her partner up, another strapping on a dildo, someone else was jacking off, still another watching. The Doctor himself was kissing a man to whom he was bound at wrist and ankle. "Well!" said someone, welcoming us back. "Are you finally going to stop playing Monopoly?"

I sat on the floor at your feet, leaning back into the angle of your open legs, my neck resting on your half-hard cock which stirred sometimes like a sleepy animal. The Doctor's party was a big erotic experiment it seemed; everyone trying something or someone new. Costumes were half on and half off, and laughs, squeals, and sighs filled the room. An unusual place to spend afterglow perhaps, but ours had not been a usual connection. Your hands stayed on me. Tendrils of energy licked from you to me, me to you. The bound man looked as big as Gulliver spread-eagled on the floor, and we watched his companion suck his cock. A pair of people fucking found their way into my lap, his head on my thigh, she atop him riding the rhythm, and still I was as aware of your presence behind me as I was of them. When I reached to cup her breasts your hands covered mine, and I answered your pressure on my nipples by squeezing hers, felt her heart beating in my hand.

The scene shifted again and I watched as you began to play with Doctor d'Amour's cock, a very responsive toy. The Doctor's hands skimmed your body and he growled, a low flute-song of pleasure from your fingering. Your expression of rapt concentration, your fine hands on his hard, pretty cock pleased me utterly. For a minute I wanted all the rest of the party to vanish, all its delights and distractions, so you and the Doctor could absorb yourselves with each other and I with both of you. But too soon the ebb and flow of the party separated you. I wandered into the kitchen, to a table filled with fruit and flowers and luscious melting Brie. I was beginning to think about leaving, and already dreaming about seeing you again.

Doctor d'Amour's party wound down gracefully as we all chatted, licked Brie off our fingers, and shared a big bottle of eau minerale. Gulliver was untied; someone had changed back into street clothes, and by ones and twos everyone joined us around the table. For the first time all evening I glanced at the clock; it was nearing eleven.

You followed me out of the room when I left to change. Words seemed a little banal now, after all we had said wordlessly: "That was so wonderful!"—"Yes, I'm so glad we had a chance to connect."—"Can I get your phone number?"—"Of course." But our eyes were still full of shared heat, our embrace warm and intimate. As I shed my damp black silk and lace stockings, as I transformed myself back into an imposter of the ordinary ready to step out into the night streets in a guise that would draw no attention, I still held your gaze. I knew we would come together again soon, hot to explore this sweet lust that cut right to the heart of things.

"And we don't even know one another yet," you murmured. I shook my head, held you in tight farewell, felt the pulse of our bodies say, *Oh, sex-cat, but when we do . . .*

Magenta Michaels

Taking Him on a Sunday Afternoon

I'm lying on the Sunday couch, dozing between snatches of the television's drone, the newspaper spread around me. My lover crosses my line of half-mast vision to get to the *TV Guide*, naked except for the white Jockeys. My eyes focus on his thighs and crotch, and, not really interested in sex at all, I murmur to him from a half-sleep, "Bring that up here and put it in my face." Startled and smiling, he does. He straddles my head, one foot on the floor, one knee beside my ear, supporting his weight on the arm of the sofa.

I arch up, nuzzling my face into the dampness of the white cotton, snuffling him, inhaling him deeply, smelling both his man-scent and the cleanliness of his shorts. I mouth his hardening front, breathing on it, gumming it with lips drawn tight over teeth. I nip the insides of his thighs, biting hard enough to make him groan, and lap at the skin to disperse the pain.

I stretch the elastic waistband far down, freeing him. I circle his tip with a pointed tongue, stabbing at it, bouncing it, flicking at its underside, and finally drawing its heaviness into my mouth. He is salty, smelling of soap, and I rotate my head as I press my hand hard against his buttocks, forcing him against the back of my throat. He groans low, sucking in air through clenched teeth.

18

I slip my hands inside the shorts and trace circles on his muscular cheeks, letting my thumb dip down to the space between his balls and buttocks, then sliding a finger up to explore the puckered mouth of his bum. He clamps up to prevent me from rubbing here, but aggression has risen in me and I press on, massaging a moistened finger at the entrance. It's slick there, and I can imagine the smell, which excites me; I know that he's concerned about the smell, too—how I'll find him—and this excites me more.

The thought pops into my mind that if I had a dick, right now if I had a dick, I would wear him out. I would stay in that puckered, slippery, sex-smelling ass as often as I could. I would dominate him, kneeling over him to rub my pubic curls against his lips as I wanted to, and not when he wanted to taste or smell me. I would be the aggressor, and he could not ask sex of me: only I would be allowed to initiate. And when I did, it would be with aching lust and probing fingers and bursting genitals. I would fuck him from behind, his cock gripped in my fist—a gleaming trophy peeking out between my lacquered fingertips—the completion of his pleasure at my bidding alone. I would ride him, standing in a half crouch, my dick slipping in and out wetly, making that squishing noise. And when I was about to come, I would jerk him very fast, his eyes closed, throat exposed, head back against me, allowing me to do with him as I chose. And then I would come, violently, with cramping muscles and teeth bared and curses under my breath, all the while jerking him off, and he would spatter his seed, shooting out a foot from his body.

I would roll the head of his cock gently between my fingers, rubbing his cum into his balls, weighing them in my hand, my own dick still curved hard within him. And then I would let him go. My dick would dissolve, my aggression would fade, and I would become feminine and docile again. And only he and I would know who we were, who we had been, in the privacy of our room.

Lisa Palac

Love Lies

The sheets soaked in sweat and liquid sex, heavy summer hung like a velvet curtain around the city. They were exhausted. At 11:32 P.M., the mercury was stuck at 82 degrees. Her hair separated into tiny strands on her forehead, a matted clump in the back: a screwball, a friend once called it. She brought her hands to her face, loving the way her fingers smelled covered in fuck. It was reckless incense that opened the memory box.

Sometimes she liked to bury her face in his armpit and breathe him in.

"Smell good?" Alex asked, amused at her weird habit.

"Mmmm . . . I love it."

It smelled like potato chips eaten on the beach.

Certain smells triggered instant Polaroid memories for Emily. Anyone with bad breath made her think of Joseph Kazinski in third grade. He was always breathing on her and exposing bits of salami and Wonder bread stuck in his orthodontic jungle. He never brushed his teeth after he got braces.

Then there was the death smell. People look out for the face of death but it's really the smell that gets to you. When Emily was a kid, Mrs. Lindenhart the landlady had been dead upstairs for a week and nobody knew. A horrible odor had wafted down into their apartment and her mother had cleaned out every closet looking for dead mice. This city smelled of dead things. There were probably thousands of lifeless old ladies trapped with hundreds of cats in sixth-floor walk-ups.

Maybe she had been a dog in a past life, or an aardvark or just watched too many *Planet of the Apes* movies where Roddy McDowell constantly flexes his nostrils, but her olfactory factory suffered from oversensitivity. This sixth sense of hypersniff was a real pain in the ass sometimes. She had to sniff everything before she tasted it, including her lovers.

Pheromones made The Chemistry. Sometimes the mix was a dud. Other times it was like drinking orange juice after brushing your teeth. Incongruous chemical reaction. But the intrinsic odor offenders were the worst. These types could take a shower and still smell like an alley in Chinatown. The only way to discover this, however, was to be in an intimate situation. At that point, escape routes are limited.

Emily got into a mess like that with an eighteen-year-old disaster from Detroit who immortalized William Burroughs and had tattooed a flaming cross in the middle of his chest. Posing fashionably as one of the discontented, he asked Emily to buy him a beer.

"What did you spend your fortune on? Performance rights for *Drugstore Cowboy?*" Emily said with a smirk.

But the bar was crowded and the idea of almost jailbait was extremely appealing. Finally, in a deliberately careless way, she let him put his tongue in her mouth as they walked through the door of her place.

His skin was white and smooth, except for the raised pink scar that ran around the edges of his torched crucifix. Immediately, Emily scanned her brain for the best consummate icon adoration position. He could be up on his arms fucking her and the cross would dive right into her eyes, then pull back again with each of his thrusts, like a sacrilegious yo-yo. Maybe she should straddle the symbol, rub her clit against the fleshy imperfection and revel in the vision of divine tattoo fornication. No! Wait! He could be reciting the Act of Contrition while she whipped his ass with a giant rosary! She suppressed her laugh and passed it off as a cough.

None of her plans were put into action because the tattoo disappeared over the edge of the bed and only his face was visible between her legs. Ah, those sweet young lips, so eager to please, so desperate to find the right rhythm. Kneeling on the hardwood floor wasn't too comfortable and he tried to change his position a few times, but she took a fistful of his hair and made him stay like a bad dog. She wasn't about to sacrifice her upcoming orgasm for a game of Twister.

When she was satisfied, he sprawled out next to her and reached for her hand, encouraging her to perform. Suddenly she realized that the foul smell she thought was last week's eggs over easy still sitting in her kitchen sink was, in fact, the throbbing teenager who now lay beside her. All those Marlboros must have covered up this nasty surprise when she kissed him in the bar.

The rude fragrance became so overpowering she could barely concentrate on reciprocating the pleasure. He was waiting for his turn. Emily could feel him squirming around, trying to bring her lips closer to his, rubbing her hand over his crotch, moaning and whispering the revolting phrase, "C'mon, baby."

Possible excuses: lack of expertise, peniphobia, fatigue, insanity.

"I don't feel too well," she said, "I think I had too much to drink. Let me rest for a second."

A second became twenty minutes. She woke up again when he slammed the door on his way out.

Then there was Alex. With Alex, it was a salty wave. Emily tugged at the little hairs under his arm with her teeth.

"Ouch! Don't bite me there!"

"I'm not biting, I'm just playing."

"Well, don't play like that."

"I'm just doing it so I can kiss it, like this, after it hurts."

Alex was thin with barely brown skin and hair that was feeding itself into dreadlocks. She followed the orange tip of his cigarette as it passed back and forth through the full moonlight, to the ashtray balanced on his chest. She'd never acquired the habit, but she loved watching others suck and blow.

"Where's the fan?" he asked. "I'll put it in the window."

"On the floor. By my dresser."

Alex got up to move the fan and she watched the shape of his body stand, stretch, bend over. She loved the curve of his ass, especially just where the cheeks began to divide. She slunk to the edge of the bed and put her tongue on that favorite spot. His hips swung forward involuntarily, almost hurling the fan down four stories.

"This city is so fucking hot, you turn on the fan and it feels like a hair dryer," he said.

She started licking the cheeks of his ass, spreading them, trying to get her tongue right on his asshole. He spread his legs for her.

"What do you say, huh?" she said, playing tough.

"Lick my ass . . . my asshole."

It was so hard for him to say the word "asshole," aside from calling somebody an asshole. But when she found out he was crazy about getting licked "down there," she demanded he voice his request. Every time. The word was a Pavlovian bell that sent shock waves into her cunt.

He bent over completely, so she could see her fingers fucking his ass. The visual was unparalleled; his submission so rare.

She made him stroke his own cock.

"Imagine it's two women fucking you," she said.

The sexual repetition was endlessly fascinating. The way he held his breath and let it out in gasps as he got closer to coming. She wanted to crawl inside his mind and watch the fantasy loops.

The artificial breeze blew droplets of sweet salty juice mixed with sticky dark air all over the place. It was like sand from the Sandman, and the darkness of dreams closed in.

Too bright sunlight hurt her eyes, creating a watery mess in the middle of an urban drought. Emily hated wearing sunglasses because they slid down her nose and gave her tiny pimples on her cheeks, but she liked the disguise. The cleats on her cowboy boots clicked against the pavement and each click brought her closer to the place where she spent 1,920 hours a year.

Every morning she bought a newspaper from Murray's Cafe. The neon sign once read TRY MURRAY'S COCKTAILS! but some of

the letters had burned out and now it read TRY MURRAY'S COCK.
The best part about Murray's was the big glass case under the
cash register filled with all sorts of ancient candy like Black Jack
gum, Mary Janes, and those wax pop bottles with colored goo
inside. Murray was a million years old, but he was always fresh
enough to comment on Emily's outfit.

"You look nice today," he wheezed. Emily was wearing Hom-
age to June Cleaver: a sleeveless yellow-and-white-striped cotton
button-up with a Peter Pan collar and a full skirt cut to half its
original length. Her red hair looked like a palm tree sprouting
from the top of her head, and thick strands of fake gold and
rhinestones dangled from her earlobes.

"Thanks, Murray," she replied. "Hey, when are you gonna get
your sign fixed?"

"As soon as somebody takes me up on the offer!" He started to
laugh, then broke into a raspy coughing fit. She could hear him
hawking the phlegm out of his lungs as she waved good-bye. The
sound made her sick. What happens to your sex life when your
body starts to fall apart and taking a healthy crap is the high
point of your day?

Cool air blasted out when the doors of the bus flew open.
Emily sat in the back on the long, horizontal stretch of blue
vinyl. Nobody could see her eyes wander behind her black lenses,
surveying the crowd. Next to her was a young blonde wearing a
beige Evan Picone suit, textured hose and silly tennis shoes. On
her lap was a leather briefcase, carrying, oh most definitely, her
schedule for "doing lunch" and *People* magazine. Emily's pro-
tected eyes rolled. Okay, give her a break. Maybe she reads By-
ron and gets turned on by the models in the Victoria's Secret
catalog. Careful clods jammed the aisle and through their polite
distances she glimpsed the other side. Fatso with a bad complex-
ion and buck teeth, Baldy with a vacant stare. God, was she a
bitch this morning!

Emily opened the paper to Jeanne Dixon, hoping for some
insight into her vile Scorpio mood, when a stifling scent floated
past. It was perfumy and sweet, kind of like the aerosol Glade
in floral scent that infiltrated every American bathroom in the
seventies. Spraying it was a dead giveaway that a horrendous

turd had just been dropped. It never actually got rid of the smell,
it simply transformed it into a fragrant Rosepoo. Where did the
term "poo" come from anyway? And why did it get tacked on
to "sham" to create something you wash your hair with? Shampoo . . . shampoo, the word lolled around Emily's conscious like
a psychotic's mantra. After days of persistent pleading, Emily's
mother finally took her to see *Shampoo* and they left after the
first five minutes. It began with Warren Beatty fucking someone.
It was a bad thing to watch people fucking. Yet everyone on the
bus existed because of people fucking.

Emily looked around for the stinkbomb and zeroed in on an
older woman with a jet black hair-sprayed do and bright orange
lipstick that went far beyond the natural outline of her lips. Perspiration mixed with powder as she patted her damp face with
a hanky. She was wearing a sleeveless dress patterned with darts
that accentuated her huge breasts. Wrinkled skin hung from her
heavy arms. Both of her hands clutched a shiny lime-green vinyl
purse that matched her sandals. With a chunky heel and wide
straps fastened too tightly by a green daisy buckle, the shoes
caused her feet to swell. Her thick toenails were painted frosted
pink.

Emily closed her eyes and tried to picture what this woman
looked like when she had an orgasm. She saw the pink toenails
go up in the air while a tongue lapped and slurped all around
between her legs. Her soft, flabby belly jiggled in excitement and
she begged under her breath for her old man to put his calloused
hands on her tits. Her fingernails dug in to the chenille bedspread
as she squealed, "Oooh, yes, oooohhhh yes," softly at first then
louder and . . .

"Oooooowee! Fuckin' hot today!" The sudden intrusion made
everyone look up.

His belch echoed loud and drunk and Emily could see the yellow stains of perspiration on his grimy white T-shirt as he gripped
the bar above her head. His teeth were gray and there was dirt
caked in every crevice of his rancid skin. This polluted menace
set off everyone's internal fear siren. Emily folded the paper and
slipped out of her seat, just in time to avoid the string of drool
from the drunk's mouth about to land on her thigh. Across the

aisle, the lime sandals shifted uneasily and the woman sighed disgustedly. Yet the thing that may have truly alarmed her went completely unnoticed.

Another stagnant day became a lifeless night. The air turned to Jell-O. Everywhere, everything moved slowly, submerged in the humidity. Beastly hot. Hot as hell.

Emily lounged on the couch in her bra, sucking on ice cubes, then spitting them back into her glass of iced tea. The tenacious heat made her fucking irritable. All day long, everyone bitched and fought and spat and you could feel the pressure build in the cooker. Millions of people swarming around like voracious ants, all cutting each other's throats. Alex was smoking and the smell was suffocating. The ashes: he wasn't tidy about his ashes and she felt like she was being buried under them. Every pore was gasping for air.

Alex sat in the window, watching the action on the street, looking for the breeze of salvation. Alex in his Ziggy Marley T-shirt.

Ziggy, she thought. Ziggy Stardust. Ziggy the Elephant at the Brookfield Zoo who killed his trainer and had a broken tusk. Ziggy the nauseating cartoon. Ziggy, Iggy, Twiggy. Whatever happened to Twiggy?

"Come sit with me," Alex said. He broke the train.

"I can't move."

Alex walked over, peeled her off the plastic couch and led her to the window. She set the iced tea down on the window ledge. He started stroking her hair and she moved her head away.

"It's too hot," she whined. But he persisted. He reached over to kiss her, but she pushed off the advance. He reached for the glass and the ice cubes clinked together when he swallowed. Emily resisted another kiss, but he grabbed her head and made her open her mouth when the cold fluid went running down her neck.

"I'll chill your ass, you little fuck."

He pulled down one cup of her bra. His cold lips circled her nipples and his teeth came down hard. She tried to push him away but he wedged her against the frame of the window.

His fingers chased the cubes around the glass and finally pulled two out. He ran the ice over her tits, on the outside of her bra, then stuck one in each cup. Then he squeezed her tits, pressing the frozen bits against her precious points. She gasped and swore while he held both of her wrists in one of his hands.

His free hand fished out another ice cube, this time sending the glass crashing to the floor. He slowly ran the cube up along the inside of her thigh, teasing her pink. His words were sharp whispers without punctuation.

"Spread your legs baby spread those legs and beg me to cool you off."

She was silent.

"Beg me beg me you whore."

He pulled her down and lay her over the windowsill like a seesaw; half her body dangling out, her feet barely touching the floor inside. Emily was dizzy from the height and her breath was ragged. Thick night steam poured into her head like cement and rivulets of melted ice mixed with her sweat and streamed up her neck, flooding her eyes. The acrid scent of rotting garbage burned her nostrils. Somewhere a radio blared the Commodores' "Brickhouse" and someone was pounding metal against metal, dull clinks that chimed with the dirty talk spilling off her lover's lips.

This lover is the one who lets her bad girl dreams rip. He's got a twelve-inch dick and an eternal erection. He is the whore's only Daddy. He fills every nasty hole you can think of and he is the only thing you can fuck in Hell.

His cock is ice cold and as thick as a baseball bat. Her cunt swallows it all. She wants to pull her legs together but he holds them apart. His tongue is long, so long it's like a whip that darts out and lashes her nipples with an arctic sting. His eyes are gleaming white and bloodshot as he pumps his frosty pole into her, keeping in sync with the pounding drone.

"That's a good bitch." His voice is distant thunder. She writhes and smiles and gets ready to be his sacrifice. His cum is a blast from a flamethrower.

She screams and shakes. She licks the fire and sticks her tongue out for more. Her body explodes then settles down like volcanic ash. The heat slowly subsides, leaving watery streaks down her legs. And Alex slowly and gently draws all five fingers out of her cunt.

The floor felt cool against Emily's feverish skin. Alex stroked the small of her back, where the ledge had left its mark.

"I hope the neighbors don't freak out when they hear you scream like that," he said laughing. "It sounds like you're possessed!"

"I was," she murmured.

But he would never know the Devil had a frozen dick.

Roberta Stone

The Journal

P-town without a partner. I look out at the bay through the window of the dark apartment. I have spent so many summers here that they all somehow blur into one another. Two weeks with Marilyn at the Beach Grass, a wild weekend with Jane at the Ship's Mast, many seasons with many lovers at the Light-house. One summer, when I had finally booked early enough to get back to the red room at Island House with Chris, the two male innkeepers ran beaming up to me with their file box. "Why, Joan and Chris, welcome back! We've been holding onto this for you since 1979." With that, they proffered a thin silver bracelet lost in the throes of a wicked night involving candles and bed-posts. I had to explain to Chris II about Chris I.

Now I am here alone. Not quite alone, I'm sharing the flat with a friend. Both of us without lovers, comfortable together in the way that friends can be; no arguments about dinner, danc-ing, or the beach. Comfortable to go our separate ways. Vicki is leafing through the P-town *Advocate* looking for who is playing where, which spots are hot, the usual stuff.

"I think I'll bike down to the Express for a capuccino. Want to come?" asks Vicki.

"Now? On a Sunday morning?" I groan.

"Sure. The Unitarians will just be getting out of church. They've got that great dyke minister there. Best cruising spot in town."

"You go," I say. "I'll cruise the Sunday *Times.*"

Vicki throws on a shapeless lavender top and a pair of gym shorts and leaves the apartment. Vicki looks great in shapeless clothes, long and languid. The same styles always make me look . . . shapeless.

After an hour of unrewarding reading my mind begins to wander to the life outside. I wish I had the energy to cruise. I can just picture what I'd be doing if I were a gay man. I pull out my journal and start to write . . .

Peter left the standing-room-only crowd feeling healthy, happy and hot. The Reverend Kate Crandall-Howard had just given another of her famous sermons, "Community To- getherness and Orgasmic Response." Peter joined a group of regulars on the steps outside of church. He disdained the tourists who packed the church during the summer months, wide-eyed lesbians, creaming their pants for a look at the Reverend Kate.

"I loved your story in the Advocate, *Peter," said Helen, a regular summer habitué.*

"Why, thank you, Helen, though most people wouldn't agree that hairiness is an indicator of gay political radical- ism."

"No, no," said Helen. "I mean the P-town Advocate. *The one about zoning in the West End and the prohibition of chintz curtains."*

Peter eyed the crowd as they chatted up the local news. In fact, all of them were skilled in this game of rhetoric and dish while simultaneously cruising the scene. Peter caught the eye of a tall, handsome man who was leaving the church. His hair was almost jet black, as were his thick beard and eyebrows. Peter quickly assessed the coloring, looking from eyebrows to beard. "A natural," he thought. As his eyes moved down the man's body, Peter could see a black tuft pushing its way out of the man's open collar. Further down, black fuzz trailed out of his sleeve around a black leather wristband. Peter quickly looked away. Although an outspo-

ken gay politico, *he had an innate shyness that most people
did not notice.*

"Nice sermon."

*Peter looked up, meeting the eyes of the man with the
black beard. "Yes," he said. "I particularly identified with
the part about 'self-love equals safe love.' "*

"Tea Dance at 5:00," said the man. "I'll be there."

*Peter turned back to the conversation on the church steps.
More talk about the abysmal crowds, the trash problem at
Herring Cove, and who was shtupping whom. "What will
I wear?" thought Peter.*

Vicki glides into the room.

"How was it?" I ask.

"The coffee was great but the cruising sucked. Writing in your
journal? My journal has turned into a goddamn novel since I
broke up with Melanie."

"It's not quite a journal. More like a fantasy."

"About sex?" Vicki grins.

"Sort of. But from a gay man's point of view. After all, it
couldn't be as boring as the last five months of my life."

"Or mine," Vicki agrees as she lies down on the couch.

"Everyone's here," she says. "Rita and Linda are at the Light-
house. Rita was Fed Ex-ing memos to D.C. from the Express.
John and Bill are at the Seaside. John was cruising every boy in
leather on the street and Bill was carrying a telephone in his
backpack."

"In his backpack?" I repeat, astounded.

"He says the Gay Center is battling the city over water problems and he has to be in constant contact."

"I hope my apartment floods while I'm here," I sigh.

"And I get fired from my job and never have to go back," says
Vicki, finishing the thought. We laugh easily.

"Who else did you see?"

"Marina, Jill and Debby are all in town—"

"Oy," I groan.

"Marina and Jill are staying with Bill and John. And John says
he can't get any sleep, what with the fighting. Debby's been

prowling around but she's not allowed to call so Marina runs out to use the phone every now and then. Marina and Debby can see each other every other day but not on weekends. Jill's—"

"Stop, stop," I plead. "Is anyone having a relaxing vacation?"

"Jessica is in from New York. She wants us to come to the bar with her tonight. Girl's Leather Night. It's a fund-raiser for the Women's Health Network."

"Great," I respond. "I brought my leather jacket. Did you?"

"I don't think mine qualifies. It's brown."

"Well, I think it looks great on you. The girls will be at your feet."

I pick up my pad again and bring it and a beach towel down to the garden. I start to write . . .

Peter spent the rest of the day in quiet pursuits: reading, "desk work," as he liked to call it, and long, rambling telephone conversations with a few intimate friends in L.A., New York, New Zealand, San Francisco, Fire Island, Washington, D.C., and Paramus, New Jersey. At 4 o'clock he went up to his room to pick out his wardrobe for the evening. He stood before the open closet thinking, "A body shirt would be very becoming." He imagined the effect of his furry shoulders and back. "Too benign," he decided. "I haven't worn my state trooper's uniform in a long time," he thought, eyeing the starched brown shirt wistfully. "But hats are definitely too queeny at Tea." Then he remembered the leather waistband on the tall, dark stranger. "Yes," he thought. "I'll call his bluff." It was going to be a cool night anyway.

Peter emptied his closet of all the leather that he owned, and placed the items ritualistically across the bed. There were the leather chaps, the leather briefs, the leather body harness, the leather collar, the leather hat, the leather vest, the leather arm bands, the leather jacket, the leather cock ring, and finally, at the foot of the bed, the leather boots. So much black leather was there that Peter had to open the shades, for the room had suddenly darkened. "What to wear," he pondered. This was not L.A. where you could walk into a bar in full regalia and be relatively unnoticed. Besides, if he were to wear everything, he would weigh an extra fifty pounds, and he was already struggling at the gym to lose the five extra he had gained this summer at Franco's.

Peter donned a pair of old blue jeans as a base. "This is P-town," he thought, and quickly slipped on the black cock ring. He buttoned his fly but left the third button undone. He then zipped into his black leather chaps, carefully arranging his basket in a most fetching way. Next, the vest, showing his hairy torso and pecs to their full advantage. The harness was too much, he decided. "One shouldn't overdress at a summer resort." Besides, if they came back to his place it would be at hand. Peter discarded the arm bands, but put on both wristbands. The cap went back in the closet as well; his brown curls were at their peak. Peter finished the ensemble with the engineer's boots he had bought at the yard sale of a retired Hell's Angel in L.A. They were a steal and would last forever. Who knew where they had already been? He quickly threw the rest of the things back into the closet, lingering over the collar. "A bare neck is so sexy in summer," he thought, and the collar followed, tossed with abandon.

As he stood before the mirror, Peter was taken with the image before him. His cock started to come alive and he could feel the cock ring cradling his semi-hard, cut hunk of meat. He got the same feeling when he stood before the mirror prepared for a fund-raiser, dressed in a well-cut tuxedo. He was ready.

"I'm ready," shouts Vicki.

"You look great," I say as Vicki ambles out into the living room. She is wearing her brown leather jacket over a black silk shirt and pants. Vicki bends down to fix her laces and I focus on the silk folds that drape her ass and thighs. God, I never noticed what a great ass she has. I'm dressed in black with my black leather jacket. It goes well with my streaked hair. As I look at myself in the mirror, shaking my hair into place, I notice Vicki behind me staring at my back. What a funny look she has. Is it confusion? Sadness? Longing!

I zip around without looking at her. "Let's go, sweets. We'll make an entrance."

Vicki and I walk into the bar together. Surveying the room we start getting into the mood of leather and lust. Women are all over the place in varying states of dress and attitude.

"We won't meet anyone like this," I say, and give Vicki a subtle salute, as I walk down to the other end of the bar. The room is hot. Women are moving close together, fingers entwined in hair, leather thongs connecting necks to waists. Two women are "dancing" together slowly, their bodies melting into one another, hands down each other's pants, mouths connected. I am being cruised by a baby dyke in a new leather jacket. Cute enough, but could I stand to wake up with her? I know I couldn't. Several older women sit in the corner wearing no particular costume, laughing among themselves.

"Drink?"

The voice belongs to a beautiful but cold-looking woman wearing nothing under her leather vest. I can't help staring into her cleavage as I mumble, "Yes, yes, a drink." The woman pulls a tray off the counter and I realize I am not being cruised. "Poland Springs, please," I say and throw some change onto the tray.

Across the room I watch the back of a woman who is dancing with my friend Jessica. Jessica is wearing white linen and getting everyone's attention. Beautiful, thin, long hair tossing wildly, Jessica looks like she's coming when she dances. As usual, she has already picked someone up. Her partner is dressed in flowing black and is shaking her ass like mad to the wild music. As I follow the woman's movements with my eyes, I feel my cunt throb. The woman's clothes are sticking to her back with sweat and I can see her luscious pear shape. Jessica is bumping her hips into the woman's cunt and I can feel the heat every time the woman's ass juts out. Suddenly they both turn with the beat. Jessica and Vicki are smiling into my eyes.

Peter stood at the window holding his Ramlösa in a butch attitude. Scanning the dance floor, he noted sweating, horny men of every description: thin, fat, muscled, soft. Balding and hairy, young and old. There was a smattering of lesbians. They always touched when they danced. Peter closed his eyes and inhaled deeply. The smell of men's sweat ex-

cited him, and he became aware again of his cock ring. When he opened his eyes his dream man was across the room at the edge of the dance floor. He was striking in his leather pants and leather vest. His black chest hair was thick and curly as he stood at the rail. Peter noticed a line of bare skin below his armpit, where the hair from front and back had agreed upon a DMZ. Peter's cock was getting hard at the thought of this white spot, and it was pushing handsomely out of his chaps. The man looked taller than he had that morning at church, and Peter realized that he, too, must be wearing heavy black boots.

They walked toward each other and met at the entrance to the dance floor. "My name is Jim," said the handsome leather man. "Dance?"

They stepped down onto the dance floor, eye to eye, moving slowly and smiling imperceptibly. Leather men always danced slowly; no wild waving of arms, no flailing feet. The boots weighed about five pounds each. "I'm Peter," he said, leaning forward. They danced through two dances before they spoke again. At the start of the third song, a Whitney Houston which precipitated much screaming from the crowd around them, Jim leaned close and said in a husky voice, "I have a room close by with some very interesting features." Peter nodded knowingly, and the two tall men in leather left the dance floor. Their space was filled immediately by two men in bicycle shorts and hats.

"I think I'm going to leave," I say as Vicki and Jessica come up to me.

"Don't go," replies Vicki. "We haven't danced yet." She grabs my hand and pulls me onto the dance floor. "That Jessica," she says in a conspiratorial voice. "She's such a flirt. She even flirts with me!"

"What's so strange about that, Vicki? You're beautiful, you're intelligent and you're single."

"Well, I'm intelligent and single," she says, her brown curls bouncing down into her eyes. "She really wants to sleep with you, you know."

And I want to sleep with you, I think. I watch Vicki dance with obvious delight. Her eyes are closed and she shakes her long slim body in bursts of movement. I drink in her every curve and can't resist putting my hands on Vicki's hips. Eyes still closed, Vicki dances closer and closer to me. I can feel the hot flesh beneath the wet silk. Vicki is moaning into me now and I can smell the sweet musk of her sweat and see it glistening along the top of her smooth breasts.

All at once Vicki stops moving and just stares into my eyes. We breathe together, just staring. I feel that I'm melting into an incredible softness and realize I'm kneading Vicki's ass with both hands.

"Let's go home," Vicki says. "Let's go home together."

As they walked down Commercial Street, Peter was struck by the man's height and his hard body. "Almost my height," he thought.

Jim was talking to him now about his room. "I rented it through an ad in Drummer. *It came fully equipped," he said. "It has some handy built-ins which I hope to take full advantage of tonight."*

Peter wondered if it was the same place he stayed in three summers ago, the one with the brass rings above the bed and the post in the middle of the room slyly disguised as a ship's mast. That was a wonderful summer. He had devised a signal system for Helen and his other friends: a black leather triangle in the window meant DO NOT DISTURB.

Jim stopped at the gate of an old, weather-beaten cottage. "This is it," he said.

It was a different house! P-town was full of surprises. Peter noticed that Jim's hands were trembling slightly as he worked the key into the lock.

We walk along silently toward the East End. Everyone seems to be going in the other direction. I am mortified. I can't believe this is happening. How could I not have known? Vicki is quiet, seemingly unfrazzled by this turn of events. "What are you thinking?" I ask, fearing I have blown not only our vacation but also ten years of friendship.

"Uh, it's a cool night. Good thing we're wearing our jackets."

"What do you think about what just happened?" I ask.

"At the bar?" Vicki asks. "It was fine. It was okay. I mean, it was great."

"Aren't you upset with me? I mean, this is P-town, you're supposed to be meeting new women, getting laid, not going home with your roommate."

Vicki stops and turns toward me. "But I want to be going home with you. I've been waiting for this to happen. Is that okay?"

"It's more than okay," I reply. "It's fabulous."

We come to the door of our inn and one of the cats jumps out of the shadows. Vicki starts to sneeze. We both begin to laugh and wait outside the door as if it will open by magic.

"You took the key, didn't you?"

"No, you had it."

"No. I distinctly remember giving it to you."

Once inside, the two men looked each other over slowly, receiving the full effect of the powerfully built, leather-clad bodies. Jim reached for Peter's hands and brought them up to his nipples, coaxing Peter's fingers to squeeze the already hard buttons.

Peter's breath hissed between his teeth as he pinched the dark protrusions. "I love a man who likes pain," he said, his face close to Jim's. "How much can you take?"

"Only time will tell," Jim answered, as he backed away toward the bed.

Peter could see that his partner's cock was hard in his leather pants. He released one nipple and slowly moved his hand down the other's body, fingering the black curls as he went. Jim's head dropped back, his chest heaving as he breathed through his open mouth. Peter could feel the washboard muscles rippling under his hand as he continued down to the man's pants. Jim brought his hands together at his zipper to help him along. Peter pushed his hands away roughly. "I'll call the shots," he said. They looked into each other's eyes evenly. There was a palpable tension in the room as the two powerful men measured each other.

"You can do what you want with me tonight," Jim said. "I can take it."

"You will take it," Peter commanded in his deepest voice,

pushing the other down to his knees in front of him. "Un-button me and take out my cock," he boomed. The black bearded man was on the level of Peter's crotch. He ran his hands up the inside of Peter's chaps and carefully unbut-toned his fly. Peter's ten inches was almost fully hard and it sprang from its constraints. "Handle it!" commanded Peter, pushing his hips out.

The black bearded man deftly grasped and squeezed Pe-ter's meat, scooping in every now and then to squeeze his balls. "It's . . . it's beautiful," he mumbled as he worked the cock, his mouth watering.

Peter's cock throbbed in its cock ring and he pulled the man's head back by the hair. "Don't be so hopeful. You're drooling," he said, looking down at him.

We enter the apartment, take off our jackets and sit down at the table. We sit in the same places as in the morning but every-thing has changed. Vicki picks up the pad that I have been using for my story.

"You've written so much. Can I read it?"

"It's just trash. Just a fantasy. Real life doesn't happen that way."

"How does real life happen?" Vicki asks.

I rise from my chair and take Vicki's hand. I lead her into the bedroom and we lie down on the bed.

Vicki starts to unbutton my blouse quickly. "I want to see your breasts," she says.

We silently undress each other, rolling around on the bed. Vicki gasps at the sight of my full breasts. She arches her body over to get them into her mouth. Moans and sighs are all that I can manage as my friend sucks on one tender nipple. I look at Vicki's back, rounded as she bends to suck. My hands move down along her spine and balloon out at her hips. In that instant I think of porcelain or some fine ivory sculpture. But Vicki's ac-tions belie the fragile feeling of her skin as now she pushes me back into the bed.

My cunt is throbbing and my skin is pink with excitement and apprehension. Will this be a bust? Will we wake up tomorrow and have breakfast together, never mentioning what went before? God, will our friendship be ruined?

"Is this really happening?" Vicki asks, breaking into my thoughts.

"It must be," I say. "I'm too wet for this to be a dream."

With that, I tumble Vicki over onto her back and kiss my way down her body. Kissing and licking, I linger on her smooth belly and settle in to enjoy the shape and feel of the small roundness. All thoughts of our curious situation leave my mind as I become more and more involved with Vicki's silky flesh. I lick and nibble every inch of Vicki's skin, roaming from belly to ribs to hips to breasts, back and forth, rolling her over as I go. She groans and giggles, sighs and gasps, feeling my tongue and lips and teeth.

My passion is growing as I lick and bite at her ass and thighs. "You are so beautiful," I moan into the warm flesh. "I just want to devour you." I lift her to her knees so that her ass is up in the air. And, spreading her legs, I lick down and into her open cunt.

"Oh, baby," moans Vicki. "This is what I want. Yes, this is what I want."

Peter pulled Jim up from his knees and instructed him, "Now that you know what I expect from you, you can show me your toys. I'll decide which ones I want to use on you."

Jim turned and went to the head of the bed. He pulled back the curtains, exposing two leather straps with brass rings at the ends. They were fastened to the wall with brass studs. Then he pointed to the other end of the bed. Fastened to the floor on either side were its mates. Jim squatted and pulled out a drawer from beneath the bed. The contents were carelessly scattered around: leather restraints, cock rings, nipple clips, two tubes of K-Y, condoms, butt plugs and dildos.

Peter was overjoyed at his good fortune, but his face belied nothing. "Those will do," he said calmly. As Jim rose, Peter pushed him face down on the bed, falling on top of him. He humped Jim's ass with delight, his hard cock sliding against the leather. Peter reveled in the subservient posture of his partner. He especially liked to top a hunky guy.

On his knees now, Peter turned Jim over between his legs. Reaching behind him, he grabbed the nipple clips out of the

*drawer. "I'm going to see how hard you can take it before
you beg me to stop." He clipped the hard rocks of Jim's
nipples, rubbing and squeezing the man's strong pecs as he
did so. Jim let out a deep breath, and Peter could feel Jim's
cock growing beneath him, under his leather pants. Peter
groped for more toys, and pulled out the soft restraints. He
grabbed Jim's hands and tied him to the rings on the wall,
looking proudly at his handiwork.*

"My ankles. Tie my ankles," whispered the man.

*SLAP! Peter's hands stung, but Jim had asked for it. "You
don't make the rules here, fella," he said in his most masterly
voice. "Put your knees up so I can have a view of your ass!"*

*As Jim planted his boots on the bed, Peter reached over
and unzipped the leather pants all the way down, exposing
a brown hairy butt hole, aching to be entered. His hand
behind him again, Peter searched for the butt plug, found
it, then tossed it away. "I'm going to fuck you like you've
never been fucked," he hissed between clenched teeth, as he
pulled out the big black rubber dildo. He started to tease
Jim's ass and balls with the rubber cock when a wave of
caution overtook him. "Better be safe," he thought, and
grabbed a condom, ripping open the package with his teeth.
Jim was writhing and moaning on the bed as Peter worked
the fine, ribbed rubber over the dildo. "Now I'm going to
shove my cock into your ass, all ten inches of it," he said, as
he prepared the way with a generous spurt of K-Y.*

*"I want it, I want it," screamed the bearded man, de-
fenseless on the bed. "Oohh, yes."*

*The head was in, as Peter twisted and turned the rubber cock,
screwing it into Jim's tight ass. "Take it, take it," Peter said
gruffly as he pumped away. "My cock . . . is in you . . . cock
. . . in you . . . yes . . . take it." His own rod was engorged.*

*"Fuck me, fuck me! Hard, hard!" Jim screamed, as white
drops began to ooze in rhythm from his stiff column.*

*Peter now took his penis in his hand and pumped away,
faster and faster. One hand on the dildo, one hand on his
own cock; they were the same, hard, stiff and rubbery.*

*"I'm coming," cried Jim. "I'm coming." And with a jolt
that felt like a bolt of lightning, the two men came together,
Jim's semen spurting wildly over his hairy chest and beard,
while Peter aimed his arrow at the matte black pants.*

* * *

Vicki is on her knees and I am behind her and between her legs, nibbling and licking and sucking her wet cunt. The sensations are so intense, the position so intimate, I know that she feels vulnerable and lightheaded. She can't stay that way much longer, balanced on her knees with only the thick damp air holding her up. But she stays and stays, taking it in. My tongue, my mouth sucking and sucking, she hangs on the tip of an explosive orgasm. I reach around and find her breasts. My other hand moves down to her clit. Her body shudders, then falls, her muscles giving way. Over she goes, across the bed, pulling me down beside her.

"I want to give you more, do you want more?" I ask as we lie together.

"I want to fuck you," Vicki mouths into my ear. "I've wanted to fuck you for so long. You'd like that, wouldn't you?"

"Yes," I say, gasping.

"You want it?"

"Yes . . ."

"You want it?"

"Yes, yes."

"Can I? Can I fuck you?"

"Yes, yes. Fuck me, baby."

Vicki covers my body with her own and kisses me deeply, a long wet sucking of my lips and tongue. "Oh, baby, so many girls, so many girls have enjoyed you. Enjoyed your luscious breasts, your belly and your wet, juicy cunt," Vicki whispers as she licks my ear. "So many girls. And now me."

I breathe shallowly waiting for it to happen. My eyes are open and I watch Vicki's head as it moves down my body. I feel the soft lips and hot breath as they move from neck to breasts to belly to cunt.

"Come inside me, Vicki," I plead as I feel the hot damp breaths on my mound and clit. "Come on, honey," I moan.

She lingers there, breathing hard into my cunt. Breathing and licking, blowing and kissing. "You taste so sweet," she says, looking up at my face against the pillows. "You taste so sweet and so juicy."

"Do me, honey. Take me," I breathe.

"I'm going to tease you first. After all, you've waited this long, haven't you?"

My thighs relax as I expel a long breath. It is out of my control now. My lover, friend, will do whatever she desires. "Oh," I gasp as Vicki's tongue pushes deep into my cunt. Hands play on my thighs, pinching and pulling the cheeks of my ass. Her tongue is thrusting and licking, hands playing and taunting.

"Please, baby, please give it to me," I groan.

Faster and faster, Vicki's hands and mouth take what they want. Pulling and coaxing, thrusting and nipping. And I can no longer tell what is mouth and what is cunt, what is fingers and what is tongue. And she is inside me, three fingers in and deep inside. Moaning and rocking, I'm so wide open, swallowing her up, drinking her in. And she is thrusting, in and in, her fingers reaching deeper, her whole hand moving and rocking, rocking and rocking as her tongue and her lips play over my clit.

"Oh, God. Oh, God. Yes, yes," I scream. My cunt balloons and Vicki can feel me taking her in and holding her in.

> *Peter fell forward over his prone companion, sweating and exhausted. Jim panted, semi-conscious and wet with cum. They lay there like that, bellies heaving against each other, hair wet and curling between them, for what seemed like a very long time. Then Peter reached down and slowly began to remove the dildo from Jim's sweaty butt hole. Jim shuddered. "Easy does it," he said. "Easy does it."*

Vicki and I lie entwined, sweat mingling under the covers. Vicki strokes my face and belly and breasts, holding me close and kissing my face. I breathe more slowly now, but the vein in my neck still pulses with the quickness of an electric current.

"Are we still friends?" Vicki asks, looking slyly at me as I lie in her arms.

"I think we're more than that now," I answer.

"After all these years it finally happened," muses Vicki.

I look back at her, tired and pleased. "It was so easy, baby. So easy."

Rubenesque

It was nearly noon when "The Mountain," as she was known to her slimmer and catty co-workers, left the confines of her eighth-floor accounting office, hailed a cab, and within ten minutes alighted at the entrance of the grand and formidable Clift Hotel.

Actually, Evie Satterwhite wasn't really a mountain anymore; these days she more resembled a sweetly sloping knoll, resulting from many months of diminished intake and nearly 5,000 miles on her stationary bike. And while many women still dismissed her as heavy and in need of a good diet, many men looked at Evie and figuratively licked their lips, finding her rounded good looks toothsome and much preferable to the brittle edges of her slimmer sisters. Evie was not unaware of her effect on such men and helped it along. No drab power suits with skinny neckties for her but rather glossed red lips, high-heeled sandals showing off gorgeously arched feet, and softly glowing hair—colored Titian Red—that she fluffed with perfectly manicured fingertips. Men dropped like flies.

And so, in small celebration of her growing self-confidence and her diminishing heft, she came each month for lunch at this fabulous hotel where, for the price of many lunches at Alex's Deli next door to her office, she joined society ladies and literary buffs who assembled to hear the authors of famous and infamous best-sellers discuss their work. And, for the price of the same ticket, have an exquisitely catered, designer lunch.

Once in the lobby, she found her way to The Redwood Room, a draped and muraled splendor heavy with tapestries and chandeliers. She was the first to arrive and the room was empty, though each of the fifty tables in the hall was wonderfully appointed with heavy pink table linen and flowers at every place, silverware and wineglasses gleaming under the lights of the chandeliers. Evie stood in the doorway for a long time deciding where she would sit, and it was then that she saw the two workmen tacking down a portion of the richly patterned carpet. They looked up when she stepped through the polished double doors, and one of them—small and trim with Mediterranean good looks—immediately smiled at her and sat back on his heels, his eyes gobbling up the bounce of her hips as she passed him. She chose one of the smaller tables with two upholstered chairs and a loveseat, set against a side wall. And while the table was not near the lectern, from there she could see everyone who entered without having to turn around to look. She settled herself, checked her watch and was immediately distracted by the arrival of a noisy group of fashionably dressed matrons; fur coats, reptile skins, and expensive perfume ruffled the air around her as they passed. Slowly the room filled, and at 12:45 jacketed waiters began to serve. Her plate was set before her: a gorgeous, spa-inspired creation of poached salmon resting on a technicolor bed of various perfect greens and raw vegetables. Freshly baked bread lay steaming in a cloth basket, and even before she could think to ask, her wine was being poured by her silent but attentive waiter.

From the corner of her eye she saw, still on his knees and very near her table, the carpet man gathering his things to go. Then, with mounting disbelief, she watched him gaze intently at her, look carefully around him, lift the corner of her tablecloth, and quickly disappear, crawling beneath its skirts. Riveted, she stared wide-eyed at her wineglass, its amber contents trembling and then sloshing with the movements of the table as the man settled himself underneath it. Glancing at her neighbors to see who might have witnessed this phenomenon, she found herself unobserved. Not knowing what else to do, she fumbled in the bread basket for the miniature loaf, broke off a tiny piece and nervously began to butter it. Somehow feeling this was not the appropriate thing to do, she lay the bread down and picked up the heavy silver fork, fluffing the salad greens on her plate. The man beneath her table had not moved.

Of course she fully expected him to come crawling out at any moment, confused, flushed, and apologetic, and she, in her excited mind's eye, would smile sympathetically and nod him away, glancing around the room at the other diners who by now would all be staring. They would shrug their shoulders ("These things *do* happen") and then turn their interests back to their exquisitely detailed lunches or the brilliant wit of the speaker who was about to take the lectern. So she waited, gleaming fork poised above the burst of colors on her plate.

But he didn't come out and he didn't move, continuing to kneel there, his breath an intermittent warming to her knees. Through the haze of her growing excitement the oddest array of thoughts possessed her: could he *see* under there? Suppose the waiter spies the tablecloth moving and drags the man out by the scruff of his neck and then calls the police? Suppose the speaker at the lectern sees his feet sticking out, stops in mid-sentence, and points, as all of the diners turn around and stare at her? Suppose . . .

And then he touched her, his hands encircling the shoe of her crossed leg, causing her to start with such violence that her fork clattered heavily to the plate, scattering bits of salmon and vegetables onto the pink tablecloth between the porcelain cups and half-filled, beveled wineglasses. Dazed, she collected bits of food and placed them on the corner of her plate. Broad, warm fingers stroked the leather of her heeled sandal and the nylon at the top of her foot, the tiny rough places on the surface of his hands catching at the silken finish of her sheer stocking. He held her foot motionless for the longest time, and when she did not move or protest, he carefully removed her shoe, slipping it off with one hand and enclosing her foot immediately with the other hand as though he wished to make certain that she remained warm and secure. Then slowly, slowly, he began to knead the arch of her foot, moving his fingers up to the ball and then to the toes. And when still she did not respond, he began to pull gently at each toe, separating and finally rubbing into the crevices between them as much as the nylon stocking would allow. Above the table, the waiter took her plate, Evie gazing at him through dreamy, unseeing eyes.

She could feel the tiny tremors of his cramped position as his mouth bent to the inside of her arch. Caressing more with teeth and tongue than with lips, he moved along the whole inside of her foot, moving his attentions slowly up to her toes, nibbling at her longer, second toe before sucking its tip deeply into his mouth. With bites and tiny caressing sucks, he made a warm, wet trail up the length of her leg from ankle to inner knee.

A rising panic made her feel that she must move her body, that if she did not she would be unable to breathe or that she might fling herself wildly from the table. To calm herself, she carefully drew her foot from his hand, uncrossing her leg and changing her position on the loveseat until she was comfortable again. He, unsure of her movements, waited until she was still again before resting his forehead against her knees. Then he wriggled his head from side to side to part her legs. She could feel the roughness of his stubble, the prominent outline of nose and cheekbones as he burrowed his face against her. She allowed his head to part her as in slow motion she watched her waiter pour more coffee, the speaker at the lectern animated but voiceless for her. "Adventure," she thought dumbly. "This is what they call an adventure," as he nuzzled his way up and up with tiny bites and little licks done with the inside of his lips, alternating between her thighs, nudging her legs farther apart. As he approached her mid-thigh, she knew that he could smell her— that the smell of saliva-stroked skin, wet nylons, and her perfume mingled with the beckoning steam from between her legs, and that it rose to his nostrils as surely as the steam from her coffee floated to her own.

Abruptly the warmth of his mouth withdrew, startling her and leaving the spots where his mouth had been feeling cold and somehow desolate. During this long instant when she felt nothing from him, she began to be afraid. Then, with the purpose and familiarity of a longtime lover, he lifted his hands from her ankles and slid them, in one smooth movement, up the outer sides of her legs, pausing only at the hem of her skirt to gauge its tightness, then swept them underneath to her hips, one warm palm on each fleshy pad. He tugged at her pantyhose and she found herself helping him, shifting her weight from one buttock to the other. He slid her skirt up and up until it was bunched up around her hips, barely hidden from view by tablecloth, napkin, jacket, and the arms of the little loveseat. When he'd finally stripped the nylon from her legs, she sighed almost audibly as though some great weight had been lifted from her body. For a moment he did not touch her, and she knew that he was looking at her, inspecting her, admiring her. It added to her excitement that he could not watch the play of emotions on her face, or that she could not control him or guide him or wiggle or thrust herself up to his lips. She was at once helpless and in total control, able to take all that he was offering without guilt or reciprocation but at the same time unable to move toward him. This last thought made her smile, because should her covering table be somehow snatched away, there she would be, skirt to her waist, legs agape, a strange man with a bag of carpet tools by his side having his way with her.

When he could get no further because of her seated position, he guided her bare right foot to the seat of one of the upholstered chairs tucked under the table, spreading her legs further to allow him room. He pressed his nose against the swatch of silk that covered her crotch, rubbing up and down on either side of the distended kernel that pressed against her panties. He put his mouth to it, breathing on it, blowing at it, and finally pressing it, circling it through her panties with the tip of his tongue. She had all but stopped breathing, the room forgotten, the speaker's voice a senseless drone. Then, with one finger, he hooked the edge of her panties and drew them to one side, and dragged his tongue in one long velvet stroke from the base of her asshole to the top of her swollen clitoris.

"More coffee, madam?" The waiter bent to her ear. She looked up at him, unable to answer as the man beneath the table worked away, massaging her outer lips between his teeth, curling his tongue in her hair, pressing, blowing, sucking time and again the little kernel of flesh. Release rose up in her, washing over her limbs like smoke, and he held her stiffened legs pressed against his sides as she covered her face with the linen napkin, pressing it to her eyes to cover her grimace. Everyone in the room was clapping, the sound coming through to her consciousness like the volume on a TV crowd scene being quickly turned up and then down. Were they applauding her? Him? The speaker?

She opened her eyes to diners, rising to go. The luncheon was over. Crumpled and exhausted she sat at her table until the room was nearly empty. He had knelt back, no longer touching her, and she knew it was time for her to decide what to do. Awkwardly, she lowered her skirts, arranging her jacket and removing her foot from the chair. Feeling with one foot, she found her shoe and swung her legs to the side to slip into it. She pushed the table back slightly and rose to go, her legs wobbly, her head light. As she stepped across the doorway, she looked back at the table, its cluttered surface and pink skirts looking for all the world like the fifty others in the room. It looked as though nothing had happened here except a lecture and a luncheon and she was tempted to go back, to raise the tablecloth to see if he indeed was still crouched underneath.

No, she would not go back. She would not look under, or wait for him to come out and approach her. Maybe it was a dream. But as she stepped toward the main lobby a woman in a fur coat whispered loudly to her companion, "I thought bare legs were only acceptable on thin French mannequins!" And Evie, looking down at her stockingless legs, smiled as she remembered her rumpled pair of damp nylons lying under the table. Queen size.

Cassandra Brent

Strangers on a Train

Alyssa stood on the platform at Osaka's Umeda station and congratulated herself for having left the university early. Maybe she'd even get a seat on the train this time. Yawning, she ran her hand over her close-cropped Afro and kneaded the nape of her neck. She scanned the group of waiting passengers and noticed the white-gloved "pushers" who stood ready to firmly but politely shove as many commuters as possible onto the waiting trains. But they weren't needed now. Not yet.

Out of the corner of her eye she saw a stumbling, drunken Japanese man lurching and reeling down the length of the platform. Two Japanese women stood directly between Alyssa and the drunk. They were speaking softly, occasionally touching each other with the intimacy of close friends. Their conversation was rudely interrupted when the drunk lunged forward and grabbed the breast of the woman closest to him. He hung on as if trying to steady himself, then moved on to her companion and assaulted her in the same way. Both women hung their heads in shame.

Alyssa was livid. The drunk moved toward her, his hands out, ready to grab her. She set her backpack down, put one hand on her hip, and motioned to the man with the other. In a loud voice she said, "Come here, I've got something for you."

The man stopped. He opened his eyes a little wider and stared in shock at the angry black woman in front of him. Slowly, he lowered his hands. He glanced nervously up and down the platform, took one last look at her and stumbled on his way.

Alyssa closed her eyes and exhaled forcibly. Before she reopened them, a spasm shot straight from the hand on her hip to her crotch. She shuddered, gasped, and then smiled. When she opened her eyes her train was pulling into the station.

She boarded the train, her legs a bit shaky. The first thing she noticed was that all the seats were taken. Two high school girls were tittering in the seat next to the door about the *"Gaijin"* with *"borondo heiya."* The second thing she noticed was the object of their conversation: a man in a gray suit standing next to the door on the opposite side of the car. His eyes were closed and his blond hair was mussed, falling across his face. His lips were slightly parted, and he breathed with the slow, deep rhythm of sleep. Alyssa stood on the other side of the door and inspected him.

His eyelids, with their long dark lashes, fluttered rapidly back and forth. His collar was open, tie loosened, and Alyssa could see wisps of wiry blond hair peeking out at the base of his neck. He had a wonderful erection. Alyssa blinked and looked away, focusing instead on the black leather briefcase at his feet.

The train stopped at the next station. More people got on than got off; the area by the doors was starting to fill up. Alyssa grabbed the handrail above her head and moved a little closer to the man to keep her view of him unobstructed.

She glanced at his face again; his eyes were still closed. Feeling safe, she let her gaze travel back down his body to his crotch. She would have sworn she could see every detail of his cock, outlined against the smooth fabric of his trousers.

He's perfected the art of sleeping standing up, she thought, smiling to herself, complete with erotic dreams.

Almost as if he had heard her, his cock twitched and strained against his zipper. Alyssa glanced up at his face and was startled to see his green eyes wide open and a crooked grin on his face. He seemed delighted to find her watching him.

Alyssa gasped and spun around, turning her back to him. She

was intensely conscious of her long, full skirt swirling against her legs.

"Caught ya," he murmured. It wasn't an accusation, but an invitation.

"English. . . ." Alyssa couldn't remember being more happy to hear her native tongue. She couldn't return his gaze, but she could feel his eyes on her. She glanced over her shoulder; the crooked grin was still there. He chuckled softly.

The train pulled into the next station and Alyssa watched to see if he would get off. He didn't budge. Alyssa allowed the crowd to move her closer to him. He was right behind her now, and she could feel his breath on her neck.

"I loved the feeling of your eyes on me," he whispered over her shoulder. "It woke me up."

I wonder how he'd like the feeling of my hands, my mouth, or my cunt on him? Alyssa thought to herself.

The train went into a tunnel and they were plunged into darkness. She took a deep breath and said to herself, "I'm gonna do it." She reached behind her and grabbed his cock. She gave it a quick squeeze, then started to withdraw her hand. He grabbed her wrist.

"Aw, don't go away," he begged, placing her palm against his erection and slowly curling her fingers around it. She squeezed it again and he inhaled with a hiss.

The train lurched and Alyssa was thrown against him. He grabbed her hips and held her there. She ground her ass against his crotch. His head slumped to her shoulder and he nibbled on her neck.

The train emerged from the tunnel and they both froze. The man exhaled slowly. Alyssa scanned the car. In her high heels she was taller than almost everyone on the train, so mostly what she saw was the tops of people's heads.

They pulled into another station and more people crowded on. This time the "pushers" were called upon to pack them in tightly. The train pulled out of the station and began to sway gently.

"No one's looking," she said. She held her breath in anticipation.

She felt him grab two handfuls of her skirt and slowly begin to raise it. She put her hands on top of his and stopped him.

"It wraps around; just part the folds."

The first contact of his hands on her skin sent a flash of panic through Alyssa. She strained to see if anyone was watching them. But they were packed tight and all facing the other door. Alyssa closed her eyes and concentrated on the tingle on her skin as his hands slid her panties down. Keeping his elbows between them so as not to jostle other passengers, he caressed the insides of her thighs. Alyssa pulled up onto her tiptoes and arched her back.

"Oh my goodness," he moaned as he encountered her stickiness. He eagerly coated his fingers. "I have to get in there!" he whimpered. Alyssa nodded rapidly in assent.

"Release me."

Alyssa paused for a moment before she realized what he meant. Then she groped behind her and unzipped his pants, leaving the waistband buttoned. She pulled his cock out and gripped it tightly, making him growl deep in his throat.

The train conveniently entered another tunnel and slowed to a crawl. He pressed his hips forward and Alyssa felt his cock between her legs. It wasn't inside her, but against her. It was wet by the juices running down her thighs. She could feel his pubic hair on her ass.

"May I?" he whispered.

"You'd better."

He pulled back so that the head of his cock was just at her opening. She tilted her pelvis back to greet him. His fingers parted the lips of her cunt and he thrust forward, embedding his cock fully inside her. Alyssa's knees buckled; he wrapped his arms around her waist and began to make small movements in and out. Alyssa rocked with him.

Suddenly, the train pitched forward into the lights of the next station. The man started to withdraw his cock, but Alyssa followed his backward movement and kept him inside her. She began to clench her muscles around his cock as if she were sucking him with her cunt.

The doors opened and a few passengers fought their way out.

The pushers peered into the car, assessing the dismal scene, and barred any other passengers from entering.

The man made a little mewing noise in his throat and started mumbling, "You're gonna do it," over and over.

"Shh," Alyssa cautioned.

He slumped forward again and bit her shoulder to keep from crying out. Alyssa held her body stiffly, her fists balled at her sides and her cunt muscles clenching and clenching. A tear rolled down her cheek. She felt the man go rigid behind her, and then his orgasm started, his cock twitching and pumping inside her. She thought he'd bite a hole in her shoulder. Then her own orgasm hit and she tensed against it, her head twitching from side to side. The commuter next to her shifted position and she let her body go limp.

The train entered another tunnel. Swiftly the man extracted his cock from her body. Alyssa felt a pang of remorse; she clutched her thighs together. The man placed his hands on her shoulders and squeezed. Tentatively, Alyssa sent her hands to join his. He kissed her fingertips, then slid his hands out from under hers. That was when Alyssa felt the business card.

"Call me. Please. Call me."

The train came out of the tunnel and pulled into the next station. The man left her. Alyssa sensed him making his way to the door, but she couldn't bear to watch his departure. She leaned against the other door and squeezed her thighs together even tighter.

When the train reached her stop, she stumbled to the exit. She walked the blocks to her apartment in a daze, her body still tingling. She unlocked her door, removed her shoes, and padded across the tatami mats to the ornate mirror in her bedroom. She stripped off her clothes and stared at herself. Clutching the business card in one hand, she ran her fingers over the teeth marks on her shoulder and trembled with the memory. She glanced at the business card, grinned, and reached for the phone.

Kate Robinson

Silver, Gold, Red, Black

Cass and Dru are fighting again, in the blindly bloody fashion of obsessed lovers. "Typical dykes," I say to no one. I recross my legs and light another cigarette.

As their voices subside into teary mumbles, I read the headline for the fourth time. Earth passes through meteor shower tonight, it announces. Good. All the crabby insomniacs created by two weeks of unaccustomed heat should have something to comment on besides my ass.

Now it's silent behind my roommates' door. Seven minutes, I predict to the sofa, checking my watch. Right again. I recognize the first moan as Dru's; long, dark, full, loud. Cass isn't far behind: fluent, young, round, undisciplined. This won't go on for long; after a fight, they're always quick and dirty.

I don't care what anyone says. Sharing a house with a couple is the best way to remember why I'm single.

I calmly finish the paper, rolling my eyes at their crescendos. That Catherine Deneuve look-alike from work crosses my mind once: I see her looking up at me mischievously from between my legs. OK. Out to the kitchen for a beer. I take my time. Cut myself a couple of slices of cheese, take little bites.

When I walk out onto the porch, Cass and Dru are coiled

together on the glider, all arms and legs and red and black hair. I lean on a post and face them, smugly single. I nurse my beer and blow cigarette smoke out the side of my mouth, poised for their disapproval. The sun sets behind me with a radioactive-orange glow.

Dru pushes back her heavy mat of black hair and says, "I wanna go to the lake." Cass and I latch onto the idea and we fan out into the house, hunting for swimsuits, zoris, and towels.

Pressed together in the front seat of Cass's Datsun, the three of us are finally headed in a single direction. Catherine Deneuve drifts up into the air and blows away.

The feeble parking-lot light doesn't reach far into the thick darkness under the trees beside the lake. There are people around us, on land and in the water, but they are as indefinite as minor characters in dreams. There is splashing in the lake. Teenage girls squeal, teased by teenage boys, but nobody plays loud music, nobody is rough or raucous.

Dru and Cass look almost comical in profile. They hold hands. Cass is short and lush; she rubs her bushy red hair on Dru's shoulder. Dru is taller, dark, and solid. I'm the tallest. I walk a little behind.

I stop when I reach the water. The meteors look like stars playing tag. I want to reach up and brush the black velvet and running mercury of their game with the blunt tips of my fingers. If I glance away, I fear I won't be able to burn this night into my memory.

Meanwhile, Cass and Dru give themselves to the water. Dru plunks herself in whole, the sooner the better. Cass submerges inch by inch, savoring each sensation. I'm stalled in the shallows.

Finally, I take giant steps, wading in. The lake is warm, womblike, from the day's heat. When the water reaches the Y at the top of my legs, I pause. Warm wavelets lap at my groin. I shudder, then take two more steps and I am rib deep. I plunge in, scissor-kicking underwater.

Amorphous shapes float around, yellowish-gray, large or small, moving toward or away from me. Some Northern-climate part of me suggests they might be frightening, but I am in far too deep to heed it.

When I surface, Dru and Cass have blended in with all the other splashing thicknesses in the dark water. I am completely surrounded and completely alone. I float on my back, watching. Meteors tumble and burst over my head. I can't help feeling loved and welcomed, suspended in the warm palm of a gentle hand.

As I float farther from shore, I hear the voices of boys on the diving platform. I have a sudden, urgent wish to throw myself up through the warm air and descend to penetrate the lake's surface. I begin to backstroke evenly toward the platform, watching the show above me. I can't look at everything: the sky blurs.

The abrupt closeness of a male voice startles me. I jackknife my body and twirl around. The platform is a dark wall in front of me. Light seeps dimly from beneath me. My daylight self pushes small points of fear into my belly; I appease it by swimming around to the ladder on the other side of the platform.

The light in the water is stronger here, more lunar. The cold should be more noticeable in this deeper area. Instead, there is a warm current flowing up my legs. The current seems to be directed at my cunt. I am disturbed and fascinated.

Far below me, something sparkles. A fish? But I know the only fish in this lake are small, planted trout. I duck my head under the water to look at the shape. It grows larger, moving sinuously, taking on form. It is lighter, less yellow and more silver/gold than the other shapes I saw around me. It is definitely human— torso, head, legs, and arms—but otherwise unrecognizable. The hair is short and the same color as the body. I see neither clothing nor indications of gender.

It is beautiful. The heat and light seem to emanate from it. It moves like the current from beneath the platform.

I am acutely aware of my surroundings—the water and waves, moon and meteors, shore and, distantly, voices—but I am exclusively involved now with the shape. My cunt swells and opens to the rhythms of the current. My breathing is as complex and re-active as the tiny patterns of ripples on the water's surface.

The shape swims up swiftly beneath me. I feel its presence on my skin before it touches me. Its hands, hot and almost dry, slide up my legs, greedily testing and comprehending each muscle and swelling of flesh. My extreme arousal seems to make me float more lightly; the howl between my legs arches my back, makes me reckless. The lake laps impudently at my nipples.

The shape's fingers explore my ass, my belly, the groove between inner thigh and pubis, before it rips away tight fabric to find my own heat. Its hands are clean and smooth and ruthless.

Its head floats near my waist—I stroke its temples, then grip them tightly. That contact releases a flood of sensation. Meteors shoot and burst on my throat, in the small of my back, across my breasts, deep in my belly, behind my knees.

The shape's hands are on my pubis now. Its fingers trail between my inner lips, invade my vagina. One hand balls up and thrusts into me, the other grips my ass.

Its fist smacks rudely upward inside me, the knuckles kneading my walls, which roll and squeeze against them. A stand-up-bass thrum descends from my uterus to my vagina.

With each thrust its arm seems to plunge deeper into me. I seem to grow to eagerly take it in. I let go of the shape's head, unable to tense any muscles unconnected with my cunt. Larger and larger, I'm hungrier and hungrier. The night is scorched by my breath. The shape's warmth and bulk fill me and burst.

My flesh is overwhelmed, I'm lost, I can't see myself. It's happening too much, too long, too hard to see. I think of a woman giving birth but in the other direction; I take it in, in, in. Short time, long time, all time disappears. Maybe one meteor streaks across the sky and flashes; maybe it's almost dawn and the lake has emptied of revelers. The sounds I make are shameless, inseparable from the ripples on the lake's surface.

When it's over, young male voices still sound above me, dark yellowish shapes still move around me. The earth is passing out of the shower now. Individual bursts are easy to distinguish.

I find myself gripping the lower rung of the platform's ladder. I am stripped and hot and glowing gold. I cannot see the shape, cannot feel it banging into me.

I check my belly. I'm surprised that it is still flat. The shape is there; I sense it radiating from me. I expect to blast the ladder and everything else around me into shadows with its brilliance. My brilliance.

Arias tempt my tuneless voice. My bowed legs itch for a footrace. I want to catch a barn swallow and feel its quickness throb in my hand. Instead, I swing my legs up onto the step, climb onto the platform in a surge of water and muscle, and stride across the platform.

The boys fade into the darkness. They see I am more virile than they. My path is clear.

I walk out on the short diving board. Feeling perfect and ready, I bend my knees, bounce up, come down once again, then rise high over the lake. I fly. I return to earth only because I choose to, insinuating my fingers, shoulders, ribs, pelvis, knees, and heels into the lake's open mouth.

Armadas of bubbles slide up my body, silver and perfect, male and female. The warm sap of my arousal charges the lake, flows outward from me with water and bubbles.

I surface beside Cass and Dru. They are floating together quietly, on their backs and occasionally touching—rafted. I roll over and join them.

When I touch Dru, she hums. I pick it up, then touch Cass and she starts her low sound. We are in unison, we make chords and dischords, passing the sound between us. For long minutes, we are a humming raft suspended between warm water and the silver-black maze of lights. When the song dies, we float silently for a moment longer, then turn to swim toward shore.

Dru and Cass do not touch on the way to the car but they are utterly entangled. Neither of them mentions my nakedness, so I do not notice it either. We are silent.

Instead of taking my customary post in the car—jammed against the passenger door—I sit between Cass and Dru. Cass presses her soft flesh against my left side; Dru imprints her mass against my right side and firmly clutches my thigh. Their touch clothes me.

The porch light reveals greenish-brown alluvial deposits on our skin. Embedded in Cass's red hair and paleness and freckles they look iridescent. They give Dru's skin a scaly texture but soft, inviting exploration.

We survey one another, then they strip away their wet clothes, leaving them in oozing piles. They race.

By the time I get to the bathroom, Cass and Dru are already in the shower. I hesitate. I want a cigarette. I feel naked.

"Get in!" Dru demands.

They meticulously soap and scrub every part of my body. Without a word and with very little movement, I direct my bath, indicating my pleasure with subtle expressions and shifts of my limbs. I make no attempt to wash either of them, but observe the sediment sliding off their bodies and down the drain. When I am spotless, Dru turns off the water, we step out of the shower and just as carefully they dry me.

Cass takes my hand and leads me toward their bedroom. We have turned on no lights, and the house is fuzzy with shadows and heat. Even in the dark, I recognize the unique combination of odors that signals my roommates: Dru's clean-edged, freshly laundered–bedding scent, and Cass' fertile, incense-and-strawberry smell. When Cass lays me down on their bed, the odor envelops me. The raspberry-colored walls and dark purple comforter turn moist and womblike in the heat and the light from the setting moon.

Cass crawls over me and sits cross-legged against the wall. She leans forward and begins to stroke me. "Hard," she remarks. "Strong!" Dru stands at the foot of the bed, watching, nodding her approval. I lie still, lacking will.

Cass's hands begin to linger in their path. My breasts get extra attention. Each time she passes from belly to thigh, her path veers more centerward.

Dru walks around to kneel beside the bed. After examining me for seconds, she slips her long arm under my legs, pushes one thigh upward and pulls her longest fingers through the thickest wetness between my legs.

Cass unfolds, hoists herself over my belly and, with her tongue, begins to stroke and suckle my breast.

The bedding under my ass is already soaked. I cannot exhale without moaning.

The shape's heat is rising in the room, and the light seems brighter, more reddish silver, than the fat, setting moon could reflect. These are my friends; I can see that in their bodies and their faces, smell it in their room. But the ritual is ancient.

My skin, my breath, my cunt did not relinquish what began at the lake, I realize; they merely took it in, transmuted it.

Dru's mouth and tongue are at my cunt now, Cass is everywhere else. I have my hand in Cass's cunt, and Dru is riding her own hand. Our voices are once again joined, more in tumult now than harmony, but just as powerful, just as sacred. I can feel Dru in me; she carries me off. I arch and arch, she pushes against me and comes into my cum again and again. My hand clutches and stiffens in Cass; she thrusts her ass against me and warbles into my breast.

We are tireless, almost ruthless. We go on and on and on, until all of us are so swollen and exhausted that we can no longer either come or move. We finally fall wetly asleep, Dru curled with her cheek still resting on my drenched pubic hair, my hand still inside Cass, Cass and Dru touching across my sweaty belly.

We wake up sticky and smug, comfortable with tired laughter but not very talkative. Dru makes a pot of coffee. Cass brings in the newspaper and we share it, sipping coffee, on their bed. I smoke, knocking ashes neatly into the ashtray that Dru has brought in; neither of them complains. We shower and dress groggily.

Before we float off to our respective jobs, I ask, "Did you dream?" They look at each other, then at me. Everybody has a secret smile. "Yes," Cass says, "didn't you?" I just widen my smile into a foolish grin.

In my dream, the shape girlishly tried on a number of familiar and unfamiliar faces and I was the shape, the girl, the faces, and my cunt was not worn out in the dream and pursed its lips against Dru's sleeping cheek.

As the bus rolls downtown, I wonder. What did Cass and Dru make of the shape in those few hours we lay asleep, linked? I wonder whose face it wore.

None of us ever speaks of the dream. When Catherine Deneuve visits, she mentions the meteor shower and we are silent. Except for the smile, of course. We share it, the three of us, and she scowls. I pretend not to notice.

Susan St. Aubin

This Isn't About Love

Ilka on the road in her yellow Volkswagen, traveling from job to job: I can see her as clearly now as I could then. Monday nights she's at City College teaching English as a Second Language; Tuesday and Thursday afternoons she teaches two sections of remedial composition at Cabrillo College thirty miles south; Wednesday nights she's thirty miles north at the College of San Mateo teaching self-defense; and Thursday nights it's self-defense again at the Women's Center, which doesn't pay much but she doesn't have to drive so far.

"I'm exhausted," she says when she walks into the university gym where the Women's Center holds its self-defense class.

We sit on the floor dressed in leotards or sweat pants. Lynne, who's gay and wears men's jeans, removes her heavy hiking boots reluctantly because street shoes aren't allowed in the gym. Patty, a sophomore math major with long red hair who says she's sick of male logic, whispers to Louise and Janice from the Women's Studies program, whose breasts float loosely beneath their cotton T-shirts, one aqua, one bright yellow.

I sit against the wall in my black leotard, my long braid of brown hair over one shoulder. We're the regulars; others come for a few lessons then leave.

Ilka dumps a green shoulder bag bursting with books and papers on the floor and pulls from it a rumpled white cotton karate suit.

"This material is so sick," she says, shaking the knee pants and jacket. "It'll last forever."

She means "thick," not "sick"; she's Swiss-German, and though she's taught English for years, her consonants sometimes slip.

A dozen years later I can shut my eyes and watch as she bends to unlace her knee-high boots, then pulls on the heavy cotton trousers before sliding off her denim midi skirt and vest. After she unbuttons her blouse, there's an instant when she stands in her pink camisole before it's covered by the cotton jacket she ties around her waist with a brown cloth belt. She wraps a silk scarf around her head to contain her long blond hair, except for the bangs that cover her eyebrows. She has our rapt attention when she's ready to begin the class. I'm not gay but my breath comes quicker, then and now.

Her green eyes, which she rarely blinks, stare intently as she leads us through our warm-up exercises.

"It's best to be a generalist," she tells us while we stretch. She's taught for years, first in Japan where she tutored businessmen in German and English, and then in California, where she specializes in English as a second language, a subject in which she has personal experience as well as a Master's degree from our university. The self-defense course is her own invention, loosely based on the karate, judo, and aikido she picked up in Japan.

"Use your opponent's energy against him," she tells us as we glide together across the floor of the gym, moving our feet and arms as she's taught us.

"These are the vital spots of the human body," she recites, jabbing her right arm with fingers stretched straight. "Eyes. Base of the skull. Solar plexus. Groin. Knee cap. Christine!" She calls to me across the gym. "Your movements are far too weak. Put some muscle in your arm, push against the air, like so." Her arm swings forward in a controlled punch. "Imagine your attacker."

After class we go to a coffeehouse called Sacred Grounds in the basement of a church where we drink espresso and listen to Ilka talk about her life on the road.

"The freeways are full of boys in delivery trucks," she tells us, her green eyes round and staring. She says she's bisexual and once told us about a woman in Japan named Mika whose body was so smooth and hairless that making love with her was like being caressed by a silk scarf. But only when she speaks of men are her eyes this big. Patty leans forward, while Lynn sits back in her chair, arms folded across her breasts.

These aren't long-distance truckers high up in the cabs of their semis with their eyes fixed on the road, these are boys driving local routes in vans and pickup trucks with signs painted on the side: Doug's Pharmacy, Race Street Fish Market, Global Paint. They honk when they pass her yellow Volkswagen, and she honks back.

"That's stupid," says Lynne. "No matter how good your judo skills are, you're defenseless in a car. What if one of those guys forces you off the road? What if he has a gun? I still say it's better to carry a gun, because if your attacker's got one pointed at you, you can't very well throw him over your shoulder."

Lynne and Ilka have a variation of this conversation nearly every week.

"If you're in control of your own healthy body, you'll never need a gun to defend yourself," says Ilka. This time she smiles, leaning her elbows on the sticky table, and adds, "Besides, you're assuming I'd be unwilling. How can I be defenseless against what I want?"

Lynne's mouth opens, then closes tight.

Still smiling, Ilka tells us about Denny, who has lips like Mick Jagger's and delivers stereo components to a chain of stores up and down Highway 101. He's a drama student at City College whose ex-girlfriend took Ilka's self-defense class at the College of San Mateo. The first time they met, he motioned her off the freeway in Belmont and bought her a drink in a bar, then took her in his company's van into the dry October hills where they made love on the floor among boxes of speakers, turntables, and tape recorders. The van's back doors hung open so they could watch the planes take off from San Francisco Airport to the north. Ilka tells us that except for his shaved face, his whole body is covered with black silky hair that's as smooth as Mika's skin.

Once every couple of weeks she runs into him—the literalness of this expression when applied to their freeway meetings makes us laugh. They always drive somewhere in his van: up to Crystal Springs Reservoir where they make love in the moonlight on the concrete steps of the Pulgas Water Temple or over the mountains to the beach where they lie in the back of the truck and watch the afternoon fog roll in.

It's 1975 and nobody's heard of AIDS. Ilka's on the pill, so all she has to worry about is that Denny might turn out to be a crazed killer who'll pull an ax from behind a stack of stereo speakers and chop her into little pieces which he'll scatter between San Jose and San Francisco. She knows if she wants to she can kick the ax from his hands and paralyze him with a chop to his Adam's apple, but still it excites her to imagine cowering before him, especially when they lie wrapped in each other's arms in the back of the truck on a deserted road in the hills at sunset.

"If there's a part of me that wants direction, I can't be defenseless," she tells us in Sacred Grounds. "The trouble is, I can defend myself too well. I feel so safe with men it's a bore."

"I wouldn't mind being bored like that," says Lynne.

When Ilka stops seeing Denny on the road, she's not too disappointed. Perhaps he quit his job or was fired. Did his boss find the red silk underpants Mika sent her from Japan in an empty turntable box? Did Denny get back together with his old girlfriend? Does he swerve off the road whenever he sees a yellow Volkswagen in the distance?

"He was very immature," she says, sipping coffee. We're all kids, nineteen and twenty years old; she's twenty-nine and we're flattered to be included in her maturity.

One night while pulling out of the parking lot at City College, she sees a quick flash of headlights in her rearview mirror. For a second she thinks the van is Denny's but this one is light blue; and when it passes, she sees no writing on the side. Inside, a man leans back casually as he drives. She catches a glimpse of him, hair unfashionably short, seat tilted back, a cigarette dangling from his lips and then he's gone.

The next week she sees him again at one of the other colleges.

Once more it's late; her night class has just let out, or she's spent the evening tutoring students from her afternoon English class. She watches his eyes in her rearview mirror all the way home. When she changes lanes, so does he: they dance together across the nearly empty highway. When she exits he's close behind, but three blocks from her apartment he pulls ahead and disappears around the corner. His license plate reads "ZIP," but she keeps forgetting what the three numbers are.

When she sees him on a Tuesday afternoon, she gets a better look. "He has a very long nose," she tells us in a whisper. "Of course, you know about men with long noses."

We look at each other for clues.

"They have long penises, too," she says.

Late one warm night in May, he stays on her tail, changing lanes when she does, getting on and off the freeway when she does. When she stops for gas, so does he, but instead of getting out of his van she sees him wave a thick, stubby hand to the attendant sitting behind the flickering light in the window of the gas station. The attendant gets up and strolls out to lean on the open window of the van before filling the tank and washing the windshield.

Ilka rolls her eyes to the side to watch without seeming to as she cleans her own windshield, and so she doesn't see much. His fingers do look short, though, which she thinks contradicts the mythology of the nose. After paying the cashier in her booth beside the gas pumps, where she sits with candy bars and cigarette packages stacked up to her ears, Ilka drives away with the mysterious van close behind.

When he passes, blinking his lights, she follows. He signals right without moving out of his lane and she signals too but stays behind him. When he actually does exit at a sign that says "Rest Stop," Ilka is close behind. The moon is so full and bright that she sees every bush, every rock, almost every blade of grass. She follows him up a winding road that ends at the top of a hill in a circle of picnic tables beside a lighted building nearly as big as a house, with two entrances, one for women and one for men. Two men come out of the men's entrance, one behind the other, and stroll into the bushes behind the building.

She passes the restrooms and parks beside the light blue van, where her pursuer sits staring straight ahead, one arm resting on his steering wheel. The arm looks heavier than his neck and shoulders, but she can't see it clearly because it's hidden by his loose jacket.

She gets out and walks around her car to the open window of the van. At first she thinks he has no legs. Then she realizes his bare feet with their clean, stubby toes *are* his hands, his heavy muscular legs are his arms. He sits in a padded, velvet-covered seat, with one of his legs resting on the open window, the knee crooked like an elbow, while his neatly manicured toes drum the steering wheel.

He laughs as she gasps. He wears bell-bottomed denim pants and a dark blue shirt whose short sleeves flap loosely. With his free foot he pulls a lever on the dashboard, which looks like an airline cockpit with lights and buttons everywhere, and his seat tilts back. He raises his legs straight up above his head, lacing the toes together like fingers as he watches her, then stretches with a thrust of his pelvis and puts his feet back down on the floor where they belong. She backs away one step.

"Why have you been following me?" she asks. With one kick she could knock him out of his van. She can't imagine an attack he might win.

He smiles at her and shrugs; without arms, the shrug seems to originate in his groin. "I could ask you why you followed me up here. What's your name, anyway?"

"Ilka," she says.

His eyes are dark in the moonlight. "Where're you from?" he asks. "Isn't that a German accent?"

"Originally Berne. In Switzerland," she answers before she can stop herself. This is more information than she usually gives the guys she picks up on the road. Her heart beats faster.

"Come for a ride with me, Ilka." The door on the other side of the van pops open when he pulls a lever.

She feels like she's been hypnotized, and knows that even if she needs to, she won't be able to make herself throw him. Obediently she walks around the front of the van and gets in, landing on a padded velvet seat identical to his. He pushes a lever with his big toe and the door shuts. She feels disarmed, and finds this intoxicating, as though she's just smoked a joint. She listens to herself breathe as she rubs her arms across the armrests. He puts one foot on the seat of his chair and moves it rapidly back and forth, brushing the velvet. The moon hangs frozen in the van's windshield.

"We don't have to go anywhere," he says, turning on a light that dimly illuminates the windowless interior of the van. There are two bunks built into each side and covered with velvet spreads to match the front seats. On one of the bunks is a fur rug. The ceiling is glued with squares of mirror; a reflection of the light glows in each one. When he swivels his seat around to face the bunks, so does she.

"Do you live here?" she asks.

"No, but I could if I had to."

He stands up and moves, half stooped in the low van, to the bunk with the fur rug, where he lies down. She kneels on the carpeted floor beside him.

In Sacred Grounds we look at each other, at her, at our cups.

She laughs at us. "You don't believe me! But his legs were so much like arms it seemed like there was nothing missing."

She tells us how he wraps a leg around her waist with a grip so firm she feels she can't escape, and pulls her down on top of him. Her hands slide across the thick fur rug. With his foot he strokes her back, then with one deft motion pulls off her long skirt, which has elastic at the waist, and her underpants. His foot slides up her legs and those toes, she tells us, her mouth slightly open, those toes know just what to do. As they lie side by side, one of the toes—the big toe, she thinks, but she's not quite sure—penetrates her while two or three of the others move around faster than anything she's ever felt before, faster than her own fingers. This can't be a human foot, she thinks, and listens for the hum of a vibrator or maybe some sort of electric arm or mechanical hand, but hears nothing. One leg holds her while the other plays until she comes with a rushing sensation she's never felt before.

"I wet the fur," she whispers to us. "I came like a man. Can you imagine?"

We stare at her, and then I start to giggle.

"I've heard of that happening," says Lynne.

The others shake their heads.

"No," says Janice, who's organizing a library of feminist writing for the Women's Center. "That's not possible."

Lynne glares at us until we're quiet.

Ilka shrugs and says, "It happened."

He rubs the wet spot with his foot and kisses her again. She's still embarrassed, but he finds nothing odd about this wetness; if anything, it seems to arouse him further.

"I don't meet many women like you," he whispers in her ear. "Take your blouse off."

While she sits up to unbutton her blouse, he lifts a toe to his crotch and pulls his fly apart with a rip to expose his erect penis. Where a zipper should be she sees strips of blue Velcro. He slides out of his pants like a snake shedding its skin, but leaves his shirt on. She's fascinated by his short, military haircut.

His leg is around her waist. He pulls her down to his penis, which she takes in her mouth and sucks until she feels he's about to come, then she pushes his leg down and seats herself on top, riding while he writhes beneath.

After he comes, she comes again, but she can't tell if the wetness is hers or his. She rolls onto her back beside him and feels with her hand, then sniffs and licks her fingers, but it all tastes and smells the same.

She sits up. "I've got to leave," she says, and is disappointed when he slithers back into his pants without comment, passing a toe over the Velcro closure. She wants those legs to grip her again so tight she can't move.

Ilka puts on her blouse, fumbling with the buttons. She imagines him reaching under a bunk with his foot and pulling out a gun, but she knows she can unbalance him easily with a kick. She feels let down.

He sits on the bunk smiling at her while she binds her hair in her brown silk scarf then crawls to the front of the van and opens the door. In her mind he jumps on her, pulling her to the floor with his powerful legs while she struggles to break free, but when she looks back, he just sits, smiling.

She jumps out of the van and runs to her car, wanting him behind her, then roars out of the parking lot in a sputter of gravel. She keeps checking the rearview mirror all the way home but he's not there.

Yet he's caught her. Ilka begins driving even when she doesn't have to—Saturday nights, Sunday afternoons, early in the morning she cruises up and down the freeway from San Jose to San Francisco, looking for an unmarked light blue van. She wants his legs wrapped around her waist again while his toes massage her spine. She imagines holding him where his arms should be and shaking him until his heavy legs pull her down. She imagines him with arms wrestling on the floor of his van, his fingers—real fingers—so tight around her neck that the light turns gray.

Did he come into the world unarmed, more helpless than most of us? Or was there some sort of accident—arms ripped from their sockets in a car wreck, arms burned to the shoulder in a fire? Did he lose them in Vietnam to a Viet Cong soldier with a knife or one of his buddies gone mad? She does research in the library on the babies born in Germany in the early sixties without arms because of a drug their mothers took for nerves and nausea, but he's too old for that; he's at least thirty. She hadn't felt his shoulders where the arms should be, so she wonders if he has some sort of residual flipper attached to each one like the thalidomide babies she sees in medical textbooks, reaching for rubber balls with sprouts of tiny hands. She closes her eyes and sees wrists and arms emerging from his shoulder stubs like plants growing in slow motion. His body is outlined in a glimmer of light that remains even when she opens her eyes again, making everything she sees look faded.

That summer Ilka teaches more than ever: Remedial Reading, English as a Second Language, and Freshman Composition at four different colleges. Twice a week she drives across the bay to teach in Hayward, where she tells us there's the possibility of a permanent job. Though her territory has expanded, she doesn't see the blue van for two months.

Then one night she says she's started seeing him on the road again, but always so far behind she has had to drive slowly to let him catch up. She sees him in her rearview mirror, the short hair, the dark eyes staring, even a glimpse of the smile, but when he gets close to her, he speeds ahead and vanishes into the traffic. She ignores the other boys in their vans, who honk and wave as she dodges in and out of traffic after the one van she can never catch.

"It's like I'm hypnotized," she says. "I can't stop." She's not smiling now; her face looks thinner and her wide eyes are swollen.

One day when his van passes she's able to follow him up the freeway, changing lanes when he does, and flashing her signal right, right, right until she herds him up to the rest stop where they met before. His license plate reads "ZIP," and she thinks the three numbers are the same. It's noon and the sun glints off the chrome of parked cars whose license plates are a map of the United States, from Maryland to Oregon, Alabama to Minnesota. Families with small children sit at the picnic tables. A man in his fifties peers at her from the light blue van. He has the short hair, the long nose, but he leans his arms on the open window of his car and says, "Lady, what the hell do you want, anyway?"

"I'm sorry," she says. "I thought you were someone else. A friend of mine has a van just like this."

"Yeah? Well, you've got a hell of a nerve trying to run me off the road like that." Turning abruptly, he climbs back into his van and drives off, wheels spinning in the dusty gravel of the parking lot.

She sits alone in her yellow Volkswagen for nearly an hour before driving down the hill to the freeway.

Though Ilka laughs with the rest of us, I think I can feel her sadness, and I curl my hands into fists under the table when I picture the unarmed man chasing Ilka, catching her, then throwing her back out on the road again so he can play with her without letting her defend herself. What good is her karate if she can never touch him again? Lynne's right, I say to myself, Ilka should carry a gun and shoot him through the windshield the next time his teasing blue van speeds by.

"Maybe you dreamed him. Dreams can often be more true

than reality," says Patty, who plans to change her major to psychology.

"No, he exists, I can assure you." Ilka takes off her silk scarf and shakes out her long blond hair, fluffing it away from her head with one hand while the other plays with the scarf. "But I did dream about him the night after that guy told me off at the rest stop."

We lean forward.

In her dream, the armless man drives up and parks beside her as she sits in her car halfway up a hill. It's not the rest stop, just a green meadow with poppies in the grass. There isn't even any road. She smiles at him; he smiles at her.

"You never told me your name," she calls to him in German.

He answers in English, "I'm one of the unnamed."

When he jumps out of his van, she sees that he's armed with a pistol held in his right foot. His Velcro fly bursts apart so that his penis, too, points straight at her, just below the gun. She's out of her car now, running up the hill. When she looks back she sees him hopping behind her, gun and penis aimed, clearing bushes in one bound. She's panting; she can't quite reach the top because the hill grows as she runs. He dances after her, faster on one leg than she is on two, and she wakes up just as she hears the gun explode.

She breathless as she reaches the end of her story. "I was having an orgasm when I woke up," she says. "It was as though the gun that woke me started the orgasm. He finally gave me what I wanted."

"Death?" I ask. My fingers are clenched under the table. "How can you think you're in love with someone who shoots you?"

"But it was like being shot to life." Ilka looks at me and sighs. "He shot his power into me. I can't explain it, there are no words in any language I know. I'm not talking about love, Chris."

Lynne rolls her eyes to the ceiling and chuckles. "Well, Ilka, that's one way of looking at it. If you won't carry a gun, suck power from his. It's not a bad dream when you think about it."

Ilka smiles into her empty coffee cup, turning it around in her hands as though trying to see the future, while Patty nods like the therapist she wants to become.

I can't find words in any language for what I want to say, either, so my mouth stays closed while I watch Ilka bind her hair up into her scarf again. Though I long to stroke the smooth light hairs on the back of her neck, there's no language in my hands for this desire. I tell myself I'm not gay and never have been, yet I know I could love her better than any man without arms, no matter what she thinks she wants. Sitting across the table from her that night in Sacred Grounds I think I can have her just by putting my arms around her, but I can't move them; it's as though all their muscles have been pulled out.

We didn't see each other much after that. Ilka had so much work in the fall she had no time for self-defense. When the job possibility in Hayward fell through, she wasn't disappointed. "One job would be as boring as one lover," she said.

She began teaching farther north at College of Marin, and moved to San Francisco to be in the center of her work. I heard she had her hair cut short, bought a black Honda sedan, and started wearing suits and carrying her students' papers in a briefcase. In this costume, she began to meet a higher class of men who drove Jaguars or BMWs instead of delivery vans. But by then I'd lost touch with her. I heard that she met the unarmed man again, but he didn't recognize her; I heard that when she saw him again he had arms, and smiled slyly at her confusion. Patty still claims the whole thing was Ilka's fantasy.

The truth is I don't know how Ilka's story ended, though I often think about the possibilities. Does she still expect to see him whenever a light blue van comes up behind her, close on her tail as she heads down the freeway to San Jose? These days, self-defense has a different definition. Is she a cautious woman who carries condoms wrapped in pink cellophane in her briefcase instead of a karate suit? Does he keep a box of them in the glove compartment below the dashboard of his van? Does he pull this box out with his toes, take off the lid, rip open a plastic packet with his teeth and, with his skillful big toe, glide the glistening pink sheath onto himself? Or does he reach his foot into the glove compartment and pull out a pistol, swirling it around on his big toe before he shoots her, just the way she likes it?

The Shape of the Feeling

When alone, I prepare for my orgasms just as I would prepare to bake bread. First, I wipe off the counter. Then I carefully lay out all the utensils I will be using. My body is the dough. I knead it in my hands like putty. I toss it up in the air and wait for it to fall into my arms like a lover.

Often, I want an orgasm so bad I feel it before it comes which prevents it from coming. For years that's what I thought pre-orgasmic meant: feeling prematurely.

Sometimes I have to take my orgasms. Like a horse extending her neck down to the trough for a drink of water.

Each time, I know exactly how far down I have to go. As if I am digging for them in the garden and can see the level clearly, like liquid in a measuring cup. They are always there, concealed in the soil, but I sometimes can't decide if it is worth the dredging. I sense I will have to dig deeply this time. To the point where there will be dirt under my nails and perhaps my hands will start to bleed. It is an important decision. Because after a certain point, there is no turning back, no matter how hard the struggle.

What does an orgasm look like? Like fish shooting out in all different directions from a pebble dropped in their pond.

The most wonderful orgasm is like popcorn popping all over.

The orgasm sometimes comes as easily as pop sucked through a straw.

I keep going back to the fireworks analogy to describe my orgasms, because each one is different and once I set it off, I can never predict the outcome. Some start out with a bang but fizzle. And some start as misfires but suddenly, way high up in the sky, just when you thought they were gone, spread out into the most brilliant umbrella.

At times I think of the orgasm spreading through my body like news spreads through a neighborhood.

The only time I can concentrate anymore is when I am having an orgasm.

My orgasms generally don't come easily.

Orgasms often play hide-and-seek like the keys I can hear, but can't find, at the bottom of my purse.

I have "slight orgasms" like I have "slight headaches." I wish two aspirins could cure both.

It takes me so long to reach orgasm I feel like I am on a freeway caught in a major traffic jam.

I always feel hungry after an orgasm, perhaps because I never feel licked clean.

Sometimes I become frustrated about orgasms in the same way I become frustrated when I am hungry for something I can't quite put my finger on. Was it salty or sweet or . . . ? Oftentimes, I won't eat or masturbate, which makes me even more frustrated. Or worse, I eat the wrong thing or have a worthless orgasm.

The orgasm was dead on arrival, a tired bubble meandering to the top of an old bottle of Calistoga water gone flat.

The orgasm teases like the fish I can feel down below, nibbling on the bait but never grabbing the hook.

It is senseless to pursue certain orgasms. I am like a kitten licking and licking the white bowl after the cream is long gone.

The orgasm looks like the sad, dark face of the sunflower.

I can't understand why my orgasms embarrass me. I don't want anyone to see me having them. When I was a little girl, I ran around Kiddieland joyfully getting on every ride while my parents stood watching me with delight. I loved them looking on as much as I loved the rides. So why am I so self-conscious now?

Upon reaching middle-age, I take an aesthetic interest in orgasms. Some nights, I even have "working orgasms" so I can write about them. Orgasms for the sake of art. Or, sometimes, I schedule my orgasms as if they were some sort of athletic event. Still others, it is as though I am shopping for the right one.

I dream that when I am applying for a job, one of the questions on the job application is: how many times per week do you masturbate? Come? Give up? I am told that corporations have discovered, through their human resources departments, that they can tell how productive an employee will be based on her/ his response to the preceding question.

At times, my orgasms seem to have little to do with me, just like various summer odd-jobs I have taken. So why pursue them?

I've concluded that orgasms are just like people; some are more likable than others.

My final orgasm always feels like an afterthought because I never know when to quit. I think the phrase "you should know when to quit" was started by someone who knew exactly which orgasm to stop on. . . .

. . . Yet I somehow enjoy the final orgasms of the evening in a different way, even though I have to search harder for them. Like looking for a memory hidden in the body. The first orgasms come to me; the final ones I have to hunt for. It is like a game of tag: I get tagged, and then I'm it.

To "achieve" orgasms I have to play both sides at once. I have to hold on and give up at exactly the same moment.

Somewhere in the world I believe there must be a dark room with a sign on the door saying "Lost Orgasms" where all the orgasms I almost had are. If I ever find that room, I knew exactly the number of orgasms I will try to claim and wonder if everyone else knows their number, too.

I have orgasms that feel like they are happening somewhere else, perhaps in a foreign country.

It is one of those orgasms, that, if someone asked me, I'd have to say, "Yeah, it's mine," though I am not sure. Like the way I feel upon leaving a party when the host approaches me with a generic black umbrella and asks, "Is this umbrella yours?" Though I know that I came with one like it and take it to be polite, I am not quite sure it is mine.

I offer my orgasms up on a bare table covered with an immaculate white sheet, higher and higher out of my body to reach the birds that peck at the invisible crumbs. I must sacrifice my orgasms in order to have them, constantly letting them go, letting go.

Serena Moloch

I Visit the Doctor:
A Tale

In this country where I live it rains in the summer and snows in the winter and I bleed every month; I have been bleeding every month for two years. When I bleed the world caves in at my stomach, I scream and keen, pain drives through me like spikes with poisoned tips. In this country where I live there are many rules: no one can touch me or check me in my pain. The rules of the family cell are very strict: no touching of the daughter's body permitted until the touch of her husband at marriage. All girls must be virgins at marriage, the certificate from the doctor must attest to that. When the cramps overtake me my mother and older sisters look at me in pity. They would like to touch me and help me, gently take up my limbs and massage them as they could when I was a baby—I do not remember this, they have whispered of it to me—but they are not allowed. No touching of the daughter's body once she is able to walk; the rules state it very clearly and the consequences of disobedience are dire.

Finally one day I stopped screaming from the pain and began instead to rip my clothes and shred my lips. Finally, it was conceded, I must be sent to a doctor, and an appointment was made for me the next day.

Only women can be doctors for women in this country and I

had imagined that this doctor would be stern and forbidding. She was not: she was beautiful. When I walked into her office I saw one woman seated at a desk with another woman leaning over her, pointing at something on a paper. The woman who had been pointing straightened up and looked deep into my eyes. She was tall when she stood, very tall; she wore a green blouse and gray skirt and her eyes were very black. Her hair was pulled back tight; her mouth was loose and full. Her might and sweetness momentarily stunned me. I had never seen a woman who looked quite like this. My sisters, my mother, and my teachers always looked subdued and pressed dry: this woman looked like no amount of wringing could ever quite sap her of her juices. I stood rooted to my spot as she walked toward me and put her hand out to shake. I took it. "Melissa Parker?" she asked. I nodded, squeezing her hand. She didn't let mine go. "I'm Dr. Simone Blackstone." We squeezed hands again. "Come this way."

We moved into a dark and woody office. All over the walls hung diagrams of pink, exposed flesh with stringy extensions and gaping, pulpy cuts. We sat down and she smiled at me.

"Before we begin, I have to ask you several questions. This is called 'taking a history.' Have you been to a doctor before?"

"No," I said. "Since the rules don't permit girls to go to a doctor except in case of emergency, I suppose that this is my first emergency."

"Yes. Well, I will take care to explain things to you as I do them. Next, the law says I must ask you if you are married or unmarried?"

"Unmarried," I replied.

"And virginal or not?" she asked. Smiling wryly, she said, "The official terms, I am required to state, are pure or tainted."

"Virginal," I responded blandly, but she had caught my interest even further. Was she a renegade?

"And what is the problem for which you are here today, Miss Parker?"

"I have unbearable pains when I bleed every month," I answered.

"Those can be difficult to endure. I see many young women like you who have the same problem. It seems to have an increased incidence under this new regime. How long have you been getting your period?"

"Almost two years."

"When do you experience the most pain?"

"The day before I bleed," I said, looking wistfully into her face which seemed so kind, so caring, and so competent to save me. "You can't know how much it hurts. I want to die, I think I am dying, but then it's never over; I have to go through it over and over again."

Her hand moved, almost twitched toward me, then rested where it was, on top of her pen. "I think I can help you. There are a variety of tests we can run and treatments I can prescribe." She hesitated a moment and sounded my eyes with her own. I gazed at her studiously. "Some of my recommendations are a bit unorthodox," she said, "and you will have to carry them out privately and secretly. You are, of course, not obliged to follow my directions, and I can always refer you to another doctor if you object to any of my practices. One final question: when was your last period? The last time you were bleeding?"

"I'm bleeding now," I replied.

"Are you in pain?" she asked sympathetically.

"I am," I answered.

"I'll do my best to help you," she said.

Her voice was mellow, deep, and melodious. I had watched her hands intently as she wrote down my spoken words; they were big, well-formed, and strong. Her neck curved away from her tied-back hair and I could see the slope of her shoulders beneath her shirt. I had never been this close to a grown woman before. My mother and sisters had to keep a distance from me, as the law commands. But the law also designates those who can exercise a "sanctioned touch," and doctors are among these chosen. Soon those hands would be on me.

She told me to go into the next room, undress, and drape myself with the white cloths on the table. I moved into a very clean and cold white room. There were counters that dipped into sinks at each end, long burnished surfaces adorned with gleaming metal objects stacked with tiny bottles and piles of small, rectangular, greenish glass plates. In the center of the room stood a narrow raised gray bed with two footrests swerving upward at one end. I took off my clothes, folded them, and neatly arranged them in a corner. I wrapped the drape around myself, and not knowing what to do about my blood, I held my hand between my legs to catch it. The doctor knocked on the door. "May I come in?" Her smooth voice nibbled warmly at the cold goose-flesh creeping up my arms and legs. I shivered and called out, "Yes, I'm ready."

She opened the door and saw me standing in the center of the room, trembling, with my hand cupped between my legs. I felt hot blood trickle onto my fingers and more blood rush to my cheeks. "Leave your underpants on for now," she said. "Here," She knelt down by my pile and rummaged through it until she reached my underwear—the sanitary pad was already sodden and she lifted it off saying, "Wait—let me give you a fresh napkin." She fished one out of a drawer and adhered it skillfully to my white underwear. She handed me a tissue and said, "Here—would you like to wipe your hands?" I accepted her offering and blotted my reddened hands on it, then stood bewildered, not knowing what to with the damp red tissue. I couldn't see a trash can anywhere. "Here," she said, opening a cabinet that magically produced one for me, "drop it in." She flipped the lid open with an authoritative slam of her foot, and we both let our bloody cloths drop from our hands into the can. She handed me my underwear and turned around so that I could put it on without her seeing me. Cramps twisted my insides and I grimaced with the pain. I climbed into my underpants and gently touched her back; she didn't start. "Okay," I said.

'First I have to weigh you," she said, "come this way." She pointed to a scale. I padded over to it and clambered up on to its rubber platform. She moved iron pieces back and forth knowledgeably; as she did so, her arm passed over my shoulder and her hand flashed back and forth in front of my chest. I could hear her breathe. "All right," she said, "now please sit on the table over there." By table she seemed to mean the bed. I mounted it and crossed my arms in front of my draped breasts to stay warm.

"Are you cold?" she asked me.

"A little," I said.

"I'm sorry. You should warm up soon. Please extend one arm so I can take your blood pressure." I gave her my right. She wrapped it in a prickly cuff and began to squeeze an oval ball in her hand. My whole arm felt constricted, my blood stopped, I felt panicked. I looked at the plastic boa she had laced around my arm. She seemed to be counting to herself. She released the ball and freed my arm from the cuff. Stooping a little to look in my face she said, "I'm sorry. That tightening feeling is frightening, I know." She lifted a sinuous instrument from her neck and placed two tubes in her ears, holding the silvery disk at the lower end with two fingers.

"The next part is easy," she said, "I'm going to listen to your heart and lungs. Please lower your drape."

I dropped it. She placed the shiny, round pendant against my breast and listened. She moved around me and placed it on my back. "Breathe out." My breasts lifted up and down, swelled and sank. "Breathe in," she said. "Breathe out."

My midriff contorted as a series of cramps momentarily distracted me from the novel sensation of a voice so close to my ears and hands so firm on my skin. Then the pain receded and I concentrated on the pinpoints of feeling her cool fingers left on my flesh. No one had ever touched me before. I had never been this close to another woman's body. Hers was a doctor's body, a sanctioned body, and a doctor's touch, a sanctioned touch. Yet in the wake of her fingers and through the supple cloth of her shirt I felt the honeyed musky heat of a woman's body, one that I recognized from my own, from having sniffed myself out, under my arms and between my breasts, as I tossed and turned on sleepless nights. My back seemed to crackle with this heat even as her calm fingers examined me methodically.

I felt uncertain, wobbly, yet on the brink of an enormous clarification. She snapped the instrument out of her ears so that it lay draped around her neck, a snaky talisman. I was still cold but I didn't raise the drape. She looked not at my breasts but into my eyes.

"Since you've never had an exam before, I'm not going to try to complete one today. Today, in fact, I will not touch you at

all. I'm going to show you in a mirror what you look like and
I'm going to teach you a way to treat yourself for your pains."

I felt strange. Her manner, her words, were very distant and
poised. But will you think that I'm crazy if I tell you that it was
love that I felt flowing between us? Love in her concern for me,
in the attentive searching and probing of her questions, her eyes,
her hands. Love in the crazy way that my heart beat so hard I
almost expected her snaky necklace to be charmed up toward it,
to lift its head up to my breasts so that I could hear it crashing
in spasms against my bones. . . . But crazy, I thought, I must be
crazy, because her voice just moved steadily on and on, "If at
any time you feel pain or discomfort, tell me and I'll stop what
I'm doing. Okay?" I nodded; what I had just assented to, I didn't
know. I lifted my eyelids all the way up to try and slow my heart
down. She raised the back of the bed so that I was sitting and
asked me to remove my underwear. She helped me get it off my
ankles and bent down again to place it with my other clothes.
Her skirt pulled tight against her as she did this and I looked. I
did look.

She brought a large purple mirror over to me and said silkily,
"If you hold this by your knee you'll be able to see your genitalia.
I'll point out the structures to you." I placed the mirror and
looked—I saw only the dark, downy skin of my thighs. "Let me
help you," she said, and placed her hand on mine to angle the
mirror. The shock of her flesh on my flesh met the shock of black
hair, masses of it swirling around purple, swollen skin, skin I'd
never seen, skin that made no sense, except for the muddy red
sap that fled from it. I was terrified.

She sat on a stool and moved between my legs to open a drawer
from which she pulled out beige, powdery gloves, matte and
sanitary counterparts to the lurid nest between my legs she had
revealed to me. She put her fist against my thigh: "You're going
to feel me touch you now." She put a finger on each side of the
purple skin and then spread it: I saw now that this eggplant-
colored, engorged flesh arranged itself into layers and folds, pyramids nested within one another. She began to point but not
touch with her finger.

"These," she said, gesturing toward the hairy billows closest to my thighs, "are the labia majora, the outer lips. They have hair on them, and that's normal." She moved in toward the deep-eyed skin, which, as I looked more closely, seemed to resemble gathered, ruffled cloth, or the whorls and swirls of fingerprints, or the windings and turnings inside exotic puff-pastries. Curiosity began to edge out my dismay and I craned my head forward to peer closer into the mirror. "These lips," she said, "which are somewhat darker and don't have hair on them, are the labia minora, the inner lips." She gestured toward the space between them and told me, "This is the vagina, the internal opening. Your hymen, or virginity, is a thin membrane partly covering the entrance to this opening. Your blood passes through it during your periods." No mention of my husband, my babies, which I had been told often enough would also pass through there one day if I was good.

My gaze drifted up from the vagina and I saw that a tiny rounded cone crowned all the other structures. Its shape exactly matched that of a ring that had been mine as a very young girl. Here it was again, between my legs, only no longer sapphire but red like the red of angry skin, skin that's been cut or burned. I watched the doctor's elegant fingers ripple along the two inner lips without touching them.

"The labia minora meet up top," she said, "to form the hood of the clitoris." She moved her hands off me—I almost clawed at her with regret—then laid them on me again, on the hair swarming on my lower belly. She pulled the skin beneath my hair up, stretching back the paler covering of the clitoris and exposing the ruddy cone more perfectly. "You see?"

"I see," I replied.

She stood up. "That's all I'm going to do today by way of a physical exam. But I would like to teach you a way to relieve your pain. By touching the clitoris you can produce sensations which may feel strange or may feel pleasurable to you, perhaps both. If you continue to touch yourself patiently and carefully, you will begin to feel a tension building up, the feelings increasing until it feels like somehow they must stop. Try touching the clitoris directly, or in a sidelong fashion; you can hold it between your fingers, rub it, roll it—there are an infinity of approaches.

You must continue to touch yourself until you feel what is sometimes called a climax. It is difficult to describe but impossible not to recognize. Afterward your heart will beat rapidly, your breath will come quickly, and you will experience a feeling of peace and well-being. Your body releases chemicals upon climax which will temporarily relieve your pain." She looked at me somewhat archly, I thought, considering how businesslike her recommendations had been. "The prescription," she said, "is to repeat as often as necessary."

All this, I knew, had to be among the things that were "strictly forbidden." For the only transgressions more serious than allowing someone else to touch you was to touch yourself. Was this a test? I kept my silence.

"I know that strictly speaking this is not permitted," she said soothingly, her voice seeping with as much assurance as reassurance. She seemed taller than ever and suddenly I forgot my pain in my hunger to let her hair down loose around her face. "But I am prescribing it to you as a medical treatment and I sanction it as such. I will leave the room so that you can practice this technique in complete privacy. Just permit me to place this cloth beneath you, to catch any liquids. Your touch may stimulate the flow of blood and other fluids from your vagina." She picked a cloth up from the side table and without being asked, I raised my hips so that she could place it beneath me. "Call me in when you have successfully completed the course of treatment," she said, "and don't be afraid to take all the time you need."

She left and closed the door behind her and I pondered my situation. Was it a trap? I could always plead ignorance, if it were, for I would have been disobeying one order only to follow another. Another screeching pain coiled within me and I decided to try. I watched in the mirror as my left hand crept down and gently prodded the clitoris she had revealed to me. I rubbed two fingers back and forth across it and felt the stirrings of—irritation? Wriggling? Tautness? Melting? Blood did begin to ebb hotly out of me and hit the cloth. I tried pinching the clitoris between my thumb and forefinger and moving it back and forth, which pushed all the feelings out along my thighs and backside and somehow made my hipbones ache. Perhaps this would paralyze me—perhaps the transgression would be its own punishment. Perhaps I should stop, but I was a bit beyond stopping already. I dared to wet my finger in my own blood and use the moisture to help glide over the clitoris more quickly. The skin between my legs began to feel hot and demanding all over and very naked, flesh with its nerves exposed instead of buried beneath the clothes and skin and laws. My whole body began to writhe and it became difficult to steady the mirror, but I held onto it rather than put it down because the scene reflected in its purple frame interested me, the blood smearing my thighs a bit now, my fingers jerking back and forth rhythmically, my inner lips puffing up even more and moving toward the mirror, then away from it, then in, then back, then in again. . . . I needed more, even more, though I also feared that I would hurt myself if I pressed harder—but the damage didn't matter anymore, no possible harm could stand between me and my rushing blood. Dark spots blotted my vision, my arm began to tire but that pain didn't matter either; I pushed harder and harder on the clitoris, which had gotten hard and rearing. I dug my fingers into it and pushed, pushed until I felt something coming, roaring through me, bursting, gushing, then dropping away and leaving me almost dead on that bed that was called a table. When I finally caught my breath and stopped hearing my heart, the rats gnawing at my entrails and stomach had begun to dissolve.

I had slid forward on the table so I shifted into a more composed position, bracing my feet against the metal supports and gliding back up. I cleared my throat and called out, "I'm finished."

The doctor pushed the door open and stood before me, her dark eyes looking closely into mine. "Well?" she asked. "Did it work?"

"I think it did," I said to her, examining her as I spoke. My rapturous and drowsy state brushed all that my eyes could see with a hazy aura. The instrument around her neck gleamed more brightly and more softly. Her captured hair looked even more inviting, her neck smoother and her mouth more lush. I tried to read her eyes to see what she might be feeling. Did she know pleasures like the ones she had just taught me to give myself?

She must, and more. Did the same country of damp russet marshes and wild reeds grow between her legs? Could I ever see it? I thought wildly of all the forbidden things I had ever heard about, the many laws and transgressions: there were words that meant things that I knew were wrong, bad, dirty, filthy, forbidden, but I only knew the words, I could hardly picture the deeds. "Kiss" was forbidden, I knew, and "fondle" and "deflower," if it wasn't your husband—all these prohibitions I had heard proclaimed in official gatherings and teachings. Then there were the whispers at school, "Put something inside you," the other, older girls sniggered, "feel you up," "do you," "fuck you" were hidden, scorching words that came back to me now. I wanted to learn more and to make this woman teach it to me. She had laid her hands on me once and I had felt my body rise, leaving its pain behind. She would lay them on me again if I had my way. Surely I could trust her not to punish me even if she did refuse my demand.

Her dark eyes caved into mine and I risked all. "Kiss me," I said imperiously, raising my arms, reaching up for her. And then a miracle came to pass. She bent her head toward mine and placed her lips against my lips, snaked her arms around my tilted neck, and nuzzled my face with hers. I pulled her shoulders toward me and stroked them through her shirt as her tongue touched my lips, my teeth, my tongue, moving deeper into my mouth and licking it inside. I did the same and felt the rough wetness of our mouths together, licking each other, sucking each other, gliding back and forth. I reached up to remove her hairband and moved my face away from hers to enjoy the cascade of dark curls. I sighed with pleasure and then asked coyly, remembering the insinuations of the girls' hallway, "Will you fondle me? Will you take me?"

She lifted her head from mine and gripped my shoulders while her eyes interrogated me. Perhaps she too feared a trap. "You know it is forbidden?" she asked.

"I know," I said earnestly, but I returned her look steadily with what I hoped was persuasive forthrightness. I twirled her ringlets about my fingers. I thought again, of how they said, "put something inside you," and "deflower," and all the trouble that could follow. But I also knew that it was doctors who provided the certificates of virginity for marriage, and doctors who could attest that they had deflowered you for reasons of medical necessity. She could do this for me: show me what was forbidden and guarantee my safety. "You could give me a certificate of medical cause," I said as respectfully as I could with my hand delving into her hair and my breast heaving. "I would never breathe a word," I said shyly, trying to bury my head in her shoulder as I murmured, "you have opened one door for me; I know there are many more. Please." I gently pressed the nape of her neck and moved to kiss her again. "Please." I heard her breathing begin to deepen hoarsely and felt her fingers grab for the drape that lay bunched around my stomach. She flung it to the floor. "Wait here," she said.

She left for a moment and returned with a candle. She locked the door behind her, turned off the light, placed the candle on the counter, and kindled it. The room's bright sharp glare eddied into mysterious half-tones; deep huge shadows hurled themselves onto the walls. She moved stealthily toward me and raised her finger to her lips: hush, she indicated, nodding, and I nodded back. As she neared me she steadily unbuttoned her blouse and then took one of her breasts out, lifting it from its corset so that it spilled forth, smooth and swollen, the soft brown nipple at its center. Her breast was no bigger than my own but as she brought its rounded expanse and sheen closer into my field of vision, it looked enormous, a polished globe approaching my hungering mouth.

She bent over me and opened my mouth with her fingers and said softly, "Suck. Lick me with your tongue and suck." I felt smothered in steamy softness and did as she said. She took my hands and placed them around her breast. "Squeeze it," she said. "And stroke it." I obeyed, gently pressing her breast as I felt the flesh in my mouth crinkle beneath my tongue and become hard and pointed. I sucked on the knob that had formed, harder and harder, and even dared to bite it delicately. Her breath rasped and her hands pressed mine harder and deeper into her breast. She leaned into me and then backed away slightly, almost tugging her breast away from my clamped teeth and suckling lips, then covering my face with it again. Where she went, I went; my mouth followed her breast and our flesh formed one fevered mass. I sucked and stroked fervently, hopefully: could this, too, produce a climax? She chuckled me under my chin and with her fingers again opened my mouth. "Let me go now," she whispered. "Let me do this to you."

The excitement had set my stomach churning and the cramps had begun to creep back through my legs. Her mouth found mine again and she grasped my lips firmly between hers as she lay her hands on me, one on each breast. She teased my nipples with a feathery touch, circling them so softly I had to strain to identify her fingers on me, teasing the ends of my breasts which began to tingle with the same naked irritation I had felt before in my clitoris. She fluted the tip of her tongue into all my mouth's moist parts and began to pinch the tips of my breasts which, like hers, had gotten wrinkled and firm. She pinched them as I had pinched my clitoris, then moved her mouth down toward them, bending over me as she stood so that she could lick at the bits of tight, tender flesh that protruded from between her fingers.

Hot blood bathed my thighs. She moved both hands to one of my breasts and gathered its plumpness up like a feast between her fingers, molding my breast beneath her hands as she kissed its tip and grazed it with her tongue, then sucking all she could into her greedy velvet mouth. Her hair draped me, deliciously, temptingly soft. Shocks came in and out of my body from all directions and I almost groaned, but remembered our vow of silence just as one of her hands left my breast to cover my mouth. I licked her fingers and stroked them with my hands, twisting and turning on the narrow bed she called a table. I took her hand and moved it down on my body.

"The cramps have begun again," I said. "Do me," I almost chanted in a low voice in the fiery, dim room. "Put something inside me, take me," I sang to her. She caressed my stomach forcefully, catching the rhythm of my pulse and meeting it with her own hands. She moved around the table so that she stood between my legs which she massaged. My hands fluttered gratefully toward her, for my legs were sore from the position imposed by the supports, but I could not please her in return; she

was out of reach. She sat again on the stool and rolled it in closer
between my legs. I ached to touch her. She looked up at my
imploring figure and said, "Put your hands up and hold onto the
table behind you. Do not let go until I say so." I followed her
order and grasped the corners of the table; my raised arms an-
chored me securely and lifted my still damp, still pointed breasts,
made my stomach stretch so that I almost thought I could see
the blood coursing underneath it, not merely feel it pass out of
me, drenching the white patch beneath me.

She moved closer in and spread my legs even further apart as
she bent her head toward my ravenous purple mouth framed
with hair as black and wiry as her own. She flicked out her
tongue and ran it between my inner lips, drawing a trail of blood
up into her mouth as she went. My hands clasped the table spas-
modically as she reached my clitoris with her tongue, drawing it
to a point with her tongue's tip, then broadly licking it. She sank
her chin in to the dripping, bloody space between my inner lips;
it fit there perfectly. She turned her head from side to side and
I began to feel sensation where her chin rocked back and forth,
sensations that met the sharper ones above, there where her
tongue pummeled my clitoris. She moved her hands from my
thighs and slipped them under my behind which I was desperately raising as I tried to push myself deeper into her lapping,
stroking mouth, her jutting chin. She grabbed my behind as she
buried her face in me, now sucking my clitoris which she had
trapped between slightly open teeth, a sugar cube for her to suck
her tea through. The blood was gurgling out of me now and the
cramps tightened their hold as if to protest their imminent si-
lencing.

"Please," I said. "Please take me now." She stopped and moved
back; the candlelight flickered and caught the blood glowing on
her chin, dyeing her teeth ruby red and flecking her cheeks in
spots. "Please end this pain," I implored her quietly. "Please take
me." She kissed my stomach, my breasts, my lips, leaving a trail
of O-shaped red marks on my skin. She stood to the side of me
and said, "Where do you feel the pain?" "Here," I said, placing
her hand on my stomach. She laid her hand flat and rotated it
back and forth, pressing my pain with the heel of her hand, then

her fingertips. "Where do you feel the pleasure?" she asked. "Here," I said, placing her free hand on my breast. "And here," moving the other and shoving it down between my legs.

"Where pain was," she sang to me, "there pleasure will be." The cramps leapt up toward the surface of my skin and vied with the joys her palpitating hands created in my breasts and clitoris. Her fingers slid into the bleeding cleft between my purple lips and slowly prodded my opening, toyed around it, then deepened their hold in me with a tiny thrust forward, circling around, then entering, while her thumb pressed my clitoris to and fro. The cramps began to overtake everything, their pain blinding me to anything I might ever have known, forcing my feet to dig into the supports, ramming my hands into the spongy table, arching my back so that I met her fingers which had moved even deeper. I felt a pain inside me, within me, her fingers pulled back and forth within me, dragged back in by my bloody ring of desire. Her thumb on my clitoris raced to match her insistent in-and-out inside me and I knew again the force which said that nothing could hurt me in my violent wish to feel that explosion once again. I hurled myself back and forth on her hand, wrenching my shoulders as I forced myself onto her fingers.

Again I felt the climax, the pain dissolved, subdued, the sleepy blindness as the candle seemed to fire up, then snuff itself out. I shuddered and relaxed my body more fully onto the table. Soon, she called out softly to me, "I'm going to remove my fingers now."

She drew them out gradually and lifted the cloth from beneath me. "Your blood is here," she said softly. "They call it virgin and deem it holy, but it is mixed with blood even more holy, the blood of your pain, the blood of your pleasure, the blood that comes, the blood that goes." She crumpled the cloth up and clasped it in her hand. Her face loomed above mine, illuminated by the candle soaring behind her. I sat up and turned my face toward her and the words I had heard so often lilted off my tongue though I had forgotten what they meant: "blood of my blood and flesh of my flesh." I licked the blood from her fingers and her chin, then pressed my cheek to her breast as my arms circled her hips. I tasted metal, salt, and savored her heartbeat.

Angela Fairweather

The Trojan Woman

Margo is staring at the telephone and feeling foolishly adoles-
cent. Her only reasonable option is to make the call. And she
can't. Nervously, she twists the copy of *Penthouse* into a roll and
releases it. She does this twice more, then sets the magazine down
in a gesture of determination and picks up the phone receiver.

"Bill Meyers, please. This is Margo Winstead calling. Hi, Bill?
Margo. I've got a problem and I need your help." She winces as
she says this. "Well, no, I don't want to talk about it right now.
I was wondering if you're free tonight and if you are, I could
treat you to dinner. . . . Okay, well, how about tomorrow night?
Great, think about where you'd like to go. . . . Oh yes, of course
it can wait. . . . No, I'm not upset, it's really kind of funny, but
I just don't want to talk about it right now. You'll understand
when I tell you. . . . Yes, I'll be home tomorrow afternoon. Why
don't you come over around five . . . sure, we can go somewhere
intimate and romantic." Margo stifles a giggle. "No, that doesn't
freak me out. So I'll see you tomorrow at five."

The next dilemma is how to broach the subject. Bill is, after
all, the best male friend she's ever had, like a member of the
family—like a brother. No, that doesn't feel right; you don't have
sex with your brother. But it isn't exactly sex. *What the hell is*

it, then? Well it's an experiment. No, it's research. Margo wrestles with this complex issue for a while then decides it's too much to think about until she must.

But it keeps creeping back into her consciousness. She's not sure she can do it. Why not? Because he's got a great body and he's my friend? Because he might not want to. Oh. Would he want to? He tried to talk me into it a few times. Yeah, but that was six months ago. Margo feels a hot rush of insecurity surge through her body. Maybe she should wear something slightly provocative to set the scene. Oh for God's sake, this is research, not a seduction! Yeah, but maybe he won't be in the mood. Is a man ever *not* in the mood? Sometimes John wasn't in the mood. Yeah, but you were married to him; that's different. Maybe.

At 4:30 the following afternoon she's still not sure what to wear. This is ridiculous—just put something on. Like your purple print dress. It's kind to your figure and the color's good. No, a dress would be too obvious. Wear pants. Pants? Yes, wear the black silk pants and your teal-colored sweater. You can wear that pretty scarf with it. But what if . . . ?

The doorbell rings. Margo throws on a robe and lets Bill in. He's dressed casually—almost Ivy League—in a button-down shirt, slacks, and a sports jacket.

Margo's not uncomfortable in her robe. After all, she's practically camped out at Bill's some weekends. But they haven't been lovers. Not that Bill would mind. The collapse of her marriage has made her hesitant. Bill is a patient man.

Margo apologizes, says she's running late. "I'll be ready in a sec," she says as she goes back into the closet and puts on the purple dress.

"You look especially pretty tonight," Bill says after their wine is served. "Problems seem to agree with you these days. What's up?"

Margo takes a sip of Beaujolais. "Oh, nothing really," she replies, trying very hard to sound offhand. "I've just been puzzling over something at work and thought you might have some insights I hadn't considered."

The waiter arrives at this moment with a steaming pot of mussels. This is helpful as they can't shell mussels and stare meaningfully at each other at the same time. It's a few minutes before Bill returns to the problem.

"So what kinds of insights could I possibly provide a medical anthropologist?"

"Well." Margo hesitates. "Well, I'm real concerned about the HIV virus spreading so quickly through the local drug community. We're seeing a dramatic increase in infected women—the women in my clinic group, for instance. They don't have much resistance—once they're infected it's only a matter of months, even weeks, before they're sick. Since most of the women have husbands or lovers who are junkies, and since some of them are also prostitutes, it's a real serious issue." Margo pauses to eat a mussel which she has carefully placed on a piece of French bread and dipped in the broth.

"At any rate, last Thursday at the clinic outreach group I asked the women if they used condoms during sex. Most of them said they didn't because their men refuse to wear them." She pauses. "Have you used a condom?" There. The ice is broken. Margo is blushing slightly.

"Sure," answers Bill. He doesn't seem the least bit put off.

"Well, what's your opinion?"

"Sex feels better without them, but if my partner felt they were necessary, I'd use them." He continues, "I don't know how guys looking for prostitutes feel, but if I was buying sex, which I don't, I'd definitely use a rubber."

"Can you tell if you have one on?" Margo doesn't feel quite so awkward now that she's broached the subject.

"Yeah. Sure you can."

"So, supposing a woman were to put one on you, you'd know you had it on?"

"Well, of course I would."

"But say she did it with her mouth. Like if she went down on you." As the talk gets more specific, the going gets tougher.

"To tell you the truth, I've never had oral sex performed on me with a condom on, so I don't know." They could be discussing suntan lotions as far as Bill's concerned. He doesn't fluster easily. All of a sudden, he laughs. "Margo, are you asking about this because of the article on the Puerto Rican bordello? You know, the one in the *Penthouse* you snuck out of my house last weekend?"

This catches Margo off-guard. "No," she answers too quickly. Then, "Well, in part, yes, I guess." She sets her fork down and looks at Bill. "Originally I borrowed it thinking the article might have insights about certain men resisting condom use, but I hadn't gotten around to reading it before group last Thursday. One of the women mentioned she heard of someone who put condoms on her tricks while having oral sex—actually, to be specific, she said, 'I heard 'bout a whore from Texas puts the rubbers on their dicks with her mouth.' "

They both chuckle. It amuses Bill to hear Margo use slang.

"So then when I read the article in *Penthouse* and the American woman talked about doing it too, I just wondered if this was fairly commonplace or not—or if it was the same woman."

Bill laughs. "Well, it hasn't happened to me yet, honey, but I wouldn't resist if I had the opportunity to try it! But how does this tie in with your problem?"

Margo giggles self-consciously. "Oh, shit. You're probably going to think I've gone over the edge, but the other night I did something really crazy."

"You tried it on someone." He gives her a wicked grin.

"Bill! Now be serious, this is embarrassing." Margo looks stern, then breaks down again. "No. After I read the article I decided I wanted to see if it was even possible, so I walked down to the all-night drugstore and bought some condoms. And, geez Louise, I had no idea there were so many kinds! You need a consumer's guide to figure out what to buy. I mean they come in different sizes and colors and flavors and there were 'pet condoms' in a special box . . . it was pretty remarkable!"

"So what did you get?" Bill asks, fascinated by his dinner companion.

"Well, it was so overwhelming I just bought some Trojans because I recognized the name." This isn't quite accurate, actually, as Margo also purchased a couple of boxes of the more exotic varieties on impulse. She isn't ready to disclose this yet, however.

"And then I went to the market and bought some bananas."
She pauses, suddenly amused at herself. Bill chuckles. "And I
brought them home, and I set the bananas on the table and
started experimenting."

"How did you do?"

"They taste terrible!" She grimaces. "I guess it's the spermicide. I don't know, I never used condoms, but at any rate, I ate
a Lifesaver and that helped."

"What flavor?" asks Bill, thoroughly enjoying her agony.

"What does it matter? Peppermint, if you must know. Anyway, I practiced for an hour or so and I finally got pretty good
at it, but a banana's a stationary object, so I still don't know if
it really works."

"How are you going to find out?" Bill looks Margo directly in
the eyes.

She blushes again and looks down at her plate. "I thought
about asking one of the girls to try it with her partner, but that
isn't very professional."

"So you want to try with me." Bill's voice turns gentle.

"Actually, yes I do." Her voice is barely audible. "I mean,
you're the only person I could possibly ask, and it is research,
after all. That is, if it's okay with you . . ."

"I'd be happy to assist with your research, Margo." Bill smiles
and reaches over and squeezes her hand, then tactfully maneu-
vers the conversations to easier subjects while they finish their
meal. He also insists on picking up the check.

Bill's house is in a hilly, wooden area of Marin. It's masculine,
artistic, and subtle. Besides that, he keeps his house orderly and
clean, a trait found occasionally in men who have lived alone
for more than a year or two. Bill builds up the fire in the stove,
puts on Coltrane, and opens a bottle of good wine. He's quite
aware that Margo feels awkward and he's doing his best to ease
things. Actually, he feels a little awkward himself. He's wanted
her for a long time, but the fantasy hadn't included being a
research subject.

Margo's doing her best to appear relaxed as well. It's been
quite a while since she's had sex; it's been a whole lot longer

since she's had sex with someone new. But Bill's not really new and this isn't really sex. It's research, remember?

Bill lights candles next to the bed, places the wine and glasses on the bedside table, then gently takes Margo's hand. This isn't the first time she's been in Bill's bed. They've literally slept together a few times when it was too late for her to go back to the city. But that was different.

Margo takes off her jacket and shoes. Bill does the same. He sits down on the bed and leans back against the pillows. Margo is still standing in the middle of the room, her purse on the floor by her feet. She feels uncertain. Should she casually take the condoms out of her purse or should she toss the purse on the bed as if purses are always taken to bed? Bill stretches his hands out to her and beckons her to him. Margo picks up her purse, walks over, and places it on the bed. She sits down, feet on the floor, next to him.

"Well, dear scientist, how do we proceed?" he queries.

"I guess we have another drink," she replies. Then she laughs, sounding exasperated. "I don't know, I guess you take off your pants."

"That's romantic. Are you going to stay clothed?"

"Actually I hadn't really thought about it. Yes, I guess I am."

"How am I supposed to get 'stimulated,' as they say?"

"Close your eyes and fantasize?" Margo offers weakly.

"I'd rather keep them open and look at you," Bill replies. "I'll tell you what," he continues, "I'll take off my pants if you'll take off your dress."

"Okay," she responds after a moment's pause. She stands up and removes her belt, fumbling with the buttons of her dress. The dress slips from her shoulders, leaving her in a black demi-bra and a half-slip. The candlelight highlights her dark hair and her fair skin is luminescent under the black silk. Bill removes his shirt, all the while watching her. He pulls off his socks, then rises to his feet, unfastening his belt and fly and slipping off his slacks. Margo looks at him from the waist up, her admiration immediately followed by a rush of anxiety. She sees her ex-husband's face and remembers his disgust at her enthusiasm for lovemaking. She remembers how he only enjoyed sex when he was in control. She tries to push away these feelings. But she knows she isn't ready for more than research with Bill. Or so she thinks. . . .

Bill removes his shorts. Naked, he returns to the bed. Margo struggles with her feelings. She reaches for her glass of wine and then sits next to him.

She opens her purse and takes out one of the "extra-sensitive" latex condoms. "You aren't going to laugh at me, are you? It's been a long time since I've done anything even remotely like this." Her voice is tentative.

"I might laugh with you but I won't laugh at you," he answers playfully, not responding to the edge of fear in her voice.

Finally Margo looks down. His penis is waiting limply. It doesn't look nearly as willing as the banana or bratwurst (which she hadn't mentioned), both of which were naturally ready. She wonders what to do. Finally she puts her hand on his penis and gives it a little stroke. It responds by moving slightly. She looks up at Bill and gives him a helpless look. He grins at her. His eyes imply that she's got the lead in this game. She looks back down at his penis and lifts it up. It stiffens only slightly, certainly not enough to slide a condom on with her hand, let alone her mouth. For a brief moment she thinks about placing his penis in her mouth. She quickly rejects that thought—after all, isn't the point to put it in when it's time to roll the condom on it?

Bill reaches into the bedside drawer and brings out some lubricant, and helps out by putting a drop on the tip of his penis. Margo removes the condom from the foil packet and prepares to place it on him. That distracts Bill enough that his penis loses what stiffness it had gained. They both laugh, albeit, nervously: she's almost enjoying herself.

Bill hands Margo her wineglass, then has a healthy drink from his. "Come here," he says reaching for her. Margo looks up at him, uncertainty clouding her face. Bill smiles and shakes his head, saying without words that there is no need for fear. He takes her into his arms and kisses her gently on the forehead. Then he traces down her face, kissing each eyelid, her cheeks, her slightly upturned nose, and her mouth. Much to her surprise, she responds willingly, and her mouth opens slightly. And then a little more.

Bill pulls her on top of him and they kiss. Without breaking the embrace, he rolls her over. Margo feels long suppressed-sensations return to her body in a great surge. She doesn't fight it. She presses her body against his and they kiss as if they have just made an amazing new discovery. Bill slides his hands down to her breasts. She doesn't object. Deftly he unfastens her bra and cups them in his hands, first one, then the other. He kisses each nipple with his tongue, then his mouth. Her nipples grow erect. Margo closes her eyes and gives in. She isn't even aware that he is ready for her research.

Instinctively she reaches down to him and strokes him, only half-aware of his erection. He responds appreciatively, then carefully removes her slip and panties. He places his hand between her legs, which part immediately, and slips his fingers into her moist vagina. An intense charge of electricity runs through her body, causing her to tense, not in fear but excitement. This brings her to her senses, however, and she slides down the bed—just like the woman in the *Penthouse* article. She starts stroking him with one hand as she reaches for the condom with the other. Cleverly, she has put a mint next to the condom and now she slips it into her mouth. Then she places the condom in her mouth, and with all the skill of the best sporting lady in the finest bordello, slides the thin latex over the shaft of his waiting penis. She runs her mouth up and down the shaft again and again, as he sighs with pleasure. She's so absorbed in the moment that it doesn't even cross her mind that he might be a candidate for the extra-long size next time.

Bill draws her back up to him, pulls her on top of his body, and slides his leg between hers. Her body willingly complies.

He massages her back and hips; long, strong, sensual strokes. Margo resonds by pressing tightly against him, arching the small of her back as his hands slide up her spine, causing her breasts to rub along his chest. She then slides her other leg over his so that she straddles him and raises her body so that he can enter her. He deftly guides his penis to her now moist vagina, teasing her by rubbing it against the entryway. Her breath catches and holds in anticipation. He purposefully enters her a little at a time, holding back, and finally he thrusts into her fully. Margo's breath is knocked from her in a sharp cry, though she is hardly in pain. For a moment they remain as they are, Margo fully straddling Bill's perfect erection, allowing herself to resonate in sensation, giving each nerve ending its erotic due. Then she drops back down onto Bill's chest and holds on to him tightly, submitting to the delight of being filled with his love.

The bottle of wine is more than half gone. Bill and Margo lie next to each other, the bed sheets and blankets in a tangled heap partially covering them. They both look happy and slightly dazed.

"You were very good at it," Bill tells her.

"At what?" she responds dreamily.

"At putting on the condom. This was really your first time?"

"Yeah, if you don't count a banana and a bratwurst."

"You tried it on a bratwurst too?"

"Um-hmmm," she says, only a little embarrassed.

Bill slaps her playfully on the bottom. "You are truly crazy and that's part of why I've waited so long for you. I knew you'd be worth every day of waiting."

"Really?" she says, her voice incredulous.

"Really," he responds. They start all over again.

The nicest part about the next morning is that they already know what they want to fix for breakfast and that they actually have things to say to each other. They've had over a year of practice together with details such as these. Bill brews the coffee while Margo tears open the English muffins and places them in the oven. She already knows that the jam is on the second shelf in the back. They separate the Sunday paper. He takes the comics and she takes the "Punch" section; later they trade.

"Did you put a mint in your mouth last night?" Bill asks suddenly.

"I certainly did. Have you ever tasted spermicide?"

"Is it terrible?"

"It isn't chocolate syrup. And I figure that if I can't handle it, my clients certainly aren't going to either."

"Are you going to teach them what you've learned?"

"Yes, but I'm not quite sure how to go about it."

"You could use the banana tricks—I don't think I'm up to performing in front of a group of hookers."

Margo looks at him wryly. "Don't worry. Now that I know it works, I don't have to continue my research. Well, at least not in front of anyone," she adds quickly.

"So how are you going to bring it up?" he asks.

"I'm going to go into group on Thursday with several boxes of condoms and some Lifesavers and I'm going to tell them you can put a condom on a man with your mouth and that the man probably won't mind. Did you mind?"

"Not in the least."

"But did you feel it?"

"Some. It felt so good to have your mouth on me that I didn't care."

"Okay, so I guess if I need to I'll demonstrate on the banana and then I'll suggest they use the technique on their men."

"What kind of rubbers are you going to use?"

"Well, I don't know. I'm thinking about approaching Trojan on Monday to ask for a donation of some better-quality condoms."

"And what flavor mints are you going to use?"

"Oh come on, Bill, what kind of question is that?"

"No, really, I mean it. Did you know that if you bite wintergreen in the dark it makes sparks?"

"Really?"

"Really."

"I don't believe you."

"Well, I just happen to have some in my desk. Let's go into the bedroom where it's dark and I'll show you how to make sparks fly."

Jane Handel

❧

The Devil Made Me Do It

Dear X,

It may seem strange that I am writing a letter to you instead of phoning, but I know of no other way to clarify my rather confused thoughts at the moment. Somehow the process of writing helps to put things in order.

As you know, a current obsession of mine is with the concept of sin. I have been trying to analyze to what extent my knowledge of sin affects my enjoyment of sex. "But love is simple," you've said, "don't think so much." And yet I continue to ramble on about my assorted transgressions, and you listen patiently—understanding that as a refugee from the constraints of Catholicism, I am caught in the crossfire between taboo and a conscious desire to violate it. I am convinced that my awareness of sin contributes greatly to the enjoyment I derive from flouting it—the old pleasure/pain principle is pretty intoxicating stuff for some of us.

I often wonder how you were able to emerge unscathed from the repeated lashings meted out to almost everyone in this culture by the Judeo-Christian patriarchal whip. How is it that, for you, fucking is as easy as quenching your thirst in a mountain stream; plunging your face deep into the crystal clear melted snow, oblivious to the hidden microbes of anguish it may contain? Why are you so able to dispense and receive pleasure without the embellishment of guilt, and enjoy it no less than one who thrives on the illicit and forbidden? I can see you shrug and smile inscrutably as you read this . . . but please indulge me as I play the role of kneeling sinner while you listen to yet another confession. With face upturned in penitent supplication, I imagine that you are licking the burning tears of remorse from my cheeks.

Nothing is ever quite as it seems on the surface, but I can assure you that the following sequence of events occurred in an environment of prosaic innocence—my studio, behind what I thought was a tightly closed door.

I had been hard at work on my painting of St. Sebastian (perhaps this scenario is not so innocent after all), and began to feel chilly and irritable. As I was contemplating the blood dripping from the saint's pierced armpit, the fog lifted and warm sunlight flooded the room, forming a golden rectangle in the middle of the floor. Drawn like a cat, I took off my clothes, lay facedown on the bare wood, stretched, and almost purred. The tension in my neck and shoulders began to dissipate as the sun's rays penetrated my aching muscles. I reveled in the sensual warmth, soporific to my brain but arousing to my body.

As the sun's aphrodisiac sent palpitations through my groin, I felt a deep longing to taste and smell you but was too relaxed and sleepy to do anything more than daydream. Perhaps I even dozed off for a while, I don't know. Admittedly, I was in a trancelike state, but whatever happened next was neither dream nor fantasy.

At first, I attributed the vague sounds to wind rustling the branches of a tree outside the window. But then I heard the floor creak and felt warm breath on my cheek as a low, soothing voice murmured, "Don't move and don't open your eyes." The voice was genderless and totally unidentifiable. It was firm, although nonthreatening, yet my heart skipped a few beats. Still, I obeyed.

Suddenly I remembered an incident that had occurred just two days before. While walking to the bank, I had stopped briefly to look in a store window, when a similar voice whispered huskily into my ear, "Hello, sweetheart, why don't you come up and see

me sometime?" I turned and looked directly into the mesmeriz-
ing gaze of a young Gypsy woman. Her eyes were like pools,
drawing me into their chasmal depths. With a half-smile that
revealed a gold-capped canine, she handed me an orchid-colored
business card. "Readings by Katrina," it said, in dark purple
letters. In the time it took me to glance down at the card, she
vanished. And now, with this voice in my ear, I wondered, even
hoped, that perhaps Katrina had tracked me down, picked my
lock, and found her way into my inner sanctum of sunlight.
Gypsies, you know, have powers a mere mortal such as I cannot
hope to comprehend, though a voodoo queen like you would
probably accept such enigmatic behavior as a matter of course.

In any case, my thoughts of Katrina and Gypsy magic notwithstanding, I was filled with an intense desire to question au-
thority and open my eyes. You know how I hate being told what
to do! But I continued to keep them tightly shut as my mind
raced with a multitude of questions. Who was it really? How
did he or she get in? Was it you? A stranger? The latter prospect
was especially intriguing. As you learned during the course of a
earlier confession of mine, I used to enjoy consummating my
then considerable lust with strangers whose anonymity remained
forever intact. Of course, this is no longer a viable form of expression, so whereas I had never felt endangered in the past, I
now felt a strong twinge of panic and began to hope fervently
that you were my mystery companion. But hadn't you returned
my key after house-sitting that last time? Unless, knowing my
secret, you'd made a duplicate for just such a purpose as this . . .
you're a trickster and capable of anything.

I lay with pounding heart for what seemed like an eternity—
awaiting either the stab of a knife or a caress. And of course this
netherworld of anticipation was visited by my old nemesis—guilt.
Because, quite frankly, the sexual arousal I felt at that moment
was far greater than either my fear of an assault or my righteous
indignation over having been told what to do. It's quite possible
that this conflict of emotions even contributed to my state of
excitation. So, despite the fact that long ago I rescinded my bid
for sainthood, this new dilemma seemed to jeopardize any viable
case for redemption.

Now I know you find this psychic can of worms to be absurd, and I, too, make these comments with tongue in cheek, but on a primal level, in spite of myself, I still worry about burning in hell. Subsequently, when nothing happened I didn't know whether to laugh or cry, and simply felt foolish. I then began to think that if tricks were being played, my own imagination was culpable—not you, and certainly not Katrina!

The wet tongue that slowly began to draw intricate patterns behind my ear and down my neck was not the product of an overactive imagination. It traversed the area between my shoulder blades, down my spine, and plunged into the crevice at its base. Lips nibbled at my flesh and teeth gently bit as my pulse raced out of control. Hands pushed apart my thighs, fingers spread my labia, then probed deeply inside as if to test the response. By this time, I had resumed breathing—rapidly. I moaned involuntarily, and pungent, sticky fingers were thrust into my mouth. "Shut up!" the still unrecognizable voice commanded. The fingers were removed from my mouth and shoved back into my vagina, while I stifled any further moans by biting my bottom lip.

It suddenly dawned on me that there was a remote possibility that my uninvited guest might be my teenage neighbor, Jamal. I had given him a key about six months before when I went away with you for the weekend and needed someone to feed my cat. He never returned it, a fact I'd totally forgotten until this very moment. I had been lusting after his beautiful young body for ages, and by the disarray in which I'd discovered my underwear drawer upon returning from that weekend, I imagined the feeling was mutual. But he was definitely still jailbait, and besides, I just couldn't imagine Jamal, the friendly kid next door, having the nerve to actually sneak into my apartment and fondle my naked body, much less having the wherewithal to order me to "shut up" while doing it. No, he was a titillating fantasy object, but it just didn't seem possible that he was capable of the sophisticated dexterity now bringing me to the point of frenzy. And, the idea of not being able to lick him in return was simply too excruciating. All around, it seemed wise to relinquish my desire for Jamal.

You can see my dilemma. There I was, being expertly transported to the brink of orgasm, unable to thrash or moan (a very difficult requirement for me as you well know), and totally in the dark as to the identity of my seducer. In some ways, I dreaded the inevitable dénouement, especially since my fate was not in my hands (no pun intended). So I really did have to rely on the kindness of a stranger. Fortunately, my guest compassionately brought me very quickly to one of the most intense climaxes I've ever had. At that point I couldn't restrain my voice any longer and let out a long, low howl as my body convulsed repeatedly.

I uncurled from a fetal position and opened my eyes. No one was there. The door of my studio was wide open, as was the front door of the apartment. Leaves had blown in off the street and were doing a crazy little dance in the hallway. The last rays of the setting sun created a sharp angle of yellow light on the wall.

I crawled on hands and knees to the front door, closed it and turned the lock. I picked up one of the leaves, admired its beautiful shape and color for a moment, and then crushed it against my breast.

Is a moment's bliss worth an eternity of flames? Let's get together again soon and find out. . . .

Fondly,

O

Moxie Light

The Company Man

My dispatcher, Mickey, used to weigh three hundred pounds until he was diagnosed as diabetic. He'd lost most of the weight, but he still ate enough for a family of four. All night long I heard him order lemon-filled donuts, Italian subs, and raspberry lime rickeys. The other drivers brought him whatever he wanted because then he would give his chosen few the best calls. In the taxi business it's known as payola. Mickey could chew while calling out addresses in a carefully modulated voice, keep one eye on a portable television, and rank out those poor drivers who could barely speak English. "Why don't you get a job as an elevator operator," he would tell them. "You can't get lost if you're only going in two directions."

Mickey oozed scorn for anyone who didn't know the city as well as he did. Before he became a dispatcher he was a radio announcer. I never met anyone who knew as many people as Mickey did: nurses and television personalities and arthritic women who depended upon him to get them to their appointments on time. Dispatchers wield a lot of power, and Mickey, for all his good points, was a megalomaniac. Once I picked up a young girl, a poet, bent out of shape that Mickey had called her "dear."

"Who is that dispatcher?" she asked. "He's got a lot of nerve. I'm not his 'dear.' He doesn't even know me."

"When he calls me 'dear,' I don't mind," I said. "Mickey is a gentleman. It probably never crossed his mind that anyone would be insulted."

"Well, I don't know him and I don't like it," she said.

"Wait until the first time a saleslady calls you 'madame,' " I said. "It's a real comedown from 'dear.' "

Another passenger told me that he'd gone to high school with Mickey. "He used to be so nice. President of our class. All sports and what a comedian!"

"He should have been a politician," I said. "He knows how to manipulate people with his voice. It really turns me on."

Indeed, Mickey's voice did not sound like Mickey looked, which was about eight months pregnant. His voice purred as if filtered through a throat of velvet, causing little flip-flops of lust in my stomach. It was a wonder I wasn't cut in half by a street-car, much as it distracted me. I picked up bits and pieces about him from my passengers who either loved him or hated him and the other taxi drivers who grumbled but never quite revolted against his favoritism.

A woman customer I had once told me: "I was mugged once, beaten up real bad. To get over it, I drank a lot. For a while. Mickey used to call me up just to see how I was doing. Every week. What a sexy voice!"

"You mean you never met him?"

"Just when I called for a cab. What does he look like?"

"Well, he's got a nice face. Really, very ordinary. His hair is brown and he's shorter than me. Did he ever ask you out?"

"No. All we ever did was flirt. You say he's short. How disappointing! His voice makes him sound six feet tall."

I never had the chance to talk to him much. Most of the time I was too tired to do more than make out my waybill. Mickey would help me with the figuring. Once, I remember dragging myself out of the cab, dirty, bladder screaming, and seat of my pants rainbow-hued with stains from blueberries and M&M's and a spilled Coke on the front seat. I ate continuously so that if anyone ever decided to splash my brains all over the inside of my windshield they wouldn't be tempted to rape me first. It's a hard, boring job, taxi-driving. When I first started, I thought it was romantic.

"If you keep that up, you're going to start looking like me, you poor little chicken," he said. I liked it when Mickey worried about me. In the beginning, he guided me as if I were flying a 747, so considerate and solicitous. When he sent me into the most dangerous neighborhoods, I never complained, never considered that a white woman in Roxbury had less of a chance than someone who could pose a bigger threat than I, even on my meanest night.

"Keep your doors locked and always keep your mike between your knees. That way you can signal me if you get in trouble, and you'll get more business by radio than by picking up off the streets. Believe me."

Mickey knew the taxi business inside out. He denied taking kickbacks but I'd seen him palming the long green in the corner of the garage when he thought no one was looking. That's when I got the idea that if I had sex with him I could make more money. I quickly put aside the thought. I was too proud, too moral. I could have slipped him a few bucks to get on his good side, if I'd wanted to, but I was never that hungry. A lot of girls I knew had sex just for fun. Not me. I wanted no involvements, no complications, no waiting by the telephone. My friends were all slaves to sex it seemed to me; dropping their personal interests when a new lover came along, wasting precious time suffering the pain of broken love affairs. I had resolved not to let it happen to me.

But I couldn't have spent as much time chasing nickels if I hadn't been half in love with Mickey. That Christmas I had given him twenty dollars. Harry, the garage manager, had given us each a canned ham. And a few of us had gathered in the dispatch room to smoke a joint to celebrate the holidays. But it was New Year's Eve we'd been waiting for. Mickey had said he would double us up with people going to house parties, affluent people who knew enough not to drink and drive, who tipped well, and were grateful for the transportation. After work I planned to stop at my boyfriend's to split a magnum of champagne. None of that domestic stuff, either. My boyfriend was no slouch even though the medication he took for hypertension made him a dud in the kip.

I didn't mind working New Year's Eve until a quarter to midnight when I broke down. I had just dropped off a young executive who'd been working late for her boss. She tipped me an extra dollar. The crowds from the waterfront were just beginning to flood through the streets. My cab sputtered and bucked until it came to a stop, hoses steaming as if it were on fire. I got out of the cab and banged on the door of the closest bar. There was a sign on it that said: PRIVATE PARTY. Nothing was going to stop me from using their phone. I banged on the door until the bartender took pity.

"I'm only three blocks away," I told my boyfriend. "I'm stuck till the tow truck comes. The driver has to stay with the cab. Isn't that awful?"

"I don't want to hear it," he said, with subtle loathing. He was sick of worrying, and didn't understand that if I got a 9 to 5 job, it would kill me faster than the traffic fumes and the constant fear of death. "I'm tired of listening to myself. You always do what you want, anyway. What's the use?"

Everyone in the lounge seemed to be having a good time, except for a few losers at the bar. At the dimly-lit tables, it was a regular bacchanal. Girls were sitting in guys' laps, shamelessly nuzzling and kissing. Lots of tongue and heavy breathing. The bartender looked at me in my grubbies and without smiling, ushered me to the door and locked it behind me. I don't think I've ever been more miserable. I felt my face tie into hard knots and felt a sudden longing for red satin underwear and feathers in my hair.

Midnight in Boston. Pandemonium reigned: kazoos, church bells, cow bells, bleating car horns. Couples carrying balloons walked arm in arm, dragging half-asleep kids behind. The revelers streamed past my cab. Teenagers with crazy hats on their heads began to bang on my fender. "Happy New Year," they called. I turned the key in the ignition and picked up the mike.

"Happy New Year, Mickey," I said. I turned the radio up for "Auld Lang Syne." A couple of kids began to shake my cab, jumping up and down on the fenders. I clicked shut the door locks and shot the kids a look of disdain. I heard the grand finale of fireworks, explosive sounds ricocheting against the buildings overhead, and thought sadly of Arthur Fiedler. Then, I reached under my seat for an old copy of *The Watchtower* which I'd found earlier in one of my pit stops, the bathroom of St. Elizabeth's Hospital.

Gloom and doom. The story of my life. New Year's had turned out to be a big nothing. I'd been out on the road all night and I had seventy-eight whole dollars, most of that earmarked for the company. Where were the big tips Mickey had promised? That liar. He'd stoop to anything. Like Thanksgiving when he'd said business would be good after the football games and it wasn't. Mickey was a company man.

It was starting to get cold. I stuck my hands in my pockets to warm them. I spent a lot of time feeling sorry for myself. My friends said I needed a team of lawyers following me to pick up the pieces. I felt sorry for the rest of the world too, the poor, the hungry. Weren't we all about to be blown to bits in a nuclear war?

I turned the radio off to save the battery and scrunched down in my seat, sitting on my hands. I was bored. The light wasn't strong enough to read by. One stretch limousine after another passed with pretty girls popping out of sun roofs. Would the masses never end? How would the tow truck be able to get through? I picked up the mike and listened to Mickey until I could cut in. "Have you forgotten me? Is someone coming? I'm freezing, in case you're interested."

"I'll give you something to warm you up when you get here," Mickey said, laughing. "The tow truck's on its way."

"Don't talk to me like that over the air. It gives me hot flashes." It was harmless banter that Mickey didn't know I really meant. Just because I was past forty didn't mean I was dead. All that raw sex back at the bar had triggered an overwhelming yearning to be touched. What was I saving it for, anyway?

Finally, with the crowd beginning to thin, I saw the tow truck slinking its way up the street. Bruce, my good buddy, who'd taken a whole night after drunken-driving school to teach me a few tricks, and driver-cum-mechanic, Joe, hooked my cab to the towline. As I climbed into the truck, a warm feeling came into my heart. Bruce and Joe could have left me sitting for hours if they'd wanted to. It was almost like being part of a family. "How sweet of both of you to give up your tips for me," I said, gratefully, in a rush of emotion.

"We couldn't leave you all alone on a night like this," Bruce said, passing me a bottle. "Take a sip."

"I'm frozen through to my bones," I said. "Thanks." Joe honked his horn and cursed out the window at the pedestrians as we slowly made our way. He passed me a joint, then the bottle, partying all the way to the garage, so that by the time we arrived, my depression had faded and something like euphoria had taken its place. I was feeling warm and lovable; kind of cute, in fact. High. My cheeks were hot and I could feel the blood careening crazily through my veins.

"Aren't you going back out?" asked Mickey, when I came in and threw my waybill down in front of him. "You need the money." A space heater in the corner blasted out heat.

"My stride is broken." Thanks to the pot and the whiskey my alter ego took charge. I could hardly believe it was me who continued: "What do you say we go to my apartment and get to know each other?"

"What do you want to know?" Mickey asked.

Mickey's T-shirt read HARVARD. I ran my finger along the edge of his collar. It was very unlike me to be so bold and I did it with full knowledge that I would never hear the end of it if the other drivers found out. The edges of his ears became bright red. I could tell I was embarrassing him, but I was too overwhelmed by lust to stop. I wanted to make love to Mickey. I wanted to watch the expression in his eyes when he came, and see him naked, beer-belly and all. I wanted to fuck him like he'd never had it before, so that every time he dispatched to me, he'd have to remember, so that if the bomb did come, we could both die with a smile. I'd been repressing my sexuality too long and too much of anything, as everyone knows, is unhealthy. We would have a last tango, a lost weekend, a brief but beautiful love affair. Once I'd made up my mind, Mickey didn't stand a chance.

"I'll go home and wait for you," I said. "You know where I live. I have a bottle left over from Christmas."

I ran around my apartment shoving kitchen clutter into the oven, swishing out the toilet bowl and shutting all the closet doors. When Mickey got there, I was bathed and perfumed, with all systems go. After a few more drinks, we undressed. As Mickey folded his clothes into a neat pile by his side, I strategically placed an unopened Christmas gift in my lap so that all he could see were my shoulders. The war against my puritanical upbringing was not yet won for all my loose talk.

"You don't have to worry about me," he said. "I have this condition . . ."

"What condition?" I asked, though I half knew what was coming. I was jinxed. Premature ejaculators gravitated to me. Some of them, I scared. Some just wanted to get me under their control. Some, I was quick to sense, were merely interested in a conquest. Most of them wanted to be mothered. What irked me the most were the men who got me all hot and bothered and left me hanging. It gives a girl a complex.

The only man I'd ever dated who knew how to please me was my boyfriend. That was the reason I stayed, but the irony of it was no sex and no money. With little in common, every day was a new challenge. Thinking of him made me feel guilty and I began to put my clothes back on.

"No, don't," said Mickey, taking my sweater out of my hands. He leaned to kiss my breast. "It's the medicine I take for my diabetes. Maybe if you're patient with me, it will work. Please?" He whispered love talk into my ear, bringing goose bumps to my skin.

"I love it when you talk dirty," I said. "But since we work together, it's probably better if we just stay friends."

"We'll always be friends," said Mickey, breathing hard, and then kissing me, hungrily. "I'll always be there for you."

"Will you start giving me some good calls instead of all the blood runs?" The medical laboratory, one of our company's biggest accounts, gave us fifty-cent tips. The specimens came in plastic bags, but we never knew if we were carrying a lethal virus or if someone would attack us in some lonely stretch of hospital parking lot. Mickey would give the plum jobs, the ones that came into the airport or the bus terminals, to the drivers who gave him a kickback.

"How can you think of money at a time like this?"

"What was all that about giving me something to warm me up?" I said. "You are a bastard. Just like the cabs this summer you said had air-conditioning. Sometimes I hate you."

"Shut up," Mickey mumbled. His face was in my crotch, hands fluttering all over my body like falling rose petals. And as much as I had all kinds of reservations, I was dizzy with desire, answering his probing tongue with the rhythm of my hips. I felt glued to his finger. The energy charged into me like Michelangelo's Adam on the ceiling of the Sistine Chapel.

"My God," I moaned, gasping. "I never wanted anyone as much in my whole life." It was true. The loneliness of the holidays had erased all my defenses, all my Bostonian reservations. My whole body began to tremble. "Don't stop!"

Mickey clambered onto me, unceremoniously, one hand still working in me, fondling his penis with his thumb. I could feel his testicles, soft and warm, knocking on my thighs. I was in a state of perpetual orgasm. Small animal sounds came from my throat. I heard them as if they belonged to someone else. I panted until I couldn't catch my breath, the sides of my throat like Velcro.

"The neighbors . . ." I managed to break away from his grasp. "I've got to get a drink of water," I said. But he was quicker, dragging me into the bedroom, the connection between us broken momentarily. He pulled back the covers and threw me onto the mattress. Shoving a pillow onto my face, he kneaded my breast with a sure hand. I could feel my thighs slick with his spit, smell the sex rising from my body, earthy and warm like peat. There wasn't a square inch on my body not begging for relief.

Mickey was indefatigable. Impotent, but indefatigable. I felt as if I were having an out-of-body experience, lost in the universe somewhere, or maybe underwater, a stranger to myself.

For a day and a half we hardly came up for air or knew the time of day. I vaguely remember the phone ringing unanswered and scrambled eggs, but for most of that time, I was in a sexual coma. Mickey's tongue rode me like a surfer, crest after crest. I was powerless to speak, think, or leave, until the pain began to leak through my miasma. I was unable to pee without a terrible burning nor look at Mickey for shame.

"You've got to leave," I said, at last, when my rationality reappeared. "My boyfriend has a key. What if he comes?"

"I'll hide in a closet."

"He also has a gun," I said. He really didn't, but I couldn't bear the thought of another lick. A razorlike pain bisected me where the skin was chafed. Mickey looked as if he'd been on a bender. He needed a shave and his eyes were bloodshot. I hated it when men gave me those puppy dog eyes.

"I've got to go home and get my insulin," he said. "But I could come back. I know you're too good for me. I'd ask you to marry me, but you could never be happy with an ordinary guy like me."

"I'll never have sex with anyone else after this," I promised, "not for a long, long time, anyway. But I feel terrible about your condition." Words. What I really felt terrible about was not sharing this part of love with my boyfriend. Maybe it wasn't too late. Maybe I could strip myself of all the manners and be a real woman. Yeah.

"Hey," said Mickey, matter-of-factly, "it's my own fault for not taking care of the diabetes when I had the chance. The important thing is, did I satisfy you? Did you enjoy it?"

I walked him to the door, my arm around his waist, leaning on him, I was so weak. "What do you think?" I rasped. What a dumb question! My boyfriend would never have been so stupid to ask. I didn't want to appear ungrateful. God forbid I should lose all of my feminine virtues and become as crass as anyone who took what they wanted, as unfeeling as if it were a shower.

"It was an experience I'll never forget. Thank you." It was as if my body had been saving itself, as if orgasms could be stored like memories. Why had I been so helpless to fight it? Why did I have this feeling that it had been meant to be? My head went into a transcendental swirl as I contemplated the universe and my tiny part in it. What rot! I was as basic as your gum-chewing

East Boston person. It took someone like Mickey to help me realize it.

"What will you tell your boyfriend about why you didn't answer the phone?" Mickey asked, concerned as always for my
well-being.

"When he sees how much weight I've lost, he'll believe me
when I tell him I've been sick." My boyfriend loved me. Of that
I was sure. As I would not deny him, he would not deny me.
We were both too conventional to verbalize this, but I suppose,
at the very bottom, it was why we had never married. Call it an
understanding. I smiled at Mickey, toyed with the doorknob,
and blew him a kiss. "Sex is a sickness, you know. I really believe
it."

As Mickey shrugged his shoulders, his eyes gleamed. He was
back to his normal jaunty self. "I wouldn't have missed it for the
world. But don't think I'm going to start giving you better calls.
Some of these drivers have been with me for years. They have
to come first."

"I always knew you were a company man," I said. I couldn't
wait to get rid of him now. "Someone has to carry those little
old ladies who make a big deal about giving a dime tip. I just
hope you don't go shooting your mouth off at the garage."

"My lips are sealed."

But, of course, either someone had seen his car outside my
apartment or Mickey's friendship with the other men included
using his big mouth in other ways. I had to put up with a million
smirks. Even Joe, the tow-truck driver, who'd always treated me
with respect, asked me to pose in some fancy underwear for his
Polaroid. When Mickey pestered me for a repeat performance, I
always said no.

After a while, he began to treat me like everyone else.

Pat Williams

Ellen, From Chicago

On the dresser was a small photograph of a woman. It was in an old gilded frame, the kind that tarnishes with age, but this one was kept polished to a warm gleam.

The woman was an aviator. I think I would have guessed that even if it hadn't been for her helmet and the upraised goggles. Her eyes seemed to be looking at a vision or at some great expanse, her smile soft but self-assured. A luster seemed to permeate her brown skin. Heroic? Adventurous? I had to smile at those impressions yet I couldn't take my eyes from her picture.

"That's Trina there," Rose's soft voice said.

I jerked my hand back, though I had barely been touching the photograph. Rose Owens smiled.

"She was one of the first colored flyers," Rose said. "Aviatrices they called them. She was the only one from around these parts."

Rose glanced at the picture a time or two while she put the extra blankets on our beds and I could see the fondness in her gaze. "We came up together," she went on. "We were both in the choir at Reverend Clark's church."

She looked about the room to see that all was in order.

Rose didn't look worn with age and there were only a few

116

strands of gray in her hair, but she did look tired. Sixty-one years of living in the South does that to a black woman.

"Everything's fine, Miss Rose," I said.

She nodded but looked around as if there was still something she thought could be done to make her visitors feel more at home.

We heard a footstep in the hallway and Ellen stepped into the room. At the same time a fragrance of honeysuckle came through the screened window on the night wind.

Rose smiled a greeting at Ellen but she came over to the dresser where I stood. "That's the picture they put in the colored paper down at Cane City," Rose said. "I'll have to show you the pictures in the album I keeps."

"Does she still live here?" Ellen asked.

"She was killed in a crash. A car crash. In France," Rose said. The smile had faded from her lips, but it remained in her eyes. "She had the . . . prettiest hands."

She looked at Ellen and me. "Well, I'll let you girls get your rest." She asked us if there was anything else we needed and when we said, "No thank you," she left.

When I had come upon the photograph, I had been looking at the things on the dresser.

It was something I'd taken to doing at the houses we stayed in. Looking at, examining, touching the keepsakes—old perfume bottles, saucer ashtrays, jars filled with marbles and trinkets, photographs. I continued my exploration of this dresser though I was very aware of Ellen rummaging in her travel case, of her footsteps around the bed.

I didn't turn around then because I didn't know what to say to her.

I am not normally tongue-tied with strangers. Every year I face a new bunch of them from the front of a classroom. Things had gone along all right with Ellen, too, at first. I remembered the moment I'd been brought up short.

We were on the drive from Mobile to Lewiston. Kenneth, Diego, Albert, Ellen, and I. Kenneth and Diego were joking with Ellen. She sat against the window and the wind lifted the collar of her loose white blouse. She was answering some comment of Kenneth's and she said to him, "Well, you know the finest black women on the planet came from Chicago, ain't that right?" And her voice was serious but she smiled and gave a halfway wink to me.

Something, some little cue in that, caught me off guard so that I couldn't speak just then. Fortunately Diego dove in with his own comment.

When I looked into the dresser mirror I saw that Ellen had put on her light-green kimono. It looked cool and soft.

There was a slight frown on her face, not much more than a deep thoughtfulness, that accentuated her easy-curving brows and her wide, full mouth. She ran her hand once across her Afro cut that in sunlight looked for all the world like jewels shimmered in it.

When she'd got her washcloth and a little bottle of something and left for the bathroom down the hall, I finally turned away from the dresser.

I came back from my turn in the bath to find her lying in bed with the sheet tucked about her and her arms folded behind her head. She watched me as I got ready for bed.

"Ka-ma-li," she enunciated my name softly. I looked at her and she raised an eyebrow in question. "What does it mean?" she said.

"It's the name of a protecting spirit," I said.

"What nation does it come from?" she asked.

"It's Mashona. From Zimbabwe," I said. She smiled slightly, watching me.

"I like the sound," she said quietly and closed her eyes for a moment. Her long lashes shadowed her cheeks. The smile still on her face. Then she opened her eyes and caught me looking at her.

I walked around to the other twin bed and let my short robe fall—I had only my panties under it—and slid between the sheets.

"Are you tired?" Ellen asked.

"It's been a long day," I said.

"Good night, Kamali," she said and there was a subtle amusement in her voice. The lamp was on her side of the bed and she pulled the cord on it.

I didn't go to sleep, I was too aware of her there.

I thought of the talk she'd given in Mobile two days past.

Ellen, Diego, Kenneth, Albert, and I were following the path of the sixties' civil rights workers through the South. We were on a more modern-day crusade; instead of fighting segregation we were lecturing on African history. Kenneth, Albert, and I all taught at the same college. We had scraped together what funding we could and set off at the end of the school year. We were speaking at churches, summer classrooms, lodges, sometimes in private homes. We stayed in folks' homes because we couldn't afford hotels. In Mobile, we spoke at a lodge hall.

Something drives Ellen when it comes to her beliefs. I would sit next to her as she stood and talked about ancient African civilizations in Zimbabwe and Egypt. I would be very aware of her then, aware of the very faint orange fragrance she wears. When she spoke I could watch her as closely as I wanted.

The light in her dark eyes burned when she made a point that she wanted her audience not just to know but to believe. Moisture formed on her neck and her brow, and when she became excited a little hoarseness came out in her voice.

I heard her breathing in the bed next to mine, and finally I slept too.

In the morning I woke to find her sitting on the side of her bed. I didn't think that she noticed me watching her right away. She leaned forward, examining her hands. All of the passion that could fill her face seemed to be gone; only a faint smile played on her lips.

"Good morning," she said, without looking up, then a moment later she did, and smiled. Caught again. I smiled back at her. "What were you thinking about?" I said.

"How quick the time passes," she said. "How few people we'll reach this summer after all. But," she said, shrugging, "I'm thankful for even small favors."

"I don't see how anyone could listen to you and not believe every word you say," I said.

There was a mischievous spark in her eye. "Thank you."

We held each other's gaze for a long time. Morning sounds came from the window and downstairs—some farm machinery droning across the fields, jaybirds hijinking out in the woods, voices in the kitchen. I think it was just then that something was decided between us. "What are you thinking about?" she said.

"You."

I lay on my stomach and the pressure against my mons felt good. My fingers pushed into the pillow. There was no mischief in her eyes now, no amusement on her face. It was open.

"Miss Rose's friend," I said, "was not from Chicago. But she sure was fine."

Ellen smiled. Uh oh, now who was shy? She bit her bottom lip just a little.

I got out of bed and put on my robe—for some reason—and I fastened it loosely. The beds were right beside each other so all I needed to do was reach out to stroke her cheek. For a moment I allowed my hand to lie on the soft, soft skin of her shoulder beneath her kimono. I imagined how her breast would feel, imagined the taste of her plum brown nipple. I was aware of her close, fresh, morning smell.

"Lady," one of us said.

I sat down beside her. "This is a long trip," I said. "And I find you very attractive."

She placed a hand on my thigh where my robe fell open and rubbed me gently. We kissed as softly as her touch.

We held each other breast to breast and played just a moment with the tips of our tongues on our lips, inside our mouths. She moaned and just then there was a sudden sound from the dresser. A loud click. We both jumped.

No one was there, but the picture of Trina had fallen over. Ellen chuckled.

"Yes ma'am, Miss Trina."

A moment later we heard footsteps in the hallway.

Miss Rose set a cup of strawberries and two glasses of cold milk in a place she cleared on the dresser. She inquired as to how we had slept and I wondered if she noticed the odor that our touching had brought.

Rose carefully set Trina's picture upright again. "Once Trina took me up in that airplane." Rose carefully raised her hand from the picture. "I was so scared. But I wasn't worried. Ain't that funny? I wouldn'a gone up with nobody else but Trina."

She looked at us and I saw, for the first time, how sharp and young her eyes were.

"This was her second home too. She was always over here. Little place where she grew up, they turned into a colored library. I have to show you my picture album before you go."

Ellen still sat on the bed but I gathered my things to go to the bathroom. I wanted to be alone for just a little time. I wanted a quiet place for my thoughts of what was happening.

Once there, I stood in front of the mirror and pushed my long dreadlocks back so that they lay across my shoulders. Kenneth called them my lion locks. I touched my face, taking account of the golden-brown skin, the cheekbones and brown eyes and assuring myself that Ellen liked them.

The fellows were downstairs. They commented on how refreshed we looked that morning. Kenneth looked at us closely— he knew something, I'm sure—and he said, "You two complement each other."

We sat next to one another, and all through breakfast my leg lay next to, barely touching, hers.

Toward the end of breakfast Rose held court. She told us the history of her house, built for the white Owens by her great-grandparents when they were still slaves. Now the black Owens lived in it.

Rachel, who ran the beauty parlor in the basement, came up to join us. She was light-skinned with gray eyes and a blond streak in her hair. She grinned as she sat back, crossed her legs, and said, "Miss Rose don't know it, but she's the state historian."

The morning lingered full of sounds and smells that I recalled from growing up in that part of the country. The morning radio gospel show from Memphis, the smell of dry grass and dust. It was already hot, and there were beads of sweat on the back of Ellen's hand.

The day grew warmer; the wind died, and touching the bright chrome on a car sitting in the sun could burn you.

We would give another talk that night, so we were staying the day. I lay across the bed in our room that afternoon, attempting

to keep cool. The curtains were drawn against the heat so the
light was dim. The door opened and Ellen came in.

She thought that I was sleeping because she moved quietly
across the room to her satchel. I watched her take out a small
book and pick up her straw sun hat from the chair. "Ellen," I
said.

She looked toward my bed and then walked over. "Baby, I
din't mean to wake you," she said.

When she sat down I reached up and touched her hair, warm
from the sun. My fingers ran easily down her back. She shivered
a little. "You're not going to let up are you?" she said.

"No."

She chuckled. "All right."

Then she whispered, "Nobody's objecting to the way this is
going anyway."

I touched my finger to her lips and she kissed it. And my hand
rubbed across her breast when I lowered it. It rested on her
thigh. And caressed her hip.

"Kamali, Kamali," she whispered, leaning over me. I pulled
her body to me. My hand on her hip stroked firmer, moving up
the fabric of her skirt. When I am about to touch another
woman, when I'm just beginning to, I can already taste her, her
sweat and her juices and I can already feel my fingers in her wet
places. Ellen had filled my mouth already and I swallowed.
"Baby," she said and she kissed me.

My hand smoothed around to the damp inside of her thigh.
"Come with me," she said, and I nodded. She laughed and pulled
back a bit more. "No, come with me to the library. It's closed
today. But Miss Rose gave me the key. She said I could spend
the afternoon there. I'm going to give them my copy of *Stolen
Legacy*."

We walked to the library, wide sun hats on our heads, holding
hands because I didn't want to lose contact with her flesh. I
listened to the sound of her voice as much as to her words when
she spoke of her passion, the ancients. There were ancient black
civilizations, people had to know that. Philosophies we had
founded at the beginnings of time were still around today.

Lies had covered all of that but we were going to uncover the truths. People had to know. *Had to*. I nodded my agreement. Her passion had drawn me to her long before I knew her body.

It was cool—almost—inside the tiny one-room library. The Trina Brown Library. We could hear the waters of a stream that passed a few feet away, shaded by the same gigantic oaks that covered the tiny building. We walked about, fingers linked, and looked at the precious old volumes.

"Miss Rose takes care of this place," Ellen said. "She brings flowers once a week. In the winter she gets them from the florist in town."

Petunias and bachelor's buttons sat in a blue vase by a window. There was a couch there, worn and old and soft. Ellen pulled me to her. I wrapped my arms around her, her breasts pressed against mine; her whole body against mine thrilled me.

We kissed long and slowly, tasting and sucking each other. I pressed into Ellen and she moaned.

I smoothed her body with my hands and she caressed me, kneading me all the way down my back, my behind. I opened the front of her dress, slowly. When we were both naked we lay down on the couch. I was wet, my clit was hard, and when her hand brushed between my legs it sent tremors through me.

She pulled me down onto her. "Is it going to be good?" she whispered and kissed me again before I could answer.

Her nipples hardened between my fingers as I pulled and squeezed them. I moved slowly between her legs. Kissing her neck and down to her shoulders. Such a fine, pretty woman, such a sweet, sweet good-tasting thing.

I remembered the sweat on her neck, I remembered her wink and the first time her leg touched mine in the backseat of the car. Fine, pretty Chicago woman. She found my mouth again, kissed me hard.

I bit softly at her nipples, slowly licked the sweat salt on her stomach, then found the juices between her legs and drank them. I licked the little bud there and heard the breath rushing in her and her moaning. I felt her hands all in my locks and when she pulled me up and kissed me roughly, clawing at my back, I loved it.

She rode me, her mons pushing deeper into mine, pressing

harder as it built up in me and I wanted to pee and I wanted to come. I shook and held her close enough to be a part of me.

I held her as her trembling eased and as I caught my breath. Her hands were already exploring my body again. She moved into me, feeling my wetness as she sucked my breasts, ran her tongue into my navel. . . .

I opened again, wide.

We went down to the stream sometime afterward and climbed in naked. The water was the coolest and sweetest.

Then we walked across the soft grass back to the library.

Ellen ran her finger down the spine of the slim little book— her favorite—that she was leaving behind; she took my hand again and we left. We joked that we should have exchanged dresses and seen if anyone would notice.

"You girls have a nice afternoon?" Rose said. She did not look up from the cake that she was decorating with berries and peach slices.

Ellen pressed her lips into a smile, her dimple showing.

I put on some raspberry tea—hot things in hot weather cool you down, so they say—and called down to Rachel and her customer to come up and join us.

Rose did show us her picture album.

Late that night after our talk, Rachel called us into her beauty shop where she had Rose on the recliner chair giving her a foot rub.

Rose had the album on her lap. "Come over here and see this," she said to us.

There was a picture of Trina in the plane that she flew down from Cincinnati. There was Trina and Rose in their choir robes in front of the church. Here was Trina and Rose caught by somebody's camera while they lay sleeping under a shade tree. Here was Trina Brown in her fine fur coat and her scarf and her genuine Spanish leather boots getting ready to leave for overseas.

"Kind of fond of that flyer, wasn't you, Rose?" Rachel smiled.

Rose looked down into her photograph album. "She's my hist'ry."

Cindy Walters

❧❧

Window Shopping

I've never been to Copenhagen but I understand the whores sit in storefront windows marketing themselves.

I fantasize that I am in a window wearing a pair of leopard-skin boots that I saw once in Paris. The heels are high, spiked, with all-spandex uppers in leopard skin that reach to my thighs. I like to sit in the window on a large chair with my back to the street. Between clients I lie back, legs around the chair, and masturbate.

To stay legal, I can't show my pussy directly to the passersby or expose a nipple to the street. So I wear a matching leopard-skin teddy, panties, and a little mask that covers my eyes with pointed ears and cat whiskers.

I lie with legs around the old chair and my back arched; head hanging so my pussy is hidden near the chairback but anyone can see my mound bulge as I jack myself off. Did I say that in this wild city I'm not allowed to expose a nipple either? It has to do with street zoning, I believe. My Danish isn't too good. Anyway, I keep ice water by my chair in the spotlit window and wet down the front of my teddy when I get hot. The ice excites my nipples till they show through the thin silky top, 3mm, 4mm, 6mm. . . .

I use my right hand on my clit, the other on my nipples. I've always been right-handed in this way. It takes only a minute or so to get my clit hard—I'm used to my own touch. My clit gets hard just as my right nipple does. I can feel it: 3mm, 4mm, 6mm. . . . I rub it side to side or rotate it and glance at the people watching me from the street. They point at me and I point to my breast, apply more ice water, and push it toward my audience.

I arch naturally, just keeping in mind not to expose my pubic hair so I don't lose my license. My pussy-water begins to trickle down my perineum. A drop of it tickles my anus. I almost indulge myself with a finger but it's risky; I lose track of what is exposed when I have my index finger up my ass, and the cops are on the street tonight. So I think about it instead and continue the little circles on my nipples and on my clit, harder now; it's so slippery I almost lose the sensation in there. My head rocks back and forth, for the clients outside who expect more movement from my excitement.

Diane and I have been window-buddies for almost a year now, and we know each other's masturbation styles. She must have seen my panties turn dark and wet because she has discreetly slipped a finger into my anus. I arch, and she nibbles my tit so it sticks out like a leopard-skin gumdrop.

I feel the luxury of three-way excitement on my clit, my iced nipple and my asshole. I come, squirting into my panties, wetness trickling down to my boot top. Diane brushes her hand through my hair.

A young man leaves the window and walks into the house. I hear him discuss the price. He asks for Diane.

Karen Marie Christa Minns

Amazon: A Story of the Forest

Because she had so recently come out of the desert I did not expect it; she carried the forest in her eyes, the greening golds and olives, the emeralds breaking apart the shattered light. I noticed when she first glanced up from the podium. The auditorium was packed, the slide show over as I dropped my Walkman with a resounding clunk. She stopped speaking for a moment, glancing up at the tiered assemblage, glancing up and finding me.

My breath caught like a stone in my throat. She said nothing, no cruel joke, no offhand remark, skipped only a beat and continued about the female deities of ancient Egypt. She kept watching me. I felt the heat rise like a touch on my face, knew my friends were stifling giggles, poking me in the ribs, nudging my feet, but I didn't care. I had entered the forest, I was already lost.

"I want to, um, to apply as a researcher with you, um, you said tonight that you were looking for someone who could make a six-month commitment. . . ." I took her hand and shook it, feeling the strength drain from my fingers as they connected with those long, cool hands she used so carefully. Both of them closed around my one, pressing back in a way that marked a possibility I'd only dreamed of since first seeing the video of her early excavations. But no, it was only a student's unabashed crush for

127

the brilliant doctor. I fumbled against the set-up bar, knocking over a bottle of cheap chablis. The undergraduate bartender scowled as he wiped up the mess. I turned to apologize but she'd already been led off by the head of the Humanities Division. I could only watch in soggy misery as her tall, dark head was blotted out by the taller, graying heads of the men of academia. I could still feel the press of her hands, could almost smell the scent of the forest.

"She's tired of the desert . . . no, really, that's a terrible thing to say . . . a poor Egyptologist joke . . . forget it. Look, I think it's exciting she's made the Amazon connection . . . if she gets MacKenzie as her guide she'll be fine . . . don't mention it. However, there is one favor . . . one of my graduate students . . . she wants to volunteer for the internship. Yes, the entire six months. Yes, of course she's good, she's mine, isn't she . . . ? Stop, that's tacky . . . seriously, now, I think she'll do well by the good Dr. Livingston. So, can I tell her it's a go or do you have to wait and confirm . . . excellent. Always said you were a fine man, Muldoon . . . best to Barb . . . will I see you in Florence . . . ? Yes, we've got the same place; what can I say? Clout . . . pure and simple . . . right, then good-bye." My adviser hung up, his grin stretching his usual hangdog face into an almost happy expression. He thumped his Mont Blanc against the blotter . . . two points . . . oh, how these guys like to rack them up with each other! Still, I had to grin back. Dr. Campbell Livingston . . . the Amazon . . . and I was going, I was going.

The air was almost fluorescent, hyper-oxygenated, alive. It was like drinking a long glass of cool spring water from an emerald cup; this was more than air. I stood over my L.L. Bean rucksack, squinting through the glare, looking for the woman of the forest. She was nowhere to be found and the edge of the runway was not exactly packed with tourists. Then, a quick shadow, a tap on the shoulder. I spun around, all toothy grin and immediate blush, "Dr. Livingston, I . . ."

"Sorry, she's downriver. I'm supposed to bring you back with me. You must be Langley, I'm Mac, officially 'the guide' . . . though the bloody Doc won't let me 'guide' so much as her bloody canoe. Sorry, five weeks in the bush with that woman will make anyone a bit cranked. Are you hungry? Last chance for some decent food. There's only the canned crap at camp and what we can trap or get from the river. Do you know how to shoot?" The big man scratched a red stubbled chin. He knew how to dress the part anyway.

"Shoot? What . . . ?" I thought Nikon, I thought Fuji.

"Shit, just as I thought, a college kid. I told Livingston to have them at least send her a boy. Shoot, shoot, like bang-bang. It's bloody wild out there, you know, and she doesn't have a little fridge at the cabin. You want fresh meat you have to go and . . . forget it . . . just forget it. We're all going to wind up fresh meat before this thing's through. C'mon, the jeep will take us to the river." Mac didn't so much as offer to pick up the pack. He blew his nose using a finger against one nostril, the other open and spewing disgustedly.

It was a bad movie with a good set. What the hell was I doing?

The river was not the roaring Amazon I'd imagined. We traveled through vine- and brush-tangled inlets, the canoe paddled by Indians wearing Nike shirts and bark loincloths. They talked some kind of presumed derelict mission dialect. Mac got along fine. They passed a long wooden pipe back and forth, but didn't offer him so much as a whiff. I was not even worth a second glance. My Banana Republic outfit was already going mildewed, my hair in tight curls, plastered to my sweating head. I trailed my burning feet in the river over the long boat's edge.

"Hey, Langley, that's how the last 'researcher' left—toeless. If the piranha aren't hungry, the giant catfish might be. Keep all appendages in the craft, now, will you? This isn't some damned Disney ride!" Mac spit into the water. Something rose from below, investigating, then, before it would show itself on the surface, blew a cloud of bubbles, all iridescent greens, and disappeared. The Indians laughed, relighting the pipe, pushing us on.

The dark was fast, a giant hand scooping the screaming orb of sun clear from the sky. Palm inward, the dark turned and fell over us. How they found the makeshift dock, I'll never know. I was barely keeping back the shakes. The night seemed to drop thousands of insects onto our heads. Every exposed inch of my skin began to itch and burn. We were, as Mac had predicted, fresh meat. My swatting and swearing was, at first, cause for instant delight, the Indians laughing and making bird whistles each time I smashed a crawly off of a leg or arm. Then, my choreography began to sway the boat. A growl from Mac and two answering glares from the men made me barely keep the creeps under control. I prayed a silent thanks as the bow of the canoe bumped the wooden dock. Somewhere, back behind the curtain of vines and overhang, somewhere was the woman that I'd come to find . . . maybe. Mac stepped out and offered a gallant hand, which I accepted out of fear and exhaustion. One of the Indians tossed my gear up with a quiet laugh. Mac shoved them off with a push of his boot. Their gentle whistles were engulfed by the night as the river turned away from us. And now it was Mac and I alone in the dark, nowhere else to go.

"You know, it's a real waste . . ." Mac moved ahead of me on the unseen path.

"What is?" I whispered, hushed as the night around us, aware that all the screaming birds and other hunting animals were silent at our approach.

"You wasting a chunk out of your best years to be in this bloody cesspool with a madwoman. I've seen her type before. You better watch yourself, missy." I could feel his leering wink even in the black.

"What do you mean by that? Seems to me that's my business. Anyway, do you realize how important this woman is, how remarkable her work . . ."

Mac stopped dead on the trail and caught me by my shoulders. "Langley, out here, it doesn't mean spit. I've been guiding hunters, researchers, Peace Corps volunteers, priests, and nuns all my life. I know how to read people. Campbell Livingston fell full-blown, complete with field gear, right out of her mum's snatch. Whatever she's got to teach I think you should consider twice about learning. Christ, the Indians don't even think she's really a human. Lost tribes . . . endangered artifacts . . . the fucking forest is going up in smoke all around her and she doesn't even notice. What she really needs she doesn't want and believe me, I've already offered. Mark my words, little girl, you be careful around this one. She's half-devil, even if she looks like an angel. You be careful." His voice dropped.

"Careful of what?" The question was all velvet hush.

I almost peed in my outback shorts! Jesus! Where had she come from? No flashlight, no lantern, blackness like the inside of a glove all around us. Yet there was no mistaking that husky voice. Dr. Campbell Livingston was directly in front of us!

"Welcome to base camp, Langley. I'm pleased you could make it, you come with strong recommendations," she said.

I could feel the sparks. Could swear little emerald stars sparkled and cracked where I knew she stood. Jesus, my legs trembled. No crush, this; just full-blown terror. I knew nothing about field research, less about jungle survival or proper technique. This was like a dream where you arrive for an exam in a class you never took. But I couldn't say any of this. Not to him, never to her. I mumbled some idiocy and followed them both, best I could, up the mucky path, toward the misty cabin light. I was home.

I was given the screened-in porch to sleep on. Campbell's room was the only one with a door. Mac had constructed his own sheltered camp out back, a few hundred yards from the tin-and-board cabin that made up the research facility. Things had obviously been a bit more than tense for them these past few weeks. And now, I was a new factor.

"Up with the sun . . . lots to do . . . downriver, about twenty miles . . . an easy paddle . . . a village with the same icons I found along the Nile . . . a kind of sea-animal, dolphinlike, only once before . . . never mind. Tomorrow . . ." Her voice trailed off. I couldn't keep my head up. Outside, only the screen between me and the night-hunting things, the forest watched. Mac watched and I fell deep asleep.

The river was almost sapphire as we paddled. The current was swift. Huge shapes moved below us, following, and then, off the starboard bow, a quick whistle and flash of pinkish white.

"It's the dolphins!" Mac hollered, his canoe following ours.

"Dolphins?" I turned to look at Dr. Livingston. In a freshwater river so far from the ocean? Come on . . . a myth . . . *pink* dolphins?

"You didn't know?" Livingston's eyes snapped olive and khaki, muddied with anger at my obvious ignorance.

"I'm an anthropology major . . . I knew you were studying the art but—" I blurted out, not wanting her to know I was there because of a favor, because my adviser wanted to prove his power and pull some strings. I was making him look mighty good by being out here.

"Good God, they told me you'd had some background in biology. Never mind, just let the river carry us. They'll follow if we're quiet." She turned from me, shielding her eyes from the morning's glare, watching the flying underwater figures as they streaked under and past.

Pink dolphins, pink dolphins in an emerald stream . . .

Once Dr. Livingston found the huge holes in my education, she relegated me to writing letters and filing papers. The smell of mildew and fungus filled my every waking hour. Occasionally I'd catch her watching me as I sat at the lone table, hunched over the ancient typewriter, pounding and cursing. Gone were my romantic fantasies, the moaning dreams at midnight. In their place came blisters, a constant case of dampness, boredom bordering on manic depression, and an increasing awareness of my own lack of genuine researcher worth. Mac would pass by, tip his khaki cap, laugh out loud, then disappear until dinner. That task also fell to me. I never realized I'd actually invent twenty-three ways to cook catfish and canned hash. This was not the lavender paradise I'd constructed. Whole days would go by without human contact. I'd type, file, sweep the cabin, try to wring out my clothes, gather cooking wood, make a smoky fire in the little fireplace, then watch the parade of animals and insects both inside and outside of the house.

Finally—it must have been the third week there—Campbell Livingston decided that Mac was intolerable. Their fight lasted until dawn, ending in two of the big cooking pots being bashed against a rubber tree and a machete thrown at the door. When the toucans began to reclaim the trees next to the cabin, I realized Mac was gone. The pit of my stomach froze. Hellion or not, Livingston wasn't big enough to protect us from God-knew-what-lurked-in-that-river. Even if Mac was a pig, he was an honest pig, he could talk to the Indian guides, he could find his way to the airstrip, he could shoot. I didn't even know for sure whether Livingston could shoot.

"Look, Langley, you have a choice, but if you decide to stay, I promise no more filing. You can come back on the river with me. All right, I'll admit it, with Mac gone, I *need* you on the river. Please?" She couldn't look at me when she asked. The hiss of the pressure lamps and the thrum of the night insects were the only sounds. I stared at her, then, standing so damned tall and straight above my sleeping bag, her smoky hair curling around her face in long tendrils, her fiery eyes low, and those glorious "David" hands stuck into her jeans' pockets. Campbell Livingston was actually asking me for something.

I pulled the bag closer around me. "Okay." My whisper was hoarse, heavier than I'd wanted it to be.

"Okay," she said, and reached out gently, one long finger brushing my cheek. "Okay."

I lay there until the moon rose, spilling liquid silver over me, ambushing me in the middle of my haunting, burning ache.

"They're almost gone, just a few dozen left." Campbell stretched her long, muscled legs in front of her, not so much as making the canoe lean to either side. "It's what made me change direction. The tomb of the Goddess, the last one . . . dolphinlike beings . . . and then, letters telling of a tribe out here with similar artifacts. I hunted a long time, never really believing I'd find more than the myth. But here they are, and the only direction is to protect them, keep them safe, here, as long as we can."

I watched the mammals surface, splashing us playfully. They knew us now, would often come close enough to nuzzle her hand, sometimes shoving each other out of the way for her attention, her touch.

"I wonder what it would be like to make love to a dolphin . . . ," she whispered as we came back.

We heard the motors before we saw the boats. All around us the dolphins were screaming.

"No!" Campbell almost bent in two as she struck the paddle deep into the seething water.

"Ahoy, ahoy! Who are you?" The Adventure Tour Guide's voice boomed over the river.

"Dr. Livingston, Campbell Livingston, and this is restricted water!" She hollered above the roar of their engines and the cries of the panicked animals.

"What? Come in closer, we can't hear you!" The guide was wearing an outfit tailored after Bogart in *The African Queen*. The huge inflatable carried twenty people, all in neon or khaki, many sporting zinc oxide on their faces; all with cameras aimed and clicking. And I was worried about piranhas. . . .

"Goddammit, Langley, paddle! I've got to get these idiots off this river!" Campbell's face was almost maroon with fury. We finally came abreast of the guide.

"Dr. uh, Livingston? C'mon, you're kidding, right? Hey, folks, believe it or not, we didn't set this up! Outrageous! What are you doing way out here in a canoe, Doc?" The snapping of shutters almost drowned out the mosquitoes.

"What are *you* doing here? I have a government permit to be on this branch of the river. I am a scientist doing fieldwork. You have no right . . ." She was almost stammering, her face contorted, witchlike. I thought she was going to climb aboard the raft and hit the guy over the head with her paddle.

"You're way wrong, lady. Look, maybe we took a wrong turn or something, but this ain't exactly posted property. Don't have a coronary! I've got a permit. Let me just get us turned around and we'll be out of here, okay? No need to spoil the day for all of these good people . . . Jesus!" The guide smiled through gritted teeth.

"Aren't you that lady scientist that was on 'Geographic' a few months ago? But I thought you studied pyramids." A large woman wearing a babushka leaned forward, her life vest reflecting orange into her face. A man wearing nothing but hair on his chest and a seedy Speedo grabbed the woman by the elbow and shouted into her face, "Maude, they've got pyramids down here too—remember 'Chariots of the Gods'?"

"Let's get out of here." Campbell pulled hard and spun our canoe around.

"Nice meeting you too, lady. Bitch!" The guide soaked us in his wake.

We fought the river all the way back.

I turned off all of the lamps. Outside, a soft, warm rain bathed the jungle. I listened to the syncopated storm as it played across the face of the river. The forest was coming closer to me, no longer the creeping green terror, no longer the monster waters. I lay there, drifting off to sleep, wondering if the dolphins listened to the rain.

I woke with a start, aware the cloudburst had passed. Outside, the sounds of the night prowlers, in the cabin something more. Then I saw her, sitting, a few feet away, watching, almost keeping guard over me on the porch.

"Campbell? Are you okay?" I rubbed the dreams from my eyes.

Her smile was sad, slow; the ache of it went straight through my navel. God, did she know her effect on me yet? The heavy, wet pull, the throb, almost like the first time I'd seen her in the lecture hall. The sleeping bag fell away from my shoulders. The cooled air stroked my flesh. My nipples went hard with the shock of air and fire of seeing her there, so close, only the mosquito netting between us.

"I didn't mean to frighten you." The hush of her voice had a ragged edge, as if she'd been crying.

I thought about wiggling down into the synthetic depths of the bag, protecting myself from her vision, sure she could see through the net, sure it was another power play, she clothed, awake, watching. But I only moved out of the fiber-filled cocoon, the rising fever washing over me so suddenly I had to gasp. She heard my breath and moved in closer.

"Thank you, for today, on the river. You didn't run, you tried to help. It meant, it means a lot to me, to the dolphins." She pulled back the edge of the mosquito net, moving inside the lacy cave.

I could not move, could not answer. Kneeling now, not in prayer but in the midst of something equally powerful, my body was clenched, poised, wired.

How many weeks had we shared this tiny cabin, barely brushing shoulders? Even in the canoes, we were careful not even to graze toes. Now she was kneeling in front of me, taller by a head, dark, a warrior come from the forest, fully dressed, touching my face with her powerful hands, and her touch burned.

My heart hammered a new language against the pillars of my ribs. I was sure if I died and they performed an autopsy, they would find her name carved in ideograms there.

She moved her palms from my face and let them drift down my neck, stopping only briefly to rest her fingertips at the bend of the great artery as if she were reading the pulse of a jungle drum, reading my desire, reading the fever and staccato yammer she caused in my heart.

All the blood in my body was focused, listening, waiting for the movement of those finely veined hands. She moved over the sensitive skin of my shoulders, rode my flesh like the river dolphins ride the water, trailing over collarbone and then, almost as if she were clasping her palms together in prayer, she moved her hands between my breasts, only the dry, smooth edges barely brushing against my skin. I closed my eyes, not needing to watch—I'd memorized her handsome, sunburned face, those emerald eyes, the fine, high forehead and chiseled cheeks months ago. No, I needed my other senses, needed to allow the sound of my heart, the sound of her breathing, the scent of rainwash and our rising sweat, the minute sensitivity of each pore, every hair as it rose in greeting to her touch. I needed the taste of her, please Jesus, I needed her inside of me.

She lowered her hands, the palms held flat as they brushed across my breasts, making the nipples rise, hard, tight, aching, and I could do nothing, nothing but feel the long, heavy wetness between my thighs, feel the tightness in my throat, the screaming ache of cunt that was going to explode, so swollen, so swollen, oh how many nights had I tried to sleep, the netting a shroud over me, witness to my wide-eyed fantasy, this exact scene played out, played out to the final cut before it could climax. Too dangerous, even for a daydream. How many nights in this same place, trembling, my skin moist in that heated dark, the edges of what I'd imagined keeping me awake for hours. Now, now her hands pulled gently on my nipples, rolling them between her fingers like two fine berries, checking their ripeness, about to

pick them to eat. She drew me in closer, close enough to feel the
heat rise from her own fever but still not against me. Still kneeling we were, but not touching except where her hands traced
new trails over my chest. I could feel her hot, moist, sweet breath
over me, a steaming cloud, it made my lips bruise like overripe
fruit. I exhaled deeply, almost swooning.

She stopped, her hands dropping from my full breasts, then,
in one startling sweep, her hands caressed my lower belly,
wrenching such a moan that for moments I didn't realize it had
come from me. Pure electric shock at this intimate touch, a full,
gentle press, her fingers memorizing my curves and cups of bone
and muscle, the flesh stretched tight, and she tracing each outline, the tips of her fingers barely connecting with the moist,
curly hair at the top of my mons. I moaned again, afraid I would
die with the tickle and wet burn. So much, so much feeling.
Never like this before, she was killing me slowly, scalding me
with her probe and press.

Her hands tangled in my thatch of hair, pulling and teasing,
the moisture now covering her fingers as she played only on the
mound, never dipping in, not having to find the eruption. Wet,
so wet, wetter even than the rain-soaked jungle only a few feet
away, her fingers traced moist circles again and again there, and
then, with only the warning of a quick, light, almost feathery
brush against my throbbing lips, she plunged one hand deep,
deep, opening me wide, splitting me even as this entire ghost
dance had split open the night. At the same instant she fell, hard,
full body pressed against me, rough denim sudden against my
prickling skin, my nipples scraped almost raw by the press of her
heavier breast, my belly smashed and yearning against her own
tighter one. Her hand moved hard inside of me, against me, and
her mouth finally found mine, her hard tongue filling me even
as those "David" hands filled me, her teeth biting at my tender-
fleshed lips, her tongue all probe and power, sucking me back,
sweet fruit, splitting me like a ripened fig, lapping me inside,
drinking me like rain, taking my breath into her own body. Her
hands pounded against the walls of my cunt, beating a rhythm
like the earlier rain outside, playing me like a new jungle drum,
forcing another huge storm cloud to build, freeing the lightning

that was running through every vein. I couldn't hold back,
couldn't think, could only let the feelings envelop and explode.
Too much, too much, oh Jesus, what I prayed for but too
much. I was in liquid meltdown, the burn one vast cloudburst of
surrender. No words, no words in a jungle of sense and sound, no
words, only the pelvic thrust and thunder, only the sparking fire
from her fingertips, the buck and grind as she forced me down,
sinking and sobbing and sucking her in, on top of me, this glorious wild beastwoman, and my hands came alive and began to
shuck the clothes from her. I needed the taste of her, needed to
suckle there. So much was being wrenched free, I needed some
back, and she took her mouth from mine, the loud, pulling suck
filling the room, our breathing ragged, hard, bestial, her eyes
flashing gold and ruby and emerald, filling the dark like spark-
lers, filling the dark even as the stars crashed and burned and
filled the night canopy over the cabin, her grinding hips beating
into me, her hands still working, hard and fast and baby slick.
How did she fit, how did she reach so deeply inside and bring
back this joy? She pulled one hand from the cuntcave and
propped it behind my head, then, rising, a behemoth, a goddess,
she lowered her breasts over my face, dragging their heavy lobes
across my burning lips, letting me nip and suck, then pressing
my face to their soft centers, suckling there like some hungry
child, but more, more, the taste maddening me, making me fam-
ished for her salty center. She felt my need, felt me move and
cry and thrash against her, my own coming caught in stop action, my clit between her fingers now, held at that one point.
Heaving back the final release, I broke loose, moved out from
under, gasping, unsure of where exactly I was, only positive I
must have her in my mouth, must have my face pressed deep in
her own jungle, must feel the soft tangle of her there. In the
midst of my own fire, the volcano in check, she, shocked at the
sudden switch, but laughing, wild, willing, allowing anything
in this night, let me strip off her sodden jeans, fling them from
the swamp of bed. I swam down, down her soaking flesh, my
face grazing at her navel, her mons, nipping, tasting, lapping
the wet from her thighs. She held my head, her hands pulling
hard through my hair, sobbing now, in surprise and shock at her

own happy surrender, watching me dive in the dark, like a dolphin, her beloved pet, but no pet, untamed, fierce. Fiercely I took her, the good, clean womanscent and marsh taste, the weighty salt and sweet-tickled burn; her lower lips almost purple in their desire, swollen, swollen, the moisture pearly in the moonlight, and I fell there, my face close and smooth, my teeth tickling the hood of her clit, my tongue another animal, swooping, flat and pressing, around and around, then dipping in, molten, making her scream, her purpled coming like a waterfall, filling me with the sacrament I'd come these thousands of miles to find. She screamed my name, fighting her own legs to stay open, and still I pressed and pushed and wanted all of it, all of her, this burning Amazon, this icon, this renowned scientist now split wide and moaning, needing me as much as I did her.

My hand found my own center, my hips thrust in time to her calls, the sleeping bag a soaking ball between my legs. I pressed against my palm, against its soft embrace. I thrust my tongue and teeth and lips into her cunt and she pressed back, her hands moving over my hair, then up to her own breasts, pinching the ache from each ripened nipple, each sucked nut, until there was no more than could be held in check. The night was ablaze, the stars beating on the roof, calling our names, calling to be let inside, and she was coming, crashing in my mouth, she was coming and bucking and taking me out over the edge with her and the storm burst inside of me, a long, slow, screaming explosion . . . the trembling deep, so damned damned deep, it seemed the hours of ache had built to this final release. The waves not over, not over, she held the edges of this makeshift bed, gasping my name as I echoed hers, my own thunder and rain as yet unstopped. We were so wet and limp and weak in this miracle.

Finally, the hush of the jungle outside a silent witness to our acts, I moved up the long path that is her body, moved over, and through and up, finally meeting her lips again as old friends. And we lay there, arms wrapped tight, legs atangle, cunt to cunt, heartpound to heartflesh, her hair a smoking halo around our heads. We lay there in helpless release. If anyone could see they would see that now, I, too, carry the deep forest in my eyes. . . .

Marcy Sheiner

A Biker Is Born

When I was a teenager, I hung out with a crowd considered by the more clean-cut kids to be "hoods." Like the other girls in our crowd, I wore black elastic pants, gobs of black eye makeup, and a fake ponytail that reached down to my ass. A lot of guys had motorcycles, and the biggest thrill for us girls was to be taken for a ride—and with some of those guys you could be taken for a ride with or without wheels, believe me.

What I love most about bikes is the exhilarating feel of the wind whipping around me and the vibrations of the machine between my legs. There's no foreplay that gets me hotter than a ride on a Harley.

I always wanted to drive a bike myself, to be the one up front, the person in control of all that energy and power. The one time I sat in the driver's seat, though, the bike immediately tipped over. Being a typical female raised in the fifties, I figured it was hopeless, and never made the attempt again.

Before I was twenty I had settled into marriage and babies with a nonbiker, leaving my "trampy" ways, as he called them, behind. As might have been foreseen, the marriage didn't last very long, and in the late sixties I became another statistic—a single mother.

Even though I now had two kids, my wild ways resurfaced after my divorce. I went out with a lot of different men, but I was mostly attracted to the type of guys I'd grown up with— leather-jacketed Brandos with heavy metal machines throbbing between their legs. I even looked up an old boyfriend who took me riding back and forth over the George Washington Bridge while I sang our old love songs in his ear.

One weekend when the kids were with their father, I took the train upstate to visit my friends Ron and Janet. Our old friend Louie arrived unexpectedly on a brand-new Harley-Davidson. Louie and I had at one time been lovers, but it was an affair doomed before it began. We're too much alike—willful and headstrong—to be compatible. In the few months we were together, we tore each other's guts out, until finally we settled on a platonic relationship.

Louie had been talking about getting a bike for years; I couldn't believe he'd finally done it. Ron, Janet, and I all went outside to admire the machine and congratulate Louie on having made it all the way from New Jersey on his first trip. He was struttin' proud in his new leather jacket and boots, high as a kite over his accomplishment. The four of us hung out, listening to music, eating and drinking, playing cards, and generally cracking each other up. There's no laughter as easy or natural as that shared by old friends.

On Sunday Louie took us each out for a spin, he asked me if I wanted to ride back with him to the city. I was thrilled—two solid hours on a bike! Never mind that it was starting to drizzle and that the driver was a novice. I felt like hot shit putting on a helmet and straddling the Harley behind Louie. I just wished I had on black elastic pants and a fake ponytail.

It was nearly summer; the air warm though damp. We set off with a roar. I held my arms tightly around Louie, taking pleasure in the feel and smell of his leather jacket, my body tingling from the machine's vibrations as we sped down the thruway.

After twenty minutes or so, the light drizzle became more substantial and I noticed that Louie had slowed down and was driving with far less confidence than before. I could feel and see the tension in his back, and every so often I sensed a slight wobble in the bike. I looked at his face in the mirror—it was tense and drawn as he concentrated on the road ahead.

I didn't know if I should talk to him or not. Given our history, a word from me could easily spark a battle, especially with Louie in his present condition. As we continued sliding down the slick road, I stared with terror at the huge boulders in the "fallen rock zone," imagining us crashing into them, our blood spattering across the highway. I envisioned Ron and Janet attending our double funeral; I was lost in a reverie of tears and flowers when Louie pulled over near an exit and stopped.

"Are you okay?" I asked.

"Don't start acting like a mother!" he snapped. As I'd suspected, he was in a volatile state. "It's just a little slippery, and I'm not that used to the bike yet."

"I thought you were doing great," I said, trying to reassure him. "In fact, I felt so secure I drifted into a daydream." I didn't tell him what kind of daydream.

Louie calmed down a little. "Yeah? Well, that makes me feel better. But I think maybe we should get off the thruway before the rain gets worse."

"That sounds like a good idea."

We set off again, exiting the thruway and getting onto a slower-paced route. For a while Louie seemed to be more in control, but soon I saw and felt him tense up again. This time he started yelling at me.

"Don't hold onto me so tight, ferchrissakes, I can hardly breathe!"

"Will ya stop leaning on my back, dammit!"

"When are you gonna learn how to lean with me on the turns?"

"Your goddam hair is blowing across my mirror!"

It was the nightmare of our relationship all over again. In the past I'd have yelled right back, but now my life was on the line.

I may not know how to drive a motorcycle, but I know that when you're tense about anything—whether it's threading a needle, having a baby, or riding a bike—you're bound to fuck up, whereas when you do something in a relaxed, easy manner, the moves come smoothly. I had to find a way to cool Louie out before we both became history.

I remembered that the surefire method of calming Louie down was to jerk him off. Of course, he became relaxed after any orgasm, but for some reason, being jerked off cooled him out more than any other sexual activity.

I'd handled plenty of hard cocks inside moving vehicles, but never out in the open air. This would require some preparation.

"Louie," I shouted.

"Whaddya want?" he growled.

"Can we turn down a side street?"

"What the fuck for?"

"Just turn, okay?"

"Ya gotta piss, right? Jeez, you are one pain in the ass!" Despite his complaints, he turned onto a deserted road. I slid my hand down to feel the bulge I'd known would be there, not from lust, but from tension. In the mirror I saw Louie crack a smile.

As we slowly drove along the rutted, narrow road I unzipped his fly, released his hard prick, and began a steady movement. Louie kept right on driving; I wondered how it felt to him to have his cock waving in the wind.

It only took a minute. He said nothing, made no sounds. Afterward, he zipped up his pants, picked up speed, and returned to the main road. All the tension had vanished from his body. In the mirror I saw his face, relaxed and confident as he easily guided the bike down the still slippery road. He reached back and briefly touched my arm; I knew it was his way of apologizing for yelling at me earlier.

Now the only problem was me—after all that, I was turned on. I pressed down hard into the leather seat with my upper torso firmly against Louie's back; with the bike tearing smoothly and effortlessly through space, all thoughts of funerals left my head. I began to fantasize myself as the one in the driver's seat; I leaned my cheek against Louie's leather jacket, shut my eyes, and envisioned myself dressed from head to toe in black leather, expertly steering the Harley through the streets of my hometown. I imagined my old boyfriends lounging against the candy store as I roared up, gave them the once-over, and selected one from the pack. I imagined driving my pick to a deserted spot outside of town. I was just about to fuck his brains out when the bike slowed to a halt. I opened my eyes and saw that we'd arrived in front of my apartment building. Inwardly I cursed; I was inches away from orgasm.

"Well, we made it," Louie said proudly as he parked in front of my apartment.

"Of course we made it. I had total confidence in you."

I got off the bike, removed my helmet and kissed him on the cheek. He lit a cigarette, leaning back on his seat with an air of pride. He looked like he'd been riding the thing forever.

He grinned suggestively. "Aren't you gonna invite me in for a drink or something?"

I looked at him uncertainly, remembering what a disaster our relationship had been. But my cunt was twitching, and Louie's air of self-confidence was an aphrodisiac. I shrugged, and Louie followed me upstairs.

The minute we were inside, his hands and tongue were all over me.

"You really turned me on out there," he whispered, scratching his rough beard against my cheek and sliding his hands under my blouse. I inhaled his strong masculine scent, intensified by the tension of our journey, mingled with the smell of leather. He slid his jacket off.

"No, wait," I said suddenly. I took the jacket with me into the bedroom where I quickly stripped off my clothes, threw on the jacket, and called for Louie to come in.

"You're gonna wear my jacket while we fuck?" he asked, incredulous.

"I wanna see what it feels like."

Louie laughed and shook his head, thinking this was another of my crazy quirks. I helped him undress, then gently pushed him to his knees and pressed my pussy against his mouth. He wrapped his arms around my ass and began to lick around my clit, prying open my wet labia with his fingers. I glanced into the mirror and feasted my eyes on myself, with my long red hair, damp and windblown, flowing down my back, the open jacket grazing my taut nipples, and Louie on his knees lapping at my pussy. Overcome by the vision, I fell back onto the bed. Louie held on, his tongue fastened to my clit. After all the stimulation

I'd gotten on the bike, it took only a few minutes before I was groaning in the throes of orgasm, gripping his head with my legs and grinding my cunt against his mouth.

He climbed on top of me and slid his rigid cock into my palpitating cunt. Slowly and deliberately he fucked me, his hands roaming under the leather jacket to fondle my breasts, his eyes locked on mine. With slow sure strokes he thrust his cock into the recesses of my pussy, and I watched his face crumble in ecstasy as he shot his cum deep inside me.

We fell asleep almost instantly. In the morning, we examined each other warily over coffee. Did this mean we were lovers again? I was terrified of the consequences.

"Still friends?" Louie asked, apparently as nervous as I was.

"Always," I answered. "But—"

"Hey," he said, "this was an unusual situation, right? Let's just say it was for old times' sake. Or better yet, one for the road."

He put on his jacket, and smiled when he caught me gazing at it longingly.

"You know," he said thoughtfully, "you could learn to drive a bike. I could teach you."

"Would you?"

"You bet. Tell you what—I'll come by next Saturday for your first lesson."

Happy as a clam, I walked him outside and watched as he climbed onto the Harley. Slowly he revved up the engine and stubbed out his cigarette. He leaned over, cuffed me playfully on the chin. "You're gonna make a first-rate biker, kid."

Jane Longaway

My Pussy Is Dead

Dido's vagina was dead. Her pussy was dead. No manner of book or finger stimulation of any sort seemed to get it going again. She went along as she had, looking the same on the outside with her body functioning much the same as it had before, except for the fact that her pussy was dead.

A young man spent over an hour licking it with his greedy insistent tongue, but she had no feeling down there at all. Her clit expanded balloonlike but she didn't even approach orgasm.

It was, all in all, an annoyance. The young man went on to fuck her, which she tried to imagine was exciting. She tried all the old fantasies; she looked at her lover who was handsome and exotic with long black Japanese hair in a ponytail. He was hep. He had expertise. He desired her. There was nothing wrong with him at all. As a man he was about as near perfection as she had gotten. But her cunt was dead.

She looked at the ceiling of the little square room and then at the mirror that ran alongside the wall next to the bed, a low sort of thing. She could see herself, flattered in the afternoon light, big-thighed, big-breasted with a pretty face like a Persian, only blond-haired. The man on top of her was the color copper with

strong, flat muscles which complimented her softness. He was
extraordinarily active. It was a pity not to moan.

She thought as she blinked his sweat from her eyes that her
cunt was directly connected to her brain and, as yet her brain
was still functioning. Those lobes concerned with imagination
had run through so many erotic scenes, flipped through old lovers both male and female. Her brain was working. She thought
her cunt should be connected not only to her brain (which still
functioned admirably) but also to her heart and there was the
actual problem. Her heart was no longer connected to sex. Her
heart had gone shrinking through the years until it was almost
beanlike, hard, not even decorative. A thing you could perhaps
trot out at Christmas and funerals. When she realized this she
rose up with a shudder which sent her lover into ecstasy. He gave
a little yell and came all over her belly, which was round and
white like the belly of a pure white cat.

Afterward, they kissed and promised to meet again. Perhaps
for drinks some boring Saturday afternoon when it was too rainy
or too overcast for anything else. He left with a subdued smile
on his face. She, however, was greatly troubled. She lay in her
bath, scrubbing away all traces of him, and thought about the
state of her heart.

Dido worked behind the perfume counter at Macy's. Mostly
she leaned against the glass behind the displays of crystal and
precious bottles that smelled of sweet flowers and wicked nights
and stared at the people who walked, dazed, through the store.
Some of the women were beautiful. More beautiful than the
women behind the counters who were for the most part chosen
for their beauty. Some of the women who passed her counter
were ugly or funny-looking and the rest were plain and wore
ordinary pathetic-looking clothing. Dido imagined them all suddenly becoming naked. The lady with the slick handbag and the
carmine lips suddenly appeared without her leather coat and
black silk suit, without her pumps or expensive pearls. Would
her pussy hair be as flaxen as her head hair or as well-groomed?
Dido had heard of such things.

It was rare to see a truly beautiful man in the perfume section.
Perhaps beautiful men had no reason to buy perfume, but Dido

thought that even the middle-aged doctor who had bought a large bottle of *Obsession* and a smaller, more expensive bottle of *Que-sais-je?*, would look much more interesting if his expensive Italian suit, his shirt, his Jockeys, all disappeared and he was leaning with a hairy, pale arm against the counter, his small, pale penis dangling between his legs like a fish.

Of course this sort of thing was no more than idleness at work. Dido loved her job and she loved idleness. She loved the women who made faces at the different scents and rubbed samples studiously over their wrists. The sight of a woman smelling herself gave Dido a tiny jolt of pleasure. But none of these people sparked desire in her, even though she did rub her thighs together vigorously when a handsome, voluptuous dark woman who smelled already of sex, death, and money, charged her purchase of a large bottle of *Opium*.

Still, she had no desire to touch this woman or be touched by her. The woman held the pretty lacquered sack close to her foularded bosom and it sank between the huge breasts like a stone. Dido truly appreciated the gesture, but it did not arouse her.

No, she figured she was lost. She had lost the connection. She twisted a fat strand of yellow hair between her fingers and studied the split ends. There had been a time when some spark might have passed between the *Opium* woman and herself, even a heated glance, but not now. Her pussy was dead.

That evening she went to dinner with her best friend Max, who loved to watch her eat. Since he paid, she obliged him. She ordered grilled salmon and asparagus tips from a waiter who made much more money than she did and who had huge diamonds on his fingers. Max always dieted, so he spent most of the time watching forkfuls of food disappear into her greedy mouth. He leaned forward as she sucked on a spear of asparagus and sighed as it slid into her pink mouth. Usually his desire and excitement charged Dido up, until she felt a thrill every time her small teeth bit into substance. Tonight, however, she merely rolled her eyes when she saw him move forward and she sighed.

"Max," she said, putting the asparagus down gently next to its brothers, "something is terribly wrong with me."

His face registered dismay when she stopped chewing and

started talking, but since she was his friend he drew himself up and folded his hands studiously in front of his plate and asked her what was up.

"It's here," Dido said, being very theatrical and clutching her left tit with such force that she almost brought it out of her dress.

"Do touch up your lipstick, Dido. It's smeared," Max said. He watched her take out a little gray plastic compact and a tube of red with which she regreased her lips.

"That's much better," he said with some relief. "Now about your heart . . . are you in love again?"

"No, that's just it. I'm impotent!"

"Shhh!" Max whispered in despair, glancing wildly around the room at the other diners. "Dear," he said with an avuncular smile, "it's impossible for you to be impotent. You might be frigid although I think in your case that's impossible, too. Perhaps you have burnt out." He closed his eyes and thought for a while, making his forehead wrinkle up. "Well," he said after a pause and then he coughed and said, "well," again.

"It's fucking horrible!" Dido moaned, smashing a forkful of salmon into some thick white sauce. "I don't know what to do about it. What if it lasts forever? When I think about how full of sex I was . . . I want to scream." She threatened him with an open mouth and then continued. "Now, even thinking of Louis, Pat, Marie Francis, or Cenzi doesn't do a damn thing for me. You could stick your fingers up me right now and I'd be dry as a bone."

Max winced at the thought of sticking his fingers anywhere in such a public place. Just then the waiter placed a dish of ice cream in front of Dido and she daintily prodded it with her spoon before she lifted some to her mouth, licking it like a cat with her little pink tongue. Max leaned back and shut his eyes in pleasure. When he opened them she was still lapping at the ice cream with her heavy yellow hair hanging around her face.

"There is always the Fabulous Tony Lee," Max said.

"Nah, it wouldn't work. It's not a matter of size. If it were a matter of size I could use an eggplant."

Max raised an eyebrow and considered the problem. "It's a

love problem, isn't it? I mean it's a love-thing. You need to feel something."

"No way, I hate being in love." She waved the spoon three times in the air in front of her. "Every time I fall in love I suffer. Every time I fall in love it's the absolute shits. I swore I would never fall in love again. Nix on that. No, it has to be something else. Perhaps I should bag it up."

"But it doesn't have to be a person. I mean think about it," Max countered, trying to think of what he meant.

"If it isn't a person . . . what could it be?" Dido asked between licking the spoon.

Dido had skin like a hot apricot and so much of it! Max had dreamed of fucking her for years but subliminated this risk into a pleasure at watching her eat. The girl could put it away. He tried to answer her question honestly, but her big brown eyes looked blank.

"My friend Jeff has one of those New Age places up in Sonoma that has workshops, mineral baths, massage, nature, lots of naked people. I think they give workshops in sensuality. Maybe you need something like that to boot you up. A few days away from the counter at Macy's, running around naked might be the thing."

"Would you go with me?"

"Are you crazy? Hell, no. But I'll pay for it and I'll loan you the Jeep if you take Bosco up with you. He's been so neurotic lately, making poop on the hard pavement. And Jeff adores Bosco."

Dido scraped the bottom of the little silver dish. Of course she would take him up on it but she didn't want to appear too eager. Bosco was not her favorite dog; he took on a high smell in close quarters because of his age. But the thought of leaving town thrilled her.

"Okay," she said.

The trip had been good, Bosco's smell notwithstanding. The minute they hit the tree-lined drive leading to Angel Springs, Bosco set up a howl and scratched with black claws against the window. Jeff Angel was waiting for them both where the road

opened out into parking. He was leaning against a signpost that
read ANGEL SPRINGS—NO CARS BEYOND THIS POINT.

Dido opened her window and Bosco tried to cram his body
through the small space while doing a wild dance on her lap
with his hind legs. She flung the dog out of the car with disgust
and Jeff was soon down on the ground with him being licked to
death.

He looked up and saw Dido's large, shapely bare legs in front
of him, then moved his gaze up her thighs to her tiny white
shorts and her sweet little belly button, hidden like a secret.
When he got to her face, he was wearing a sappy grin.

"I could do him," Dido thought, "but so what?" She smiled at
him anyway and he got to his feet, brushing the dog away with
his hands. It wasn't that Jeff turned her off but he didn't interest
her. She felt glad that she had her Ray-Bans on because it was
easier to be polite that way. Jeff carried her small suitcase down
to a cabin and waited for her to put her things down so that he
could show her the place. Apparently there were not only the
sulphur baths and sauna, swimming pool and nature trails but
also classes in yoga, t'ai chi and various forms of meditation and
movement. The list in her hand was so long and involved that
she sat down on the bed and wished that the place had a bar
instead of a Vegi-rite juice concession.

She took off her shirt which was sweaty from the trip and
wiped her breasts with it. Jeff hovered in the doorway like a bee.
He had one of those cute California ponytails, a thin, fierce face
and a bulge in his pants like a fist.

"Well, let's go," she said.

"Ah, you can go totally nude if you like," he said, and something in his voice led her to believe that *he* would like it very
much. Anyway, she wanted to keep her shorts on because it had
been a struggle to get them on in the first place and for her
money they could stay there the rest of the trip. She put on a
straw hat and a pair of zoris and they went off side by side to
explore the resort. It wasn't crowded, being the middle of the
week, but the people there seemed happy and languid. A number of them were playing volleyball; another group sat in a circle
talking while others lay out in the sun getting brown as toast.

"Max told me you were having some sort of problem," Jeff said.

"Ah, Max!" Dido kicked at Bosco who was running between their legs trying to tackle either. The dog was in heaven.

"The baths are down over here and that big brown building is where the classes and massage are; over here, if you follow this path, is the swimming pool." He took her by the elbow and walked her over to a small clearing surrounded by bushes. "Over here, that cavelike thing where the towels are hanging is the sauna. Max said something about you having sexual problems and I want to tell you that we have a sexuality program you're welcome to join. It's on the handout I gave you. I think you might like it."

Dido looked at him and lowered her sunglasses. "I am impotent," she said, and seeing him about to protest her use of the word, she put one hand over his mouth lightly. "I am. My pussy is dead. I can only have mechanical orgasms. Men don't interest me, women don't interest me and I don't interest me. That is my problem." Saying this she removed her hand and wiped it on her shorts.

"Well, maybe you just haven't had the right lover," Jeff offered.

Dido let out a laugh that sounded like a bark and put her sunglasses on; she walked toward the sulphur baths with Bosco at her heels and Jeff had to trot to catch up with her.

"You don't have a towel," Jeff yelled and she shrugged her bare shoulders in reply. He watched her ass strain the white cloth that bound it and let out another feeble protest. "Dogs aren't allowed near the baths."

"Take him back then," Dido said, turning toward him momentarily. He looked like someone whose ship had left the harbor leaving him behind as she turned again and strode away, big fat white butterflies circling her head.

There was a group of young men sitting on a low rock fence. They looked like computer programmers or young executives although they were as naked as savages. One stood up in a mock bow. Dido stared at his pale prick, half-swollen in greeting. She knew herself to be an object of desire and stood there for a mo-

ment with her big-nippled tits pointed right at him. Three of the
men looked away but the one she was aiming at boldly came up
to her and introduced himself as Eric Maybear. He was young
and eager with a sort of doggy look to him and his dick kept
hitting her on the hip. She pushed it aside with her hand but it
kept bobbing back. Eric didn't seem to notice since he was busy
talking about himself. He followed her right up to the disrobing
room and watched while she took off the tight little shorts and
folded them up into a white little square. He lunged for her then
and there, grabbing one soft breast in each hand and holding on
for dear life while she swatted at him with her hands.

"We could do it right here," he said a bit breathless. "It would
only take a minute."

"I'm sure it would." Dido swished past and left him in the
dark damp room by himself.

The tub was huge and smelled slightly sulfuric. Six eyes fastened on Dido as she carefully put one foot then the other into
the hot churning water. It was delicious to slip into the slick
warmth which covered her to her neck. As soon as she finished
sighing she noticed the three people who were watching her
through the steam. One was a black woman who smiled lazily
at her. The other two were a couple who immediately started
kissing each other. Dido simply relaxed and shut her eyes, opened
her legs to the pulsing jets, let her heavy breasts bob up weight-
less in the water, and felt the tension of the trip leave her body
bit by bit. The heat made her body feel like a flower opening
out and out, hugely pink and soft. Just as she was sinking into
the luxury of her sensations another person entered the tub, setting up a wake of water. Dido opened her eyes and right beside
her was a large man with the sharp features of an American
Indian, eyes like live coals and black hair tied back in a ponytail.

He edged a little away from her, then sank down in the water
so that only his eyes were revealed. They were dark eyes and
they didn't look at Dido but seemed to be focused on some distant point. When he surfaced, his profile was handsome, strong
and imperial, the nose fine and noble. Dido was looking at this
face when she felt a hand (and it could only be his since it was
not her own) move gently up her thigh and right between her

legs. It seemed extraordinary at first. The fingers moved into her cunt like a hermit crab looking for a new place to live. Dido opened her legs wider.

The man didn't change his facial expression one bit but continued to stare straight in front of him with his eyes half closed and a rather stoic look to his mouth. Dido was pleased when the fingers rubbed her clit, and shifted her body so that he could hit the right spot. It was bizarre but it actually excited her.

His hand seemed quite sure of itself.

The other people were unaware. The black woman continued to smile at Dido and the couple stayed wrapped in each other's arms, the woman occasionally nibbling on her lover's ear.

When Dido tried to touch the man's cock with her hand, gliding between his smooth thighs, he stopped her abruptly. He put her hand back on her own turf, so to speak, and then and only then continued his rubbing and searching of her hidey-hole. She abandoned herself to his attentions, all the while keeping her eyes wide open, staring first at the black lady who smiled lazily back and then at the couple who, for the most part, ignored her. The finger moved against her clit-button until she was ready to explode; she bit down on her underlip and moved against the digit. It rubbed and stopped, rubbed and stopped, and then just stopped. Before her impending orgasm the finger left and for a while her legs scissored the water in desperation. It felt like her cunt was on fire with no firehouse in sight. A quick rub with her own hand brought almost instant relief, although she moaned so loud that the couple were clearly startled. The Indian, however, did not respond at all to her dirty looks but stared straight ahead at nothing.

Dido put a little distance between them. Her pussy still smarted as it had been a violent orgasm—comparable to an umbrella opening up inside her and catching fire. Well then, she thought to herself, it is happening anyway. I started to get all loose and shivery, open and wet before the bastard pulled his finger from my pot. Maybe it's nature or the hot water that's making me feel more relaxed, or maybe it's because this man is still staring at nothing at all and so, in effect, I had sex with a finger and not a person. Dido pondered this for a while until the warmth of the water submerged her into a long laziness where she thought of nothing at all.

The couple left the tub and two men entered it, talking rapidly and intensely of draperies. Dido felt she had spent enough time in the water so she got out and showered. The woman from the tubs followed her into the shower area and once again smiled at her. It was a rather provocative smile. The woman began rubbing her own body vigorously with a loofah sponge so that her skin began to take on a coffee-colored sheen. Her nipples were large and she rubbed those tender things with the loofah as well, causing Dido to widen her eyes. The woman turned and offered to rub Dido's back for her, which felt very nice indeed, but when the woman began to swack Dido's meaty bottom with the loofah and rubbed it almost raw, Dido pulled away. The woman pulled her back by her blond pussy hair, laughing a low sort of "ha ha" real far back in her throat, and whacked away until Dido's ass felt inflamed.

Drawing Dido toward her with her incredibly strong arms the woman fell to squeezing and massaging Dido's titties, rubbing her own full warm body against her. Dido figured she had landed in a strange place indeed. Although her ass cheeks stung from the loofah, she felt wild heat grow inside her and once again she longed to play with her partner. But the minute she reached out to touch the woman's large soft breasts the woman removed her hand. Dido allowed herself to be alternately fondled and spanked for some time until the woman gave her a final love bite on the neck and left to dry off with a large turkish towel.

"Wait a second," Dido called out, but the woman only smiled and disappeared with the towel slung low over her hips.

"Damn," Dido said aloud, finishing up her shower. She walked back to the little room where her shorts and sandals were and bent over to pull the tight shorts over her aching cheeks. In that moment, and it was so sudden that she gasped, an arm was around her waist and a large, smooth cock was working in and out of her pussy. She was shocked at first and began to protest but the cock felt so right going in and out that soon she was moving herself to accommodate. Feelings were opening up inside of her that were extremely dangerous. Her pussy was flooding with moisture, and the urge to let go completely presented itself to her like a flaming imperative. Just as she started to moan and respond to the thrusts of her unseen partner, he withdrew, leaving her trembling on the little cot. She turned to catch sight of him, but all she could see was one sandaled foot leaving the door.

At this point she was pissed. She lay down on the cot and played with her cunt which was engorged and frustrated. Her fingers were wet with the juice and dipped in and out of her sex; she felt insatiable. Still she couldn't come. She wanted to suck and lick something so she put a finger into her mouth and tasted herself.

Although she tasted quite good, big tears were running down her cheeks because she wanted someone. Her pussy was on fire for someone and even with masturbation the orgasms didn't satisfy. She calmed herself with her fingers, then pulled on the little white shorts, put on her sandals and sunglasses and went out into the sunlight. There was no one in sight so she walked on in the silence of nature until she came to a creek where she sat down and stared at the water.

The sun was very hot so she stretched out on the ground. It was an idyllic spot with a tiny white stream, low-hanging trees, wild grasses and the smell of hot sulphuric springs and warm earth. Barely into a nod she felt someone nuzzle at her crotch. She leaped up screaming, "No, you don't . . . not this time, you bastard," only to find it was Bosco. Jeff was right behind the dog, standing on a rock and looking fondly at her. He had a bottle of juice which he offered her. She sipped at the drink while venting her anger at the manners of the clientele he had at Angel Springs.

Jeff scratched his smooth face while Bosco played with two tiny orange peels. "Well," he said after some thought, "you did get turned on. You did get heated up."

"But not satisfied!" Dido protested.

"Then come with me to the quiet room," Jeff said lowering his voice.

"I don't want you!" Dido said rather unkindly. But Jeff was undaunted. He insisted she come with him and told her that he would do nothing that would in any way upset her. Reluctantly, she followed him to a small low building with shuttered windows. They left Bosco outside.

Inside it was dark. Thick tatami mats and several futons were on the floor and pots of incense filled the air with dark fragrance. Bodies were in supine positions, and in the dim light Dido could see that they were either sleeping or meditating. The couple from the hot tub clung together in a corner.

"I don't need a nap!" Dido hissed but Jeff gently pushed her down on a futon and told her to take her shorts off, which she did. Then he told her to close her eyes, which she also did. She heard him get up and leave. In a while she relaxed and started to enjoy the quiet; then she felt someone rubbing her feet softly and gently. This felt wonderful so she kept her eyes closed and enjoyed the nonintrusive massage. Another pair of hands began to work on her breasts, touching as lightly as insect wings brushing against her nipples. Hands were now working up her thighs, opening her legs. Her nipples were covered with lips and were sucked on until they were stiff. She could make out the profiles of the people who surrounded her but she couldn't see their faces clearly, nor did she want to. A tongue was in her cunt, licking her wet. A big thick cock was placed between her lips and rubbed over her teeth. She sucked like a baby on it. It excited her to be handled by so many at once, so many fingers, mouths, tongues, lips, cocks and pussies, hands, hands all over her body. Her pussy was flooded, hot and honey-thick with juice.

A cock went into her pussy while fingers played with her clit and pink asshole. Her mouth was engaged with a warm cunt all buttery sweet and Brillo-pad wild with hair. She felt herself lifted up, turned over and penetrated from behind. No longer was she bound by her ego or her skin but expanded into pure sensation, every cell trembling and on edge until the orgasms started rolling through her, making her fling her arms around the hips of the dark woman who straddled her face and burying her face between those strong thighs; moaning and cursing into that dark sweet hole.

The fucking went on long after her orgasms came to a stop. She was flung from one level to another, not closing up but opening more and more until she reached the absolute limit of her pleasure. Wet and exhausted, she struggled from the embraces of her lovers, which she now realized numbered four. Her body idled like an overheated car and she fell into a soft dreamlike state and thought about why the anonymity of her lovers excited her so much. Somehow it had made her regain her sense of wholeness. Perhaps it was because there was no shred of relationship, no need to be anything but alive in her own body and complete in that.

She dozed in the darkness, listening to the sounds of the couple making love in the corner. She gave herself up to the darkness.

Margo Woods

Wheelchair Romance

It still hurts to talk about my affair with Richard. I met him at a birthday party for a mutual friend. All I noticed at the time was that he was quite good-looking, gray-haired, and that he lived in a wheelchair.

Several months later our mutual friend approached me, saying that Richard was accustomed to paying for sex, and that he had noticed me at the party. The friend knew I was desperately broke, had exchanged money for sex in the past, and probably would not be freaked out by a guy in a wheelchair. He asked me if I would agree to see Richard.

Hey, no problem. After I saw Jane Fonda do it with Jon Voight in *Coming Home*, I realized that functional legs were not necessary for sex.

We met in a bar. I wore an orange silk blouse that made my reddish hair look redder and showed off my small, round tits. I wore blue jeans to show off my little ass and long legs, boots to make me look even more sexy, and several necklaces fell between my breasts. I towered over his wheelchair until he invited me to sit down. Then we were equals. He remarked about my braless tits right away, and after a couple of drinks asked me to come home with him. He offered me $100.

159

He drove a yellow Cadillac equipped with controls. He opened the door for me, wheeled himself around to the driver's side, heaved himself into the front seat, and leaned back over to his chair to fold, lift, and slide it behind his seat.

His apartment was small with an entry directly off the street. I was learning what it is like to live in a wheelchair: no stairs, no rugs, lots of space between furniture. He had exquisite taste, however, and the apartment was beautifully decorated, filled with plants, and blessed with a sound system that made any music a mystical experience.

So we drank a little more, listened to music, and I smoked some grass. He said his favorite drug was coke, but he was out at the moment, and he refused my grass because he said it made him sick. When it came time to go to bed, I watched him heave his body from the wheelchair to the bed, then grab his legs and haul them over. His torso and hands were well-developed from all the lifting they had had to do, and they were as handsome and attractive as his legs and pelvis were strange and withered. Attached to his left leg was a heavy plastic bag connected by a tube to his lower belly, apparently emptying urine.

I jumped into bed beside him, curled up in his arms, and began to kiss him.

I'll always remember Richard's mouth. In addition to having a remarkable sculptured shape, it was also the most pliable, sexy, delicious mouth I have ever encountered. We must have kissed for hours; long, deep kisses in which I easily became lost. I love the feeling of drowning in a kiss, of disappearing into a sea of sensuous feeling. It's a magical experience for me, in which I stop thinking of myself as a person or my partner as a person and am conscious only of the rushing, rolling, and trembling of sexy feeling in my body caused by the connection of two pairs of lips.

And I remember his arms, which held me and caressed me and kept holding me like the everlasting arms of God the Father. I loved the way he held me.

"Play with my tits," he said after a while. "I haven't used the lower half of my body for so long that all my sexual energy has moved to my tits." And it was true. Not only were his pectoral muscles well-developed, but his nipples were as big as my own. And very sensitive. He liked to have them sucked, of course, but also twisted, rubbed, and pinched. He went into ecstatic states when I teased and played with them.

But he kept steering me away from his cock. "It doesn't work," he said. "My back is broken in the lumbar area." So we concentrated on my body and the top of his, and I forgot about his crotch for a while.

He was extremely good at sucking my tits. He was so sensitive to my reactions and able to tell whether and when to do what. When my hand slid down between his legs again, it was greeted by a very long, hard cock, with a slight bend on the end. I was startled and confused, because he had told me it didn't work, but I really wanted that cock in my mouth or in my pussy. Reluctantly I let him guide my hand away from it and back to his tits and his mouth and his godlike arms. Why wouldn't he let me have it? His cock wasn't necessary for orgasm, because I could come with him eating me or sucking my tits while I played with myself, but I wanted his cock too, and I hoped I would get another chance at it.

The next day I was still in a glow from being so well-loved. I was deeply satisfied with this man, and I was waiting for the next phone call. The $100 wasn't bad either.

In the following weeks and months we got together many times, almost always at his place, occasionally at a bar. He refused all my invitations to movies, drives in the country, or any other sort of entertainment, and he never took me out to eat except breakfast after we had spent the night together. It was just too much trouble for him to get around. He had his world arranged around him—his stereo set, his magnificent record collection, his multiple cable channels, and his VCR. I didn't mind sitting for hours with him, appreciating the sights and sounds that came out of this equipment. But what really endeared him to me was his lovemaking.

Recently a new lover asked me what I liked in a lover. I replied, "Tenderness and enthusiasm." Richard had been both tender and passionate, making me feel like I was the most desirable and sexy woman on earth.

I'm quite sure that I take sex more seriously than most people. An affair without sex, or without good sex, is disappointing compared to one which is garnished with sexual energy. I am always confused and chagrined when a lover makes sex unimportant. And I am very likely to cross him off my list if he doesn't have lots of other interesting characteristics to recommend him. So Richard was high on my list at that time.

He really did love coke. He sent me running all over the county to get little piles of white powder with which we laced our lovemaking. Of course it meant we were into all-night stands, and of course it meant that I didn't see his cock get hard again after the white powder appeared. Once in a while in the morning, before he did his first lines, he would get semi-hard, about half of what I had seen before. But he always dragged my hand away when I tried to do something with it.

One time I turned him on to mushrooms. I have always experienced them as a positive drug and I hoped to wean him away from coke so that he could have more erections. However, far from being a positive experience, the mushrooms made his legs twitch violently—a natural condition for a person with his problems, which he corrected by continual use of Valium. Something about the mushrooms overrode the Valium, and instead of enjoying the trip, he twitched uncontrollably for hours. He was very angry at me and turned his back on me for the entire night, making me feel abandoned and paranoid. Luckily the next morning the symptoms were gone, along with the anger.

Toward Christmastime he started getting very romantic with me, saying I was his lover, and telling all his friends he had a lover. I took the bait, and waited for his phone calls. Christmas night, after the festivities were over, I went to visit him. We drank champagne and watched the Playboy Channel. He confessed he had no money and asked if I would let him pay me with his love. Of course by this time I wanted him so much that the money was just a little frosting on the cake, and of course I hopped into bed.

I was going to New York the next morning to visit a friend and get away for a while. The trip had been planned for a long time. Over breakfast Richard moaned, "How am I going to get along without you?" I assured him that I would return.

One of the things I do when I travel is look back at my home and think about what's going on there. I think about my work, my writing, my kids, and my friends and lovers. In New York I thought a lot about Richard. It was clear that he was no longer a client, this was a love relationship. I missed him terribly and called several times to tell him so. We were both very gooey over the phone.

I thought a lot about his cock. I wanted another chance at that tall member with the curved end. I had been a consulting therapist in a sexuality clinic a few years before, and I knew that men with spinal cord injuries sometimes get erections when their cocks are played with, even though they have no sensation in their genitals. Then the doctors give all sorts of drugs to regulate the body and its processes, many of which inhibit erections. They often don't tell the patient about the side effects, or give him any choice as to whether to take the drugs. With large quantities of alcohol, cocaine, and Valium laid on top of an already weakened sexual response, Richard's sword didn't have a chance, except in the mornings when some of the drugs had worn off, and on that first occasion, when there was no coke, and we had the added excitement of the first time. I wrote him a gentle letter, explaining these things, and also asking him for money to help me rent an apartment.

When I got back from New York, I called to say that I had returned. He was friendly, but he didn't ask me over. Nor did he call me in the next few days and weeks. I was crazed. "What is happening? What have I done? Was it something about the letter? I shouldn't have asked him for money? I shouldn't have talked about his cock?" I resisted calling him for three weeks, and then finally dialed his number to timidly ask if anything was wrong. He said no. "Then why haven't you called me?" I shrieked. "I don't know," he said. "No special reason." What could I do with a response like that? "All right then," I said. "I'll leave it to you to call me."

He did call once, several weeks later, and asked me over. I was nervous and confused, and my heart wasn't in it. We did everything we used to do, deep kissing, holding and hugging, lots of tit play for both of us, oral sex for me. My body reacted as usual, proving that it does have a life of its own, but my heart was in pain. I was surprised that I could make love to him with my body and not my heart, and I wondered if he could tell. In some ways our lovemaking was the best it had ever been. If he had been able to explain what was going on with him in the last few weeks perhaps we could have bridged the gap and been open to each other emotionally. As it was, he paid me and I left. He never called again.

For weeks I tried to sort it all out and recover from the shock of being dumped. Was it the money? Was it my references to his sexuality? What was with this guy and his cock? The very last time we made love, up to our eyeballs in coke, he grabbed his soft cock and whipped it furiously for a long time. It was the first time I'd seen him touch his cock. I found it very erotic and told him so. Most men like to hear such things.

But Richard gave me only the barest notion of what was going on in his head during our affair. Still, he couldn't hide the reactions of his body, and I know his heart participated for a while.

But that was the last time I saw him. I imagine that by now he has found another woman who hasn't fallen into a personal relationship with him, and he is paying her $100 each time they get together.

Tea Sahne

There's More of You

We were getting ready to go to bed. As always, Alex, who slept naked, was quicker than I and was already under the covers when I was still getting into my nightgown and robe and brushing out my long hair. " 'He had unusually short forearms,' " I said; "that's my first line."

"What do I care?" Alex said. "I'm cold, and I want to make love. Can't you come to bed?"

"Nope, not quite yet," I said, putting my brush and hairpins down on the mantel, checking that the fire screen was tight around the last glowing embers of the fire and picking up the sheaf of paper from the table beside my side of the bed. I settled into the wingback chair in the ring of light from my bedside lamp. "Not until you listen to what I wrote tonight," and I read. . . .

He had unusually short forearms. Though he was a very big man, nearly six-and-a-half feet tall and burly, his hands could barely reach down around the cheeks of her buttocks when they made love. More than a foot shorter than he and less than half his weight, she perched on him, arms and legs furled around his barrel chest and round belly like a small fragile spider tackling

165

a great furry bumblebee. His raised thighs pressed hers higher against his sides and wider apart, pulling open her vulva, vagina, anus.

As he strained to reach lower, into her wet, open cunt with his thick fingers, his shoulders were drawn down hard against hers, compressing her breasts against his. If she hunched her back then—hollowing her chest—and squirmed sideways, she could make their erect nipples—hers cold, hard, almost damp—brush. Sometimes she came then, shivering, before he had let his penis even touch her.

But she preferred to wait, moving her hips up a little and forward, willingly offering her genitals to his probing fingers. His short arms would press harder, crossing back past her waist and under her hips, as his fingers reached from behind for her labia, pulling them aside to insert first his right forefinger, then his left as well, into her vagina, feeling his way into the ridges and folds, at the same time filling her with his hands and pulling her wider and wider open, exposing her clitoris too, to contact, until she felt a channel being opened up through her fully exposed self into the pit of her belly—even higher, up through her abdomen and past her navel, hands opening and making her open, beyond mere sexual parts, even up into her gut.

His fingers worked in and out of her bursting vagina until her breath came in gasps, drawn faster and faster.

"What do you want?" he would ask hoarsely. "Tell me what you want now."

"I don't know, I don't know," she would moan. "Put your cock in, too—don't take your hands away!"

And he'd say, "No, not yet. Come for me first. This way."

"No," she would wail hopelessly.

"Yes, yes, like this," he would hiss and he wouldn't stop. Arms straining across her buttocks, he'd put his full hands over her then, one thumb first slowly, carefully worming its way into her anus, and then the rest of his fingers into every spreading fold of her vulva, working his hands forward and back rhythmically between her legs, higher and higher forward, harder against her pubic bones, and deeper, too, under them, more insistently,

stroking, kneading, pressing out, stretching out her clitoris into
its blazing, screaming, naked miniature erection.

"Come," he'd whisper; demand. "Come, come now!"

And when she couldn't stand the pain ballooning from her
agonized clitoris up through her belly any longer, she always
would, whether she wanted to or not, pulled wide open yet en-
capsulated in his hands—crying out—sometimes laughing
wildly—bucking upward from his torso, then collapsing into it
. . . coming, coming, fully into his hands.

I was still sitting in the armchair beside the bed, but Alex was
out of bed now, too; half kneeling before me, half into my lap,
not at all caring, as I had teasingly hoped and intended, about
whom I had been writing. We had done this before—reading
aloud what I had written or (it turned us on just as much) what
someone else had. For both of us, words made what we were
doing more intensely real, doubly lived through whoever's experience mirrored ours in the prose. Subsumed into that undif-
ferentiating world of passion, body pressed against mine, not
caring by whom or how I might have imagined being turned on
as I wrote, Alex cared only about being with me here and now,
part of the acts themselves.

I looked down at the wisps of Alex's black hair against the
pink of my robe, the tan-peach glow of my flesh where my nightgown was raised aside. Darker, glowing rosier than my skin,
darker even than the purplish-rose of my engorged cunt, Alex's
blunt fingers pried into me. Even in that detail Alex's hard, athletic definition was a vibrant contrast to my pliable softness.

"Wait," I said, my voice muffled in the growing confusion of
sex, of Alex's mouth now devouring me, "and listen."

Sometimes he came then, too, before entering her, and without her ever having touched his penis. He loved feeling her come
into his hands that much. But it didn't matter. He was amaz-
ingly virile. After she had recovered her breath and giggled, she
delightedly snuggled herself around his torso and under his chin
while he lay with one protective arm around her, peacefully sniff-
ing and licking the fingers of his cunt-gored other hand. If she

so much as licked his neck or eyes or the corner of his mouth, his penis began to harden again. It would bulge upward suddenly if she slid down along his side and licked and nibbled one of his nipples. She could turn her head sideways and watch, or put a hand down and feel it happening—she could do that until his penis was fully, enormously erect again, listening to him suck in his breath if she closed her teeth on a nipple, flicking her tongue quickly against its trapped, sensitive end-pores. He would press his hands harder against the sides of her waist or the small of her back then, pressing her into himself; but she would make him wait, as he had her, swelling in gradually less controllable spasms of increased pain and ecstasy.

Then, in one quick move, she would shift her weight over him and bring her vagina down unerringly around his engorged penis. Or she would draw out his pleasure and pain longer, moving her body away from contact with his, kneeling beside him, then slowly, without touching him with her hands, take first the tip, then more and more of his penis into her mouth, mimicking his hands as she rhythmically worked it further and further, teasingly, inch-by-inch down her throat until its tip touched her epiglottis. She could not feel what happened when that contact was made, but knew that this gag-reflex bit of her flesh must do something when his penis touched it, because it always made him sigh and moan and clutch for her hair and breasts or face. If she withdrew very far then, his hands always sought her cheeks and chin and lips, touching his penis, too, urging her to take it back deeper into her mouth. She would, bit by bit, wrapping her tongue around it from one side, then the other; and she would touch him then with her hands, too, one cupping and rolling his testicles, the other sweeping over his belly and chest, tweaking a nipple and swiftly moving on flat-palmed, inserting a finger, then two, then three into his mouth.

Always, as more parts of her body became engaged with his, she would feel herself swelling and moistening again, no matter how completely she thought she had already come. She would want then to make him say, "Please, now!" as she sometimes begged him when she felt she could not bear not to come, but could not bear either to come unless his penis was inside her. But he never did then—or she did not give him time to. She would hear his breaths coming faster, and drunk with the craving to have his semen inside her, with one strong, last, base-to-tip-long suck, she would release his penis and swing herself over and down onto him. Their genitals were like magnets to each other. Without the need for groping hands, his penis always slid firmly, solidly, completely into her vagina, and, as their arms gathered their bodies into one another, he—crying out in half-groans, half-grunts (and often she again, too, crooning, whining)—would come.

He liked to talk to her afterward; nonsensical, half-enunciated, affectionate clichés as likely as not. Lying with his eyes closed, his arms around her loosely, they felt the gradually diminishing, warm, after-shock pulses in their still-joined bodies. Their couplings always reached climax so quickly that neither of them lost arousal immediately, and sometimes they began to move again against each other almost without meaning to, as if in an initial rather than last stage of intercourse. A few times, they did indeed within a short time resume, slowly, serenely, for the sheer pleasure of the motion in and out of each other, without at all expecting to come again; though once, to their delighted astonishment, they both did. More often, one or both of them fell asleep while they were still joined. But usually they waited drowsily for his erection to subside and his penis to slide out of her. Her small "Ohs" of dismay as it did might have seemed a mere ritual if both of them had not known it was a shared loss and regret she expressed.

And then they slept. Often for the first hour or so, she was still at least partly on top of him. If her body was in an especially awkward position, she would waken and move to his side, and in his sleep he would automatically draw her back against him. If they slept then all night, still they would waken in the morning touching. If she stirred first, it was to lift her head and look at his face; and he, without opening his eyes, would draw her head down against his chest. She would wrap her small self against him so hungrily that she wakened breathless. And then, however it happened, it would all begin again.

* * *

I shuffled my sheets of paper together and lay them aside. Rammed into the chair on top of me, nakedly beautiful and small, her knees dug in on each side of me between my thighs and the chair's arms, cunt to cunt and all the rest of her body pressed to mine, Alex seemed to be asleep, exhausted with the simultaneous experience of what I had read and what had happened between us. Her arms were around my shoulders, her forehead against my neck. Her curly hair bristled against my cheek. I put my arm around her and kissed that rough tousle.

"I love you," I whispered. "Nothing I write is as wonderful as you are—none of it's more than a hairsbreadth or forefinger joint to you. It can't be . . . Alex?"

"I know, I know," she answered groggily. "How could I care if it were? Love you—*have* you. Come to bed now."

Catherine Tavel

Claudia's Cheeks

Claudia had a problem. Some women might not have considered it a problem, but Claudia certainly did. You see, Claudia had a beautiful ass. A big, bouncy, beautiful ass. And everywhere she went, people wanted to fuck Claudia in her big, bouncy, beautiful ass. Truck drivers said lascivious things to her rear end as it innocently crossed the street. Gray-haired dykes had an overwhelming desire to spank her bottom. Whenever Claudia met people for the first time, that was the first thing they noticed— her plump and pretty posterior.

There were drawbacks to having such a juicy, jangly behind. Claudia hated wearing panties, but whenever she didn't wear them, she would cause a commotion. There was never a doubt in anyone's mind that she was panty-less under even the loosest of skirts. Her ass enjoyed the freedom and insisted upon jumping out in all directions. Strange men would smile, follow her, and tell her to have a nice day. Even the constriction of control-top pantyhose did no good in quelling the allure of her sweet cheeks. And a garter belt? It greatly enhanced Claudia's already-dangerous curves. Tight stretch pants, the current fashion rage which other women seemed to wear with no problem, resulted in minor traffic disturbances when Claudia wore them outdoors.

Claudia didn't know exactly how to take the praise which was lavishly bestowed upon her rump. She liked it when men looked at her, even when the spittle collected in the corner of their mouths. She thought random erections were the greatest compliment a man could give a woman. But to be labeled and lusted after solely for her pear-shaped ass? There was so much more to Claudia than that.

For instance, she had an adorable face, expressive brown eyes not unlike a sad cocker spaniel's and soft ruby lips that more than one gentleman had referred to as a "cocksucker's mouth." True, Claudia's breasts were minuscule, a handful at most, but they were unique nonetheless. They were topped with dusky dun nipples that poked out more than a half-inch when she was hot. And she was hot very often.

Claudia was slim with long shapely legs that seemed to go on forever. They looked especially nice locked around someone's neck in missionary position when her cocksucker's lips were open and panting, and her sad eyes were heavy and dark with passion. That's when Claudia looked her best, when she was being fucked. Her lovely feet were topped with toenails that were always painted bright red and her left ankle always sported a thin chain of white gold. When Claudia watched her legs propped up upon a fellow's heaving shoulders, she felt especially naughty and slutty. And she liked that.

Then there was the matter of Claudia's cunt. It was an exceptional cunt, decorated with pudgy outer lips and fudge-shaped folds within. Like an exotic flower of some variety, if you pushed the outer petals apart with your fingers, you would see that Claudia's cuntlips graduated to a rich shade of pink. A two-toned cunt, a lover had noted. And Claudia's slit was so, so tight. Sometimes too tight. If you slid even one finger inside, the resilient walls of her pussy would cling and suck on that thin digit.

Claudia had a tiny clit at the top of her pussy. You really had to work to make it come out and play, because it was hidden under small flaps of flesh. But Claudia's clit loved to be kissed. If you nursed on it just right, then it would get stiff and stand out like a delicate corn niblet. Sometimes it took a great effort to make Claudia come, but when she did, it was well worth it.

To see her writhe and moan and spasm was quite a magnificent thing. You could feel her demure pussy throbbing against your face, as if gulping and gasping for air. Claudia's pussy would throb for a long time after she came. Men thought it particularly wonderful to stick their prick inside while it was still pulsing, wet and gushy.

But alas, many men didn't take the time to get acquainted with the intricacies of Claudia's pussy. A few licks, a few pokes, a few fondles and they wanted to dig their fingers into her butt-hole, flip her over like a one-hundred-and-fifteen-pound pancake, and dive into her derriere. Or else they wanted to fuck her doggy-style so they could at least gaze at her glorious orbs jiggling with each stroke. Then they could play with her cheeks, knead them like warm bread dough and grapple with them to their heart's content. Sometimes they would even pretend to fall out of her cunt and then try to put it back into her ass, thinking she wouldn't notice. But Claudia knew all of their tricks.

Claudia had a few tricks of her own. She was skilled at deep-throating cocks way down to the hairy balls. Her favorite fellatio posture was on her knees. She especially liked to lick a man's testicles while her throat engulfed his boner. Men liked this too, but usually in combination with squeezing her firm hindquarters in both hands. If a guy stuck a finger up her tush, Claudia would stick her finger up his. He usually got the message—dry digits weren't much fun.

Claudia was also very good at being on top, but rarely did she get the opportunity. Although the man could occupy himself with twisting and tweaking her sensitive nipples and cupping her bouncing ass cheeks in his hands, he generally wasn't thrilled because he couldn't actually *see* Claudia's ass bouncing. Thus, her enthusiastic performance would be trashed. Sometimes the fellow would ask her to turn around so that she was still on top but with her back facing him. Claudia didn't like this position because the man couldn't see her eyes smoky with desire. Not only that, but he could easily pretend that he was with someone else. Claudia felt very unconnected, and it seemed almost an impolite posture. Plus, it was both uncomfortable and unnatural. The walls of her vagina went one way, the curve of his erection went the other. Claudia could feel the rock-hard cock pushing the wrong way inside her. It grated upon her nerves, almost like fingernails on a blackboard. Perhaps it was a good position for women with wide cunts because it might make them feel smaller. But for Claudia, it seemed to go against nature. Like ass-fucking.

Few men knew the significance of Claudia's rump-humping aversion. Whenever she tried to relate what a terrible experience the first time had been, instead of feeling sorry for her, guys would get incredibly turned on.

When Claudia was eighteen, she had dated Mike McCall, who was twenty-eight. There was an edge of nastiness to him, but they always seemed to have hot, rough sex. Maybe it aroused him that she was so innocent and that he was only her second lover. Perhaps this is why he fucked Claudia so hard. Perhaps he just had a mean streak, but Claudia, who liked to give people the benefit of the doubt, thought he acted like that because he was afraid of falling in love. The rougher he fucked, the less it felt like love.

In any case, Mike could munch on Claudia's almost-virgin pussy for hours. He enjoyed making her talk dirty, too. Their faces just inches apart, he would pound her like a sledgehammer with his short, fat prick. Claudia would let loose with a litany of filthy phrases, which Mike liked a great deal. She would bite his neck and he would bite hers. It was a purely physical relationship. That was evident, but Claudia kept trying to make Mike fall in love with her. She had been raised to believe that making love was far superior to fucking. Actually, both were pretty good, but thanks to people in her past like Sister Elizabeth and Sister Mary Colleen, Claudia couldn't appreciate sex for sex's sake. Not yet, anyway. The truth of the matter was that Mike saw Claudia as just another chippy. Mike McCall couldn't see women any other way, but Claudia, for one, was much, much more. She just had to realize it herself.

Claudia and Mike worked at the same newspaper, him driving a truck and her behind a typewriter. On occasion, he'd dry-hump her against a nearby mailbox. One time, he even lured her into the back of his panel truck and had her suck his cock.

It was wintertime and it was freezing. Claudia took a while to find the shriveled little sausage buried in his long johns. Eventually, she did and she slurped at it until he came in her mouth.

One day, when they were at his place, Mike McCall said to Claudia, "I'm going to fuck you in the ass." Claudia didn't feel strongly about this one way or the other. She had never given much thought to her anus. It was an erogenous zone which she pretty much ignored. But that night, she told Mike okay because she figured it was about time to give her asshole a test drive. Maybe it would even make him fall in love with her.

What happened next was somewhat foggy in Claudia's mind, especially since her back was turned during most of it. She seemed to recall a jar of Vaseline on the floor. Whether it was ever uncapped or actually used remained a mystery. Perhaps it was only there as a prop. There was little in the way of anal foreplay. Claudia didn't even recall Mike sticking a finger up her behind. The next thing she knew, his stumpy, chubby penis was wedged up her rear end. Or at least it was trying its best to get up there.

Another thing Claudia remembered—it hurt like hell. Mike hadn't been the least bit considerate. Both of them were on their knees on the floor. He pressed her face against the daybed's mattress so that she could hardly breathe. This upset Claudia to some extent. Breathing was an extremely important function to her, especially during sex. As she struggled to get out from under his iron grip, she was almost crying. Mike's penis tore at her virgin orifice. Yet somewhere behind the pain, somewhere behind his lack of respect for her, it felt almost good. Then came the sensation that she had to go to the bathroom. Very intensely.

"I have to go to the bathroom," Claudia told Mike.

"No, you don't," he said. "That's the way it's supposed to feel."

Claudia wanted to ask him how he knew this tidbit. Had he ever been fucked in the ass? But whether it was supposed to feel that way or not, one thing was for certain: Claudia had to shit. "No, you don't," Mike insisted, pumping into her posterior without missing a beat.

Claudia started to cry. "If you don't let me go, I'll shit all over you." But Mike wouldn't listen. The more Claudia begged and struggled, the harder and faster he thrust into her tushie. "I swear . . . ," poor Claudia sobbed. But Mike didn't seem to hear. He was lost in a tight, dark, ribbed tunnel otherwise known as Claudia's asshole.

Claudia dug her elbow into Mike's chest. She cursed and cried some more, but nothing seemed to work. Mike only stopped reaming to pull out and shoot his cum all over her bare bottom. Then he collapsed on top of Claudia and sighed, "Oh baby," in a soft voice.

Claudia couldn't shit for three days.

Most men had the same reaction when Claudia finished telling this sad tale concerning the ravaging of her rosebud. Instead of it acting as a deterrent, they wanted to bang Claudia in the butt even more. It wasn't that the men were cruel or heartless (which all humans often are), but that Claudia was so unintentionally titillating in her guiltless candor. It was the *way* she told the story that got them so aroused. The sorrowful saga describing how Mike McCall squeezed into Claudia's cheeks always gave listeners blistering erections, which they tried to mask with their fists. Instead of the story illustrating how carefully one must approach an anal encounter, it made guys want to tear at Claudia's heinie, and then some.

Claudia's friend Jerry had a slightly different reaction, however. Jerry was a porno actor and had performed unsafe sex with the best of them. Although Jerry wouldn't have minded bopping Claudia in the buttocks either, at least he could be a bit more objective. He burst out laughing at her anal sex story. "That'll teach you to let a guy named Mike McColon near your asshole."

The episode with Mr. McCall left Claudia with a memorable souvenir—hemorrhoids. Once upon a time, her bunghole was a cute, puckered, winking thing, but now it was swollen and quite deformed. Even when she told her many admirers about his misfortune, they still didn't care. They still wanted to boink Claudia in the behind.

Since anal sex seemed to have such a fan-club following, Claudia decided to try it again this time with a gentler man, Charlie. Charlie didn't particularly like assholes. "It's dirty up there," he told Claudia with a grimace.

"I know," she said, "but so many people like to fuck them, they must have some sort of charm."

Reluctantly, Charlie lay on his back while Claudia positioned herself above him. She lowered her ass cheeks onto his stiff pole. It went in fairly easily and it hurt less than it had with Mike McCall, but it still couldn't be called a pleasant sensation. And just when Claudia was getting the hang of it, she looked at Charlie's face. It was all scrunched up, as though someone were forcing him to eat raw liver. Claudia stopped pumping. She felt like an anal rapist. After she wiped Charlie's dick with Ivory soap and a blue washcloth, she gave him a blow job. He seemed much happier then.

Claudia hadn't had anal sex since that time, but she was constantly on a quest to broaden her hinder horizons. She read about women who masturbated with broomsticks and chair legs up their rectums and couldn't understand why. A liberated kind of nineties gal, Claudia tried getting off a new way. With the middle finger and forefinger of her right hand, she made a fleshy V and invaded both her pussy and her posterior at the same time. It felt . . . interesting. She was especially intrigued with being able to feel both digits moving through the thin membrane of skin between. Very adventurous, she also got her thumb into the act and employed it by rubbing her clit. A confusing configuration, to say the least. Claudia felt like a circus juggler but did manage to have an explosive orgasm. Her clit was wiggling. Her pussy was spasming. Her asshole was twitching. It was a well-coordinated effort, but not something she could enjoy as a steady diet.

More than anything, Claudia wanted one special boyfriend, but there was no one. It was a never-ending odyssey. Claudia was becoming tired of guys only wanting to fuck her in the ass. She continued to meet new men who wanted the same old thing. She was tired of having to tell the Mike McCall story over and over again. She was tired of being recognized by former boyfriends from the rear. Although she had the perky kind of behind which women sought to achieve through ruthless repetitions of Jane Fonda workout tapes, Claudia didn't see herself as fortunate or blessed. Beneath her bouncy dream butt, there was a warm, loving lady. But no one could ever see past that protrusion. There were other things about Claudia which were pretty wonderful, but men often ignored these numerous niceties. She was tired of being judged solely by one beautiful body part.

In a perverse way, she saw the AIDS epidemic as an escape. No one in their right mind would want to butt-fuck, no matter how tempting, no matter how perfectly pear-shaped the behind. She was right, in part; still, far too many men were willing to use a condom to get into a cute behind like Claudia's. But she found even this repulsive.

So Claudia spent many nights at home alone. She sat in front of the TV and watched reruns of *Dallas* and *L.A. Law*. She made buckets of microwave popcorn and topped them with gobs of butter. She munched on Chocolate Babies and Doritos while flipping the remote control. And when she was horny, Claudia masturbated with a cute guy in an X-rated video who alternately lifted weights and jerked off. He didn't see Claudia as a body part. In fact, he didn't see Claudia at all.

Pretty soon, Claudia's thighs started rubbing together when she walked. She had to buy queen-sized L'eggs pantyhose. She favored skirts and pants with elastic waistbands. In a few months' time, the smallest actions—even shaking Jiffy Pop popcorn over the stove—exhausted her. Soon, she couldn't even bend to paint her toenails a bright, slutty red. The polish eventually chipped off. The white-gold ankle chain didn't fit around her ankle anymore.

There was no doubt about it. Claudia was on the road to becoming humongous. She didn't care about much except stuffing her face. Food became almost like sex to her. It was practically orgasmic to stick a fluffy Twinkie between her lips, to lick the melted puddle of Häagen-Dazs from the bottom of her dish. It gave Claudia great pleasure to spoon sour cream straight from the container into her mouth, just as it did to devour crunchy peanut butter, marshmallow creme, and all the rest. Men finally stopped calling Claudia on the telephone. They finally stopped seeing her as a body part, because now she was a blob. Claudia was one huge body part.

Before long, Claudia realized that the person she was hurting most was herself. Her cholesterol level skyrocketed and so did her blood pressure. Sure, the guys had liked Claudia's stream-lined frame, but more important, she had liked it, too. And she missed it. Claudia didn't hate men. In fact, she craved them, but she just hated the way they treated her sometimes. She also hated the slaughtering of seal pups and the destruction of the rain forests, but she wasn't about to leave the planet.

So Claudia went on a sensible diet. The sight of a Twinkie soon made her gag, as did soggy Oreos in milk. Claudia bought a membership at Jack LaLanne's. Gradually, she was able to bend and paint her toenails once again. Claudia worked her way up to three sets of a hundred sit-ups and mastered the Universal machine. Many months down the road, as she pedaled the ex-ercise bike, she noticed the eyes of the male patrons at Jack LaLanne's intently studying the curves of her ass as she rode. But it didn't bother Claudia as much this time around. Claudia had already decided that she wasn't going to be the victim of her own ass any longer. But then, throughout her life, she had al-ways seemed to be a victim of one thing or another.

One evening after work, Claudia went to a neighborhood pub to enjoy a white wine spritzer and to relax. The bar stool framed her once-again gorgeous butt alluringly. An entire softball team seated at the table behind her gasped in adoration every time she moved. This didn't upset Claudia. It did just the opposite. Claudia squirmed in her seat as often as she could just to torment them. She now realized the power she possessed in her cheeks. She had something that other people wanted.

Before she was halfway through her spritzer, a handsome man walked into the establishment and sat a few stools away from Claudia. From where he sat he couldn't even see her buns nestled snugly on the vinyl seat. All he could see were her long, delicate fingertips toying with a straw and her serious, abandoned puppy eyes. Very politely, he introduced himself as Al. Very soon, Al and Claudia were engaged in friendly conversation which touched upon everything from Hemingway to dolphins to Billie Holiday to the names of the Teenage Mutant Ninja Turtles. Claudia refused a second drink, but couldn't decline the invita-tion to an impromptu dinner next door at East China. Slithering from the bar stool, she took note of the expression on Al's face when he saw her ass for the first time. It was a look of surprise and delight. But instead of feeling angry or hurt, Claudia felt proud.

After pungent mu shu pork and curried shrimp that tickled her tongue, Claudia took Al home with her. His kisses tasted faintly of jasmine from the tea. It had been a very lovely evening and a very long time since Claudia had been with a man. She lured Al into bed. When she peeled off her sensible businesswoman's skirt to reveal black lace G-string panties, Al sighed loudly. Then he said, "Wow."

"Wow is right," Claudia told him. They kissed and groped hungrily. Al palmed Claudia's nether cheeks as though they were fabulously fleshy basketballs. "Mmmmm," said Al.

"Do you like my ass?" Claudia asked. And before Al could answer, Claudia was stroking it. He watched her with a thin smile on his lips. She rested on one side, like a pensive Cleopatra, taunting him with her motions, with her words. "Touch it some more," she cooed. He did. "Spank it." He didn't.

"I don't like hitting people," Al explained.

"But I'm asking you," Claudia emphasized. "*Telling* you."

Al still didn't move, so Claudia spanked herself. It didn't hurt, but sort of tickled. Red blotches stained the meaty surface. Soon, you could decipher her palm prints. "Don't you like to watch it jiggle?" she asked. And Al nodded.

"Kiss my ass," Claudia whispered to him. "It's beautiful."

"It is," Al agreed. "But I've never been a 'butt boy.' "

"You will be," Claudia said. "Starting tonight." She drew herself onto her knees like a lace-clad kitten. She cupped one warm, firm globe in her hand and traced a feathery circle onto the skin. It felt very, very nice indeed. "Come on, kiss it," Claudia told Al.

The commanding, yet gentle tone of Claudia's voice surprised even her. Al's eyes were glazed with lust as he listened. He seemed almost hypnotized, and did just as she said. There was a little thread of spittle in the corner of his mouth. Al took each of Claudia's hips in his hands and drew her ass toward his face. His kisses were feather-light, yet they penetrated her to the core. She felt a sea of goose bumps rising on her flesh. Al softly spread her cheeks apart and soon, Claudia's chocolaty sphincter muscle was winking around his tongue.

A few moments of this made Claudia's pussy hairs very damp. "Don't you want to fuck me?" she asked. It was a rhetorical question, but Al answered anyway. With a grunt into her rosebud. From the nightstand drawer, Claudia pulled a string of condoms and ripped off one with her teeth. (She was horny, but she wasn't stupid.) Al's dick was rock hard with anticipation. Claudia rolled the lime green rubber onto his long, slim rod, careful not to snag his pubes. With her legs spread wide apart, Claudia offered Al her milky, white globes. Instead, he slid into her pussy. "No. Up here," she said, gesturing to her tongue-moistened crack.

Al bit her neck. "I've never done that before."

"Do you want to?" Claudia wondered. He was tugging on her nipples now.

"Yes," he answered, but it was more like a gasp.

"Then I'll show you how." Claudia carefully backed onto Al's sheathed prick. For a moment, she almost laughed, feeling like a truck backing into a tight parking space, but the wave of pleasure, intensity, and almost-pain stopped her. It tingled and tickled and twitched. Al didn't move. He just groaned and made small gurgling noises, his hands still at his sides. Claudia moved her rump up and down on his cock. Slowly. Deliberately. For the first time in her life, she felt that *she* was doing the fucking and not getting fucked. And Claudia liked it. She liked it a lot.

Every so often, a droplet of Al's sweat plunked onto her back. He reached around and stroked her clit, taking it between two fingers, almost jerking it off like a tiny cock. And then a strange thing happened: Claudia came. While gasping and sobbing and collapsing onto her belly, Claudia somehow managed to wiggle a finger into her pussy. She felt it throb and contract. She also felt Al's friendly dick through the membrane of her perineum. And do you know what it felt like? It felt like power.

You see, Claudia had finally learned how to get on top using her bottom.

Molly Brewster

Double Date

"Look at those bedroom eyes," Nadine whispered, taking a long swallow of her drink.

"Where?" I asked, gazing around the bar, trying to be unobtrusive. Though exceedingly nearsighted, I never wore my glasses when Nadine and I went out on a Friday night. The idea was to be devastating and maybe meet the love of my life, so glasses were left in the car. "I don't see him."

"Jill, I can't point him out, you know," Nadine spoke, barely moving her lips, ostensibly staring off into space. "He's at the end of the bar. The one with the sandy curls. A mustache. I can't believe you don't see those blue bedroom eyes. You are truly blind. And now he's looking right this way." Nadine spun around on her bar stool, facing now into the room and away from the bar.

"Oh, yeah, I see," I replied a little too loudly. He wasn't only looking this way; he was looking at me. I felt myself flush under his inspection. Not my type at all, I thought. Attractive, well-muscled, but too macho. I liked more softness in a man. Besides, I never liked mustaches.

"Stop staring," Nadine hissed. "Turn around. You're missing some other nice sights. Look at the tall one in the green sweater.

182

Looks like a lawyer. I bet he's rich. I'm so sick of men who can't afford to buy me a drink, much less dinner."

"I'd rather they were nice than rich," I replied.

"You are so naive. Don't you think a rich guy can be nice? Besides, if he were rich enough, I might not care how nice he was." She lit a cigarette and took in the whole bar in one sweeping glance. "Oh, here comes Bedroom Eyes. But he's practically a dwarf. He sure is cute."

He was making his way through the crowd, heading in our direction. Nadine, having dismissed him as too short, was now in animated conversation with a thin man with a beard. The man with the sandy hair and compelling blue eyes got closer, two bar stools away now, and was looking right at me. Into me was more like it. I was helpless to turn away. I stared wide-eyed, with my heart pounding and a flush creeping up my neck. He was nearly a head shorter than me, but that didn't seem to matter.

Just as he reached Nadine, she hopped off the bar stool, and grabbed the arm of the thin, bearded man. "Let's dance. I love this song." The two of them moved toward the dozen squares of parquet that passed for a dance floor, and Bedroom Eyes slid into the seat Nadine had vacated. I pretended to be unaware of him, but that was the biggest lie. My eyes ached to look at him.

"You are the most beautiful woman in this place," he declared in honey tones.

Oh God, what a line, I thought, but his voice was even more compelling than his appearance. I glanced nervously at him, scarcely able to breathe, and found the deep blue eyes looking steadily into mine.

"You are, you know. All these women"—he gestured, dismissing the crowd around us—"they'd kill to have what you have."

"What's that?" I asked, trying to modulate my voice in what I hoped was an aloof-sounding way.

"Sex appeal. You are the sexiest woman I've ever seen. Those long legs. The way you move. And your mouth when you smile. I can hardly stand it. You're gorgeous."

As he talked, my mind kept saying, What a line. No subtlety at all. How come no one else has ever noticed how gorgeous I am? But my entire body melted as he talked, his voice hypnotizing me and his blue eyes caressing my limbs. I glanced at his hands and noticed the small blond hairs above the knuckles. He didn't push a pencil with those strong hands. I couldn't help imagining what it would be like to have his hands on my body.

"You sure like to exaggerate," I said with a smile and a flip of my long hair. I drained the last of my glass of wine.

"Oh, darlin'. The way you toss that hair around is really turning me on. What's your name? Here, I'll buy you a drink," he said, gesturing toward the bartender with my empty wineglass.

After he paid for the drinks, he moved his bar stool closer to mine. I felt his warm breath on me and my head spun with intoxication at his nearness. His name was Lee.

I don't think I ever drank that glass of wine, because the next thing I knew I was standing in the parking lot with Lee's hands sliding up under my sweater. His head was buried in my breasts and I pressed up against him. He ran his hand down my thigh, making low sounds in the back of his throat. "Oh, I want to wrap those long legs of yours around my neck."

"You don't mind that I'm taller than you are?" I panted.

"Mind? Oh, darlin', I've dreamed of legs like yours. I love your legs, your whole luscious body." He grabbed me tighter and pressed his mouth to mine. Was he swallowing me or was I swallowing him? His tongue moved about my mouth exploring and caressing. When we broke apart gasping, his mustache was covered with our saliva. I reached over and touched it, deciding I liked the mustache after all. He pulled my finger into his mouth and thrills raced up and down my body.

"We need a bed," he purred. "Let's go find one." With hardly a moment's hesitation, I climbed into his pickup truck and moved close to him. As he drove out of the parking lot, I slipped my hand onto his thigh, and he groaned with longing.

As soon as the door closed behind us in the motel, he began undressing me. "Oh, what breasts you have," he hummed as he held them in his hands, his tongue tracing circles around my erect nipples. I unbuttoned his shirt and pressed my bare breasts against his hairy chest. He unzipped my skirt and it fell to the floor. He began working my pantyhose down, kneading the flesh

on my thighs and buttocks. I pressed against him and felt his
hard cock straining against his pants. As I pulled the zipper
down, he moaned with anticipation. His pants down, his cock
was released and moving against me. For a short guy, he sure
had a large penis.

Pushing me onto the bed, he separated my legs and caressed
the inside of my thighs. He moved his mouth toward my moist,
willing lips. His tongue moved around the outer lips, toyed with
the clitoris, and then thrust deep into me. I was panting and
giving out little cries of pleasure. What a tongue. Raising my
head, I looked down my body to see his curly head between my
thighs, his sandy mustache, now covered with vaginal juices,
sweeping the dark curls of my pubic hair.

"Oh, I want to feel your whole naked body against me," I
cried, my fingers in his hair. He rose up and lowered his body
to mine, and every pore of my flesh opened to receive him. His
fingers now reached deep into my vagina, his erect cock pressed
urgently against my belly. Then he raised himself, lifting my legs
into the air, and plunged his swollen penis into me. I cried out
with a sound that brought tears to my eyes. He moved fast and
hard, thrusting deep, then pulling almost all the way out, then
plunging all the way in again. His muscular arms encircled me,
pressing us together. I grasped at his back and moved in rhythm
with him. Flesh against sweaty flesh, cock into cunt, climbing
to the peak, both of us crying out as he came, pulsating, filling
me with his cum.

We lay in a sweaty heap, panting and gently moaning. After
a few minutes, he propped himself on one elbow and ran his
other hand up and down my body. "Oh, Jill, you are somethin'
special. I could make love to you all night."

"You're something special yourself." I smiled at him, thrilled
that he wasn't the kind that fell asleep and snored in the afterglow. I fingered the soft, curly hair on his chest, and watched
his hand moving on my skin.

We talked and cuddled, and after a while his cock swelled
again in my hand. I sat up and bent my head toward this wonderful cock, first gently licking, tasting, exploring the soft skin,
then opening wide and taking him deep into my mouth as he

writhed and moaned on the bed. Soon, he leaped up, pushed me back on the bed, and entered me again, with such force that it was as if we had not made love only a short time before.

In all we made love, I think, five times that night, snuggling, giggling, and talking in-between. It was incredible every time.

As we reluctantly got dressed, I remembered Nadine back at the bar, and that we'd gone there in my car. I looked at my watch; it was long past closing time. Oh, well, Nadine was resourceful. Besides, she liked going in my car, so she wouldn't be encumbered with me if she found someone she liked. I usually drove home alone, being less bold than Nadine.

Lee, now dressed, looked at me deeply and stroked my face. "Jill, I know this sounds like a stupid question, but did you come?"

"You mustn't worry about that," I said.

"I want you to have every possible pleasure. Pure ecstasy is what you deserve."

"You've given me that in spades, love," I replied.

"But did you come?"

I shook my head. This man could see right into me and wouldn't be fooled by the usual evasive answers. I had to look away to think. "I don't come with fucking, so don't worry about it."

"How do you come? I'll do anything for you."

"So far just with a vibrator," I replied. Why was I telling him all my secrets?

"Well, next time I see you, we're going to try that vibrator out, and after a while, you're gonna come lots of ways. I think you just need more attention."

"Whether that's true or not, I love your kind of attention." I wondered if Lee was right.

"What's your phone number?" he asked, tearing the corner off a piece of motel stationery. I gave it to him, but I thought that this had been too good to be more than a one-night stand. I'd probably never hear from him again.

But it was only a few days later that he called. "Oh, darlin', I've got to see you. I can't stop thinking of your long legs and your sweet honey pot. Do you think your friend Nadine might want to meet my friend Tom?"

Saturday night Nadine and I sat waiting in my living room. Both of my children were with their father for the weekend. "Did he say how tall his friend was?" Nadine asked.

"Six feet plus. They must make a funny pair." I smiled, wondering if I'd still like Lee as much.

"Well, I hope Tom's good-looking, and not some kind of weirdo."

I heard their steps on the stairs and felt my panties grow moist. I opened the door and there they stood. Tom was a regular Tall, Dark, and Handsome, but I saw only Lee, and had all I could do to keep from ripping off his clothes.

After introductions, we settled down for some awkward conversation. Nadine and Tom sat at opposite ends of the couch. I poured wine into four glasses, then sat on the floor. Lee sat down next to me with his arm around me. He was obviously as hot as I was. Why had he insisted on bringing Tom to meet Nadine? She was being outlandishly rude, as only she can be when she doesn't like someone. Why she didn't like Tom, I couldn't tell. He was certainly attractive and seemed like a nice guy, too. Not rich though. Both Lee and Tom were truck drivers. After argumentative attorneys who made love in the dark, and boring intellectuals who thought sex was a five-minute sport, I liked making love with a truck driver who really loved sex and could do it all night. Both Lee and Tom were pretty macho, definitely not Nadine's type. For the first time, that didn't sound bad to me.

Tom tried to make conversation with Nadine but she put him down at every turn. Meanwhile, Lee's hands became more and more aggressive. Nadine turned her back on us, which meant she had to face Tom, who appeared to take no notice of our heavy breathing and moving hands. Lee, his breath hot in my ear, whispered, "I want to see your bedroom." I protested, gesturing toward the duo on the couch, but he pulled me to my feet. "Just for a few minutes."

Once in the bedroom, we tore off our clothes and were on each other, in each other, fucking like maniacs. I was hungry for him, insatiable. There could be no "few minutes" for us. At one point, I thought I heard Nadine leaving. On and on we went, touching, sucking, licking, tasting every inch of skin. After we exploded with cries and moans and his hot cum gushed into me, I remembered Tom in the living room. I didn't think he'd left with Nadine, so what was he doing? I became self-conscious thinking about him sitting out there listening to us, but Lee showed no sign of leaving my side. He was holding my breasts in his hands, alternately tasting the nipples and nuzzling my neck.

"What about Tom?" I asked.

"Oh, he'll be okay. I'm not done with you, not by a long shot. Maybe he and Nadine are getting it on."

"She left. Didn't you hear her slam the door?"

"Jill, when I'm making love to you, the only thing I hear is your sweet moans." He was moving his hand up and down my thighs, barely brushing my moist outer lips. Involuntarily I moved toward his hand and he obligingly slid two fingers inside. "Oh, what a beautiful cunt you have."

"What a beautiful cock you have."

"The better to fuck you with, my dear." With that his cock grew hard and he moved on top of me again.

I heard a footstep in the hall. Tom was definitely still in the apartment. "Lee, I think you should go see about Tom. I feel bad about leaving him out there, while we're in here . . ."

"Okay, okay." He sat up and thought a minute. "Jill, I have a favor to ask you." He paused and took my hand. "Would you . . . go to bed with Tom? It would mean so much to me if you would. You are sooo fantastic. You'd do so much for him. Would you, please?"

I sat bolt upright. Entranced as I was with Lee, the idea of having sex with Tom didn't interest me very much. But what the proposal said about Lee really excited me. I took a deep breath and began hesitantly, "Well, there's only one way I could do that." He didn't say anything, but he turned his blue eyes on me eagerly. I couldn't look him in the eye. "Have you ever been three in a bed?"

"Oh, darlin', wait right here." Depositing a kiss on my mouth, he grabbed his pants. "Back in a flash."

When Lee returned to the bedroom with Tom, I felt too exposed. I pulled the sheet up around me and let my hair fall across my bare breasts. "Oh, no, Jill, I've been telling Tom how beautiful you are, so don't go hiding under a sheet." Lee slipped out of his pants and climbed back into bed. Tom sat down on the other side of the bed, at the very edge. I looked at him and smiled. Slowly he took off his shoes and set his glasses on the nightstand.

"Are you blind now?" He nodded. "That makes two of us. I guess we'll just have to feel our way along," I said, smiling and reaching for his hand. He moved a little closer and I worked at the buttons on his shirt. Tom was more than good-looking. He was an extremely sexy man. Dark, dark eyes and shiny black hair. Long, thin, but muscular limbs. I felt myself becoming aroused as I touched his smooth, nearly hairless chest. Or was I just so turned on to Lee that I was hot for any man who happened along? I leaned forward and touched his face. He kissed me, at first tentatively, but when I slipped my tongue between his lips, he opened wide and thrust his tongue deep into my mouth. I savored the new sweetness of his mouth, a different flavor from Lee.

As Tom struggled out of the rest of his clothes, Lee drew me to him, "Oh, Jill, you're fantastic. Look at the hard-on I got, just watching you kiss Tom." Lying on my side, I wrapped my arms around him and lost myself to kissing him. I felt Tom slip into bed behind me and move up against my buttocks, pressing a very hard cock against the backs of my thighs. Lee's equally hard penis pushed against the front of my thighs. Surely this was heaven.

As I continued kissing Lee, I arched my back and lifted my buttocks to allow Tom to enter me from behind. His large hands moved up and down my legs and buttocks, and he moved his penis in and out, slowly and deliciously, making me writhe and pant, which seemed to excite Lee as much as if it were his own organ sliding in and out of me. Our three sets of legs became more and more entangled, and hands were touching and caressing and loving every which way. So much skin, all moist and sensual, like a dream, only this was really happening.

Afterward, we sat up in bed and smoked cigarettes, talking of our pleasures. How rare it was to find a man who wanted to talk about sex at all, and I had two who wanted to do it and talk about it and then do it some more. We giggled and told tales of our sexual adventures. They told me about the time Tom left some woman's house so rapidly that he left his shorts behind. Lee insisted that I was so fantastic he couldn't remember any other women. I told them about another time I'd been three in a bed, but that time with a man and another woman. They went wild, wanting to hear all the details. "I like this better. Two men all for me. I can't think of anything nicer. Have the two of you ever been in bed together like this before?"

"Not quite," Tom replied. "Almost, though, one time. Remember that redhead, Lee?"

"Oh, yeah! Too bad she chickened out. Me and Tom have been buddies a lot of years so being in bed together—with you that is—seems natural in a weird kind of way." Lee was busy caressing my inner thighs as he talked.

"Yeah, it is," Tom agreed. "When I first walked into the bedroom, I thought: I can't get into bed with Lee, but somehow once I got my clothes off, it felt fine, even when sometimes I wasn't sure whose leg was whose."

As the cigarettes died in the ashtray, Lee and Tom began caressing me, and before long I was aroused again. "Where's your vibrator?" Lee asked matter-of-factly. "I want this time to be just for you."

No man had ever done this with me. I was nervous but eager. Reaching under the bed I pulled out the already plugged-in vibrator. Before I could explain anything to Lee, he had taken it from me and was applying it gently to just the right spot. Tears welled in my eyes as he brought me quickly to the edge of coming. Tom was pressed against me, his cock once again hard and eager. Lee just looked at me with those incredible blue eyes and kept the vibrator humming. Like inching to the edge of a waterfall I moved toward orgasm, building, swelling, breathing hard, opening, and then up and over the edge and into thin air with a cry. "Oh, Lee . . ." I breathed as he tossed the vibrator aside and climbed on top of me while Tom caressed and kissed me. After having made love with Tom and then come with the vibrator, my vagina was juicy and hungry for Lee's tireless cock. We grinned at each other as if we'd invented sex.

"Too bad Nadine missed all the fun," I said.

"Well, I don't miss her," mumbled Tom.

"Nadine who?" quipped Lee, still moving in and out, kneading my buttocks with his hands.

Then there was no more talking, as Lee moved toward his climax as my body opened wide to receive him. Tom's cock in my hand was hard and excited, and the three of us moved together on the bed, higher and higher, electricity shooting through us, then gasping and crying out with bliss.

We lay quietly, three happy people, now tired as the sky started to lighten. I drifted off to sleep, curled up against Lee and with Tom wrapped around me from behind.

Martha Miller

Seductions

We watched sun dogs in the winter sky all the way down I-55. Every now and then the wind blew up dark clouds, and then they passed. I looked at Elli. She was smiling, swaying gently, sometimes humming with the music from the tape player: "Diamonds and Rust."

I had talked to my friend Judy that morning. I'd told her about my ex's new Mustang, my shattered self-esteem. She said her first husband took a European vacation when they broke up.

I said, "I feel like I've been abandoned. Even though I threw her out."

"K.C. *made* you throw her out. You didn't want to."

"After she started the new job she was angry all the time," I said. "She treated me awful. It felt like she was my worst enemy and I never did anything but try to love her."

"It sounds like she wanted out and didn't know how to do it."

That hurt. Judy was right. But why? What did I do? K.C. had always told me I was special. Was that just another lie?

I rubbed the ring imprint on my finger. It had taken four years to get there. I wondered how long it would take to go away.

Stubble fields sped by. They were dotted with snow. It was mid-January.

Cahokia had been Elli's idea. I think.

I had said I wanted to see the new museum on one of her visits. She suggested we leave my kids with their father and go today. She'd driven two hours north to pick me up and now we were headed south again. We would see the museum, have dinner, and drive home. Six hours on the road. Was she that interested in the mound builders? It seemed extravagant. But, in the past weeks I'd come to think of Elli as just that.

I looked across the car at her. She was small.

My ex and I were both large women. K.C. was shaped like the Venus of Willendorf. I'd found beauty in that. Never thought of wanting anything else. Elli was shaped different: round hips, slim shoulders, small hands. I was three inches taller and probably outweighed her by fifty pounds.

I'm going to sleep with her, I thought. If I can figure out how to bring up the subject. How had I done it with K.C.? I tried to remember. A voice in my head said, "Stop it. She's just being friendly. You haven't had sex for a month. Your thinking's distorted."

Okay, I thought. I won't sleep with her. I don't want to mess up a good friendship by hitting on her. I need all the friends I can get right now. Besides, she always had much younger lovers. I'm not her type.

"Look, there's another one." Elli pointed at the sky.

On either side of the sun were spots of rainbow colors.

I looked at her round thigh, faded jeans, western boots. Maybe if I said, "You just broke up with your lover. I just broke up with mine. We could help each other out."

"Do you have any Carole King?" I asked, shuffling through her tapes.

What if she were horrified? Put me out beside the road? I decided to wait until we were home before I brought it up.

I remembered our conversation a week ago in a restaurant. We talked a lot about sex. She kept bringing me back to it. What did I like? How often? Did I think it was too soon? "She wants you," said a voice in my head. No, I thought, you're reading sex into everything. Chill out.

It was late afternoon when we pulled off the interstate. A

strong gust of wind blew an empty paper bag. It turned end on end in front of us, then fell behind the car.

"I'm going to sleep with Elli," I had told Judy during one of our daily conversations.

"That's nice."

"Do you know anything about seduction?" I asked.

"Sure."

"How does it go?"

She laughed.

"I'm serious. I want a flow chart."

"You mean if 'yes' then . . . , and if 'no' then go to . . . ?"

"Exactly."

"How soon do you need it?" She was still laughing.

"Tomorrow. Cahokia."

"You think the mounds will get her in the mood?"

"They'll remind her of cunts," I said. "Everything reminds her of cunts."

"You don't need to seduce *that* woman."

I watched Elli walk ahead of me toward the museum. Her round hips bounced with her quick dykey stride. Her body went in where K.C.'s went out. It was distracting. I tried to imagine her naked. Tripped over a curb.

"Okay," Judy had said. "First you give her long looks. Lots of eye contact. Then you find things to laugh about. Do lots of laughing together."

I listened, thought about Elli's visits, the things we'd done and said, the things we'd found to laugh about in spite of the pain.

"Then," Judy went on. "You have long talks. Not about sex. Anything but sex."

I remembered the conversations about our children, our break-ups, our ex's.

"This doesn't sound like seduction," I said. "This sounds like the story of my life."

"Trust me," Judy said. "Next you get her alone. And have a long conversation about sex."

I thought about dinner the week before. Could Elli be seducing me?

"Go on," I said.

"Then you get her in a vulnerable position and *don't* take advantage of her."

I remembered the night after the restaurant conversation. I thought she was going to sleep with me and was a little scared. At bedtime she'd made up the couch just like on every other visit. And I lay alone in my room, hurting, wanting.

"Don't?" I asked.

"Right. Then, when she feels pretty sure you're not interested—move in. Start by changing the way you touch her. Make it suggestive. Usually by then she'll be so off balance that she'll be trying to figure out how to seduce *you*."

"You've tried this?"

"Works every time."

We sat next to a family with at least three children under the age of four in the museum theater. K.C. would have said, "See what happens when straight people fuck?" Elli simply smiled and scooted closer to me to make room for them. The lights went low.

I'll just say, "Look, we're both without lovers. Neither of us wants to get involved with someone right now. But people need sex."

Her thigh pressed against mine.

A little girl behind me leaned forward to see the village campfires as a tape played night sounds. I could feel the child's moist breath in my ear. It felt nice.

The night before I'd been on my way home from work as the sun was setting. I'd been thinking about Elli. Things didn't feel the way they had with K.C.

The sky in front of me was turquoise and coral. The clouds were gold. It occurred to me that I would never love the same way again. For the rest of my life, K.C. would be the most in love, the most invested I would ever be. And it was over.

Maybe it was a good thing, I'd thought. I would always hold a piece of myself back. I would never hurt this bad again.

Tears turned the sunset into a kaleidoscope. I had to pull the car over.

The worst had been the day she had come for her bookcase and albums. I set them outside the door and watched her load them in the truck, K.C. and her new roommate, heads close together over Janis Joplin. I watched them through the window, the pain exploding inside me. I couldn't imagine my life without her.

We wandered through the exhibit. In front of the flint knapping Elli stood close to me. I could feel her body heat.

The voice in my head was going on about how she was a good friend, and if we did have sex where would that leave us? Suppose it didn't work out. How could we be friends then? "Lover" was certainly a more vulnerable status then "friend."

Look, I said to the voice. I'm going to forget this and go to the bar. Maybe I could pay somebody.

We found a Mexican restaurant for dinner. The food was too hot and the prices too high. Elli seemed in a hurry to head home. It was dark by the time we pulled back on I-55.

The trip home was quiet. There was a knot of fear in my gut. What if she says no? Is insulted? Leaves and doesn't spend the night?

At home I made a pot of coffee and put on some music. We sat in the living room and talked. I had trouble paying attention. There were awkward silences. The voice in my head tried. "Say something nice to her. Tell her she's attractive, that you like her boots." I looked at her boots. They were nice but not—

"You want to go somewhere?" She interrupted my thought. "Do something?"

"Not really."

Silence.

"Get the conversation back to sex," the voice said. "Remember the restaurant. Ask her what she likes? How often? Does she think it's too soon? I looked at the clock. Time seemed to crawl. She picked up a magazine and thumbed through it.

What if she's insulted? What if she just walks out?

"Don't be silly," chided the voice in my head. "She's two hours from home. She's been on the road all day."

"Are you hungry?" she asked.

"No."

The ticking clock drummed in my ear. An hour had passed.

"You must be tired," I said.

"Yes, a little."

"That's it," went the voice. "You waited too long. Even if she wanted to, she's too tired now."

I stood to get a blanket. I tried to accept that we would be sleeping in separate rooms again.

She stood. Walked toward me.

I looked at her.

"You know," she said, "I've been fond of you for a long time. I was wondering if you would be willing to share some pleasure with me?"

I let out a sigh. "I've been trying to figure out how to bring that up." I reached for her, and pulled her toward me, never really saying yes.

She pressed her lips to mine. Her tongue darted into my mouth. I returned the kiss, holding her.

K.C. and I had been monogamous. Before K.C., my lovers were mostly men. Elli was the first other anybody for years. The pain of wanting washed over me.

"It's been a long day," I said. "I want to take a shower."

"Don't," she said.

I looked at her. I'd just learned something else about her. Or had I? Maybe she didn't understand. I was suddenly afraid. I didn't want to screw up.

"*I* would feel more comfortable," I asserted.

"Quickly then," she said.

I lit candles in the bedroom. I looked at the bed K.C. and I had bought together, made promises in, had our final fight in. The knot of pain tightened.

"Get on with it," the voice in my head said. "It will be good for you."

I turned and saw Elli silhouetted in the bedroom door.

"Lovely," she said.

I looked down at myself. My body was still damp and warm from the shower, wrapped in a black towel. I blushed. Shit, I thought. This feels like high school!

"Please take your clothes off," I said.

She stepped into the room and started to unbutton her shirt.

"Don't just stand there," said the voice. "Help her." I stepped toward her.

"I need to know," she said as the shirt fell off her shoulders, "if you usually come one time or several?"

"Once," I said, thinking that probably on the first night with her even once would be a miracle.

"I'm multiply orgasmic," she said evenly.

My knees felt weak. I sat on the edge of the bed.

She unzipped her jeans and stepped out of them. Her body was beautiful, ivory and glowing in the candlelight. I took a deep breath. I'd never seen anything quite like it. Her breasts were smooth, nipples erect. Her waist was small, hips round. The black hairs of her cunt glistened, inviting me to touch them.

Oh God, I thought. Then she ripped the towel away.

Our bodies pressed together. Our breasts. Our cunts. I ran my hands down her back as we kissed. I was fascinated with her ass. I wanted to touch it, knead it, bury my face in it.

We rolled all over the bed. Each time I made a move she made another. She was clearly in charge. My cunt was throbbing as I twisted away from her.

"I want to go down on you," I said.

"You do?"

"Yes, that would please me."

Who would do what, and when, had always been a power thing with K.C., so when Elli rolled off me, threw her arms over her head easily and said, "Then do it," I was surprised. It upset my sense of routine. My timing. There would be no struggle about it. What would I do with the energy I'd always put into that?

Go down on her, that's what.

I planted tiny kisses on her mound. I washed my tongue slowly over her swollen labia. She moaned. My tongue found her clitoris, firm, waiting. I worked slowly, applying what felt like perfect pressure. My tongue felt like an extension of her fragrant cunt and we both received pleasure. My lips were covered with the faint taste of the sea. My hands massaged her ass.

She moaned again and again. Louder. I was glad the kids were at their father's, remotely wondered about the neighbors. She cried out and pushed my head away, holding it in place, inches from her throbbing cunt.

"Well, how many do you think multiple means?" The voice inside was breathless.

Good question, I thought.

"We know it means more than one," the voice said.

Right. As she relaxed I started the tiny kisses again. She spread her legs. Gently, I ran my tongue over her wet vulva and found her spot. The second time was quicker. Her moans were louder. My face was wet. My tongue and lips were hot and tingling.

She pulled me alongside her. Her hand found my cunt. Then three fingers were inside me, writhing like the hairs of Medusa, her thumb pressing my clitoris. Each place she touched felt on fire. She thrust her fingers slowly. I arched my back. Met her thrusts. She kissed my shoulders, found a nipple, and began sucking. Then in one swift motion, her fingers still thrusting inside me, her lips were covering my clit and she was sucking with the same sweet pressure. It pushed me over the edge so quickly that I was stunned.

When I found my voice, I said, "How did you know I like penetration?"

"The restaurant," she said, and started moving her fingers again.

"I only . . ." I couldn't think straight. The words were lost.

"Am I hurting you?"

"No."

"Do you want me to stop?" Her thumb moved across my clit.

"No. Don't stop."

She went down on me in earnest then. Her fingers moving harder. I rocked, meeting her thrusts. At first I was sure I couldn't come. Then the sensation rushed through my veins right to my fingertips.

"Oh God!" I cried as I pushed her away.

She moved up and lay on top of me. I held her, trying to catch my breath. My heart was pounding.

"How did you know I could come again?" I asked at last.

"Lucky guess," she said.

We lay there kissing and holding each other.

"Twice." The voice inside me was excited. "You came twice!"

Well, it's been a long time, I told the voice.

"What's she doing now?" the voice said.

She had straddled one of my legs and was moving slowly.

"What are you doing?" I asked.

"Do you have any lubricant?" she answered.

"Ah . . ."

"That will do." She had spotted a bottle of hand cream on the nightstand. She reached for it and spread it on top of my leg, cold and slippery. She pressed her cunt against me and started moving.

"What . . . ," I murmured.

"It feels so good." Her voice was soft. "You want to try it?"

"Die!" It was the voice inside me. "You're going to die right here in this bed!"

"Sure," I said.

She put hand cream on her leg, then my cunt. I held her. Face-to-face and we moved. It felt pleasant. Intense. I could touch her. Kiss her. Hold her.

It was late. Elli lay in my arms. I watched two candles flicker on the dresser. Remembered the sun dogs. Cahokia. The day.

"I wonder why they're called sun dogs?" I asked lazily.

"Sun dogs?" She raised her head and looked at me. "I don't know."

"Where did you first hear them called that?"

She thought for a moment. "I think it was my second husband. It must mean something, otherwise they'd just be called spots in the sky."

One day, I thought, I'll say to a lover about something, "It must have been K.C. who told me that." And K.C. will be just someone who used to be part of my life and isn't anymore. Someday.

"What are you thinking?" Elli asked.

"Oh," I sighed, "I was just trying to figure it out."

I looked at her then. Her face was aglow in the candlelight. Her eyes met mine.

We looked at each other for a long time.

At last she sighed, "The thing is, kiddo, some things you never do figure out."

ABOUT THE AUTHORS

CASSANDRA BRENT has always had a thing about locomotives. She is an avid calligrapher, and her favorite place to spend an afternoon is in the Tactile Dome at the Exploratorium in San Francisco. She is working on a collection of her short stories, some of which have been previously published in *Open Wide* and *Aché*.

MOLLY BREWSTER is the pen name of a Northern Calfornia woman who lives in the woods. She is an accountant for small businesses, as well as a writer of both fiction and nonfiction.

*ANGELA FAIRWEATHER has been writing for the past two decades, primarily about education, health, and food.

WINN GILMORE grew up in the South, was schooled in New England, and lives in Calfornia. Her writing has appeared in *Aché*, *On Our Backs*, and *Sinister Wisdom*, and the anthologies *Unholy Alliances* and *Riding Desire*. She has a short-story collection entitled *Trip to Nawlins*.

*This author has stories that appear in *Herotica* (Down There Press, 1988).

JANE HANDEL is a writer, visual artist, and most recently, publisher. In early 1990, she founded SpiderWoman Press, whose first release was *Swimming on Dry Land: The Memories of an Ascetic Libertine*, written and designed by Handel. She lives in San Francisco with her husband and daughter.

AURORA LIGHT has contributed stories, nonfiction articles, and poetry to a variety of publications, including *Woman's World, Country Woman*, and *Broomstick*. She is a contributing editor for an international Meniere's Disease newsletter and publishes a haiku magazine.

*MOXIE LIGHT is the author of many journal articles and has recently received her MFA degree. She has also been involved in establishing a women's shelter in New England.

*JANE LONGAWAY is a writer, printer, and longtime San Franciscan who believes imaginary excess is the answer to safe sex.

MAGENTA MICHAELS lives on the coast south of San Francisco with her husband and parrot. These are her first published short stories, coming from a writing class and her personal journal.

MARTHA MILLER gets up at 5:30 A.M. and writes; then goes to her bank job where she is frequently late. She's a lesbian who's allergic to cats, a writer who can't spell, and a perfect example that nobody's perfect.

KAREN MARIE CHRISTA MINNS has been published in such diverse places as Britain's *Sex Maniac's Diary, Sinister Wisdom*, and *On Our Backs*. One of her two published novels, *Virago*, was nominated for a 1991 Lambda Literary Award.

SERENA MOLOCH maintains active ties to the women's health movement. She dedicates her story to Princess Snatch.

*This author has stories that appear in *Herotica* (Down There Press, 1988).

*LISA PALAC lives in San Francisco, where she also works as a freelance sex journalist and leads sex writing workshops. She performs carnal and comical monologues under the name Lisa LaBia.

CAROL A. QUEEN is a San Francisco writer, sex educator, activist, and adventurer. Her work has appeared in *On Our Backs*, *Taste of Latex*, *Frighten the Horses*, and other publications. She is committed to and inspired by exploring nonnormative sexualities, kissing and telling.

KATE ROBINSON is a thirty-nine-year-old lesbian separatist bisexual who harbors fantasies of roaring through the halls on a Harley at her Yuppie job. She writes and edits for business, technical, and community publications.

TEA SAHNE is a coffee addict, gardener, freelance writer, teacher, and widowed mother of two sons. In her forties she earned an advanced degree in medieval literature.

*SUSAN ST. AUBIN is working more and writing less these days, writing an occasional erotic story as a way of relaxing and preserving her sanity.

*MARCY SHEINER is fiction editor of *On Our Backs* and is still riding on the backseat of motorcycles.

DAPHNE SLADE didn't even realize what she was writing at first—this is her first venture into writing erotica. She has been a member of a political satire troupe and several improv groups, performed stand-up comedy, and written prose. Her day (and night) jobs have included waitressing, stockbrokering, and currently, technical writing.

ROBERTA STONE is a fifteen-year lesbian activist living in Boston. When not going to meetings she likes to relax with a notepad, pencil, and her own dirty thoughts. Her stories have appeared in *Bad Attitude*.

*This author has stories that appear in *Herotica* (Down There Press, 1988).

CATHERINE TAVEL is an erotic scribe of fiction, nonfiction, poetry, and adult video reviews. Although she usually writes under a number of *noms de porn*, this happily married former Catholic schoolgirl from Brooklyn, New York, gained notoriety after joining forces with Robert Rimmer to assist sex industry stars in writing their autobiographies.

MAGGIE TOP is a poet, essayist, and performance artist. This is her first erotic short story.

CINDY WALTERS enjoys Eros in reality and in fantasy, alone and with partners, or any combination of the above. This is her first published story; her earlier writings were for her college storytelling class.

PAT WILLIAMS, born and raised in the countryside of west Tennessee, now lives in Berkeley, California. She reads a lot of science fiction, fantasy, and ancient history, practices yoga and writes science fiction.

MARGO WOODS, a writer, student, and lover, has two adult children and one published book, *Masturbation, Tantra, and Self-Love*.

JOANI BLANK is the author of several sexual-awareness books for children and adults, and the founder/owner of Good Vibrations, San Francisco's unique vibrator store. She is also the publisher of Down There Press, which brought the first *Herotica* collection into the world.

SUSIE BRIGHT is the author of *Susie Sexpert's Lesbian Sex World*, editor of the first *Herotica* collection, and former editor of *On Our Backs*. She is the mother of Aretha Elizabeth. In addition to her writing projects, she is a connoisseuse of X-rated video.

More....more....more!

"Some women want the stars, some the sleaze; some desire the nostalgia of the ordinary, some the punch of the kinky. And some want all of it."

These are the words of Susie Bright who edited the first book in this series, **Herotica**. Readers and reviewers have proven her right!

*"There is a feminine power in the honesty of these stories. The women in **Herotica** are aware and willing to express their own sexuality."*

San Francisco Chronicle

"Unpredictable and well-crafted, raunchy and sensitive, this collection is an excellent addition to the growing body of women's erotic fiction."

New Pages

"It's a pleasure to read erotic stories whose authors are not trapped by political correctitude or narrow stereotypical sexual recipes."

Louanne C. Cole, Ph.D.

So, if you enjoyed the sizzling stories you've just read in **Herotica 2,** and you want more, you're sure to delight in the original **Herotica.**

Ask for it at your local bookstore or order direct from:

Down There Press
P.O. Box 2086-NAL
Burlingame CA 94011-2086

Enclose $12.00, which includes
UPS shipping and handling.